A SECRET
MUSE

A SECRET MUSE

①

MANDY JACKSON-BEVERLY

CRICKET PUBLISHING / U. S. A.

Jackson-Beverly, Mandy.
A Secret Muse / by Mandy Jackson-Beverly. — 1st ed.

Paperback edtion
ISBN 978-0-9965088-1-0 1. Art —Fiction. 2. Humanities —
Fiction. 3. Witches — Fiction. 4. Vampires — Fiction.

I dedicate this book to my mother, Doris Joan Jackson, for instilling in me her fearless independence and infinite courage. And to my father, Dr. Bill Jackson, for sharing with me his deep passion for the arts, and reminding me, that no matter what hurdles get in my way, to always, always, follow my heart.

The motto of the Allegiance

SINE VIRTVTE OMNIA SVNT PERDITA

(without courage, all is lost)

As humans, we are bound by fate to encounter a profound moment while on our journey—an instant when a choice is presented and we either accept the challenge, or carry on with life as we know it.

CHAPTER 1

Professor Coco Rhodes contemplated the image before her: a female cloaked in a shadowed background, her eyes closed—and a man standing in the foreground poised in a defensive stance. Both were drenched in tones of deep crimson. Blood tones. Had one of her students painted this picture, Coco would have perceived that the artist was hiding something, holding back from her full potential, or afraid. But Coco had created this image and it signified her personal creative interrupta. She hadn't painted anything in three months, since the headaches and visions of blood had begun. That time also marked the initiation of the nightmares in which she searched continually for something she had lost.

Splatters of red paint, once bright in hue, had dried on the cement floor of her studio classroom and had become dulled beneath the heavy foot traffic. Coco became transfixed by the splatter marks, which seemed to pulse outward and then suddenly contract. She froze as the image of a woman's bloodied face flashed in her mind.

A sharp pain pierced her neck, followed by a tingling sensation that crept over her skin. These symptoms acted as precursors to the migraines that had recently plagued her.

"Not again!" Coco spoke through clenched teeth. She picked

up her purse and tucked the painting under her arm. Then she walked briskly past the seven cubicles, which had once housed still lifes, landscapes, and abstract pieces painted by her graduate students, and went to stand before the window overlooking the sculpture garden. It never ceased to amaze her that this sanctuary stood right outside the building where she worked. Here in the sprawling city of Los Angeles, in a university that had a population of over thirty thousand students, she could walk fifty feet outside her office and stand face to face with sculptures by artistic virtuosos such as Richard Serra, August Rodin, and Henry Moore.

When Coco had entered the university as an undergraduate student fourteen years before, the art department had fueled her love of drawing and painting. She had earned her MFA before taking time off to paint and teach private lessons in the studio at her loft in Westwood. When her alma mater offered her a teaching position, she took it. But she had not expected a thick wall of creative resistance to assault her each time she held a paintbrush in her hand. She took another look at the painting of the couple, sighed, and headed for home.

Ten minutes later, she reached the loft complex that she owned with her brother, Christopher, in Westwood Village. She entered, greeted by her thirteen-pound cat, Thalia, weaving between her legs. Coco placed the painting on an easel in the studio area of her living room, squeezed the back of her neck, and dug through her purse for a bottle of Ibuprofen.

"Another school year completed… summer classes over… and I'm losing my mind," she said, and then downed two pills with a glass of water. She collapsed onto the sofa, closed her eyes, and hoped for sleep. This increased sense of anxiety and lack of sleep seemed to have dominated her life over the past few weeks. A chime alerted her to the arrival of a text message. It was from Christopher.

Congrats on completing another year, little sister! See you in D.C. tomorrow night.

She groaned and fell asleep.

An hour later, Coco heard a familiar tuneful knock on her front door. She got up and opened it to Layla, her best friend and Christopher's girlfriend.

"Are you okay?" Layla said, with concern in her heavily Italian-accented voice. "You don't look very well."

Coco made herself comfortable again on the sofa. "More dreams," she said, and gestured at the painting. "He's the cause of them—whoever the hell he is."

Layla looked at the painting.

"Any ideas about his identity, doctor?" Coco asked.

"Do you?" Layla said as she sank into a nearby chair.

"He feels familiar. I dream of him, paint him—I feel like I know him—but I'm pretty sure I'd remember meeting a face like that."

"So, he's not someone you feel you've met before?" Layla asked. "Maybe someone from your undergrad years?"

"Having you pop in like this reminds me of being back in the dorms," Coco said. "But no—I haven't got a clue as to who he is." She stood up. "Are you down for a run?"

"It'll be dark soon," Layla said. "Let's go out to dinner instead and run in the morning before we leave for the airport." She took a closer look at Coco's face. "Have you eaten at all today?"

"I had a protein shake for breakfast. Give me a minute while I change." Coco grabbed a blanket from the sofa and threw it over the painting. "I like the idea of walking somewhere local. Is that okay with you?"

"Sure, ready when you are."

Layla studied Coco, whose shoulders dipped as she walked up the stairs to her bedroom. What had happened to the vibrancy in her personality? And her eyes, too. Normally a stunning lavender flecked with amethyst, now they appeared dim and tired. When she heard Coco's bedroom door close, Layla lifted the blanket and took a photo of the painting with her cell and sent it to Christopher:

Have you seen this? Coco's latest painting...from three months ago.

She kept it at work. Says she has no idea who he is.

She doesn't look well.

Walking to dinner.

Seconds later Christopher sent a reply:

First time I've seen it. I've forwarded it to Gabriel.

Security switched up a notch—others on their way. Cxo

O

Coco watched the numbers on her digital clock flip over to 4:35 a.m. The wine she drank at dinner had done nothing to help her sleep and the tingling sensation that crept over her skin earlier had amplified. Her nerves felt raw. She felt confined. She couldn't handle another migraine. She threw back the covers and got dressed into her running clothes. When she arrived at the front door, Coco felt an urge to text Layla, since using the buddy system was an old habit of hers. She looked in her purse for her phone and on the counter while the tension in her neck grew stronger, causing her muscles to twitch and a cold sweat to run over her. But her phone was nowhere to be seen. Thalia's meowing became incessant.

"Thalia—stop it!" Coco squeezed her eyes shut and took in a deep breath. "Shit, I'm sorry, kitty." She bent down and stroked the cat. Then she gently pushed her out of the way and slipped into the darkness.

Damien had watched Coco walk through the sculpture garden and head back to her home before she left for dinner with the sexy Italian woman. Once Layla and Coco returned home, he had parked across the street from Coco's loft in his latest acquisition, a black BMW 320i Sedan. The car didn't rate as his first choice, but the model seemed popular in the area and when the time came it would suffice. His parking spot gave him a clear view of the side gate and garage to the red-bricked building adorned with green ivy. The Rhodes family lofts stood behind an iron fence with a heavy wooden gate.

During his high school years, Damien had ranked as one of the fastest runners on the school's track team, and after monitoring Coco's daily running routines, he mentally gauged her endurance to be better than most Olympic marathon runners. He had noticed the stares of longing from her students and heard the sexual innuendos from her co-workers. He saw what they saw—the woman was hot. He had a few more hours of darkness before Coco appeared for her morning run. She'd be dressed in her tight running shorts and sports bra—her body firm and muscular. This thought brought tension in his already tight suit pants. He pushed back his seat, got comfortable, and undid his zipper, grateful for the heavily tinted windows.

Distracted by a clicking sound, he looked up to see Coco open the gate, glance up at the security cameras that monitored the perimeter of the building, and take off down the street. She ran past the BMW without a glance.

He waited until Coco reached the end of Le Conte Avenue before starting the car and following her. He noticed the time on his Omega: 4:40 a.m.

"What the hell's she doing running this early?"

He tracked her to the beach at Santa Monica. If she turned around then he would be out of luck—the beach area was not conducive to what he had planned for her. But when he saw her cut down to the bike path, he knew what he had to do. Coco had chosen to run the sixteen-mile loop. Solo.

"Today's your unlucky day, luv."

For months he had timed this part of Coco's run. She never failed to complete the section from the bike path at Santa Monica to the Temescal Trailhead in twenty-four minutes, and the trail she ran in the park took another fourteen. He set the timer on his watch and then drove up toward Temescal Canyon, where he would wait for her to return to Sunset Boulevard.

Damien was grateful for the red streetlight ahead. It gave him time to admire his thin leather driving gloves. The sheen of the gloves caused his mind to drift to past assignments for his high paying client. The abortion clinic incident in Kansas City came to mind, and the art gallery in Manhattan. Do it quickly, do it right, and get the hell out of the country. That was his motto. His incentive to kill this beauty was five million U.S. dollars. In twenty-four hours he would be back in Monaco, on the Cote d'Azure, with his unsuspecting wife and kids.

Layla awoke to a sporadic flashing light and low buzzing sound. She immediately checked her iPad, which was connected to the alarm system for the entire building. Instinct took over and she grabbed her cell and called Coco's number.

"Pick up, Coco," Layla whispered while turning on the speakerphone. She navigated through the hi-tech security system to the pertinent recorded film on the iPad, stopping when she saw Coco exit the side gate and look at the camera. Layla's skin tightened and the tiny blonde hairs lifted along the side of her arms. Her fourteen years of training and experience as a psychologist had taught her to read people. As she stared at Coco's face, she saw confusion and sadness. Words flashed on the top of the screen:

Power surge at 4:40 a.m.—Temporary system failure.

Her hand trembled as she dialed Christopher's number.

He picked up immediately. "Are you okay?"

"The alarm on the security system woke me up," Layla said, shoving her feet into the closest pair of shoes and grabbing her purse and car keys. "Coco left through the side gate at 4:40 a.m."

"Twenty-five minutes ago? She didn't call you?"

"No," Layla said as she bounded down the stairwell.

"Did you forget to set up the security last night?"

"No!"

"Then what the fuck happened?"

"You're breaking up. I'll call you when I find her."

She ended the call.

Layla jumped into her Tesla and brought the engine to life. She retraced the route that she knew Coco would take, hoping to find her on her way home along Wilshire Boulevard. When she saw no sign of her, Layla put her foot down and tested the car's speed.

"*Merda!*" she cursed. She remembered how distant her friend had seemed at dinner and how she'd been complaining of a headache. "What the hell are you thinking, going running on your own in the dark?"

The second the Temescal Park entrance came into view, Layla pulled up onto the sidewalk and bolted out of the car without bothering to lock it. She had run this loop with Coco many times, so she headed for the section of road that intersected with the trailhead. She heard movement fifty feet ahead. Moments later Coco emerged from the trail.

A pair of bright headlights flashed on out of nowhere. An

engine roared, and a sedan accelerated toward Coco. "Coco!" Layla screamed. But before Layla could reach her friend a large feline shape leapt from the trail and into the car's path. The animal took the full force of the bumper, causing the car to swerve to the left before it sped off. Rather than swiping her directly, the car clipped Coco's thigh hard and sent her cartwheeling through the air. She landed in a heap on the ground next to the mangled body of the large cat.

Layla had a 911 operator on the line by the time she reached Coco's side. She watched for the rise and fall of Coco's chest, hoping for a sign that she was breathing. "My friend's been hit by a car—this is an emergency situation! We're on Sunset Boulevard, near the Temescal Canyon Trailhead parking lot—please, hurry!" She switched the cell phone to speaker and placed it on the ground so that she could evaluate Coco.

"Is your friend breathing?" the 911 operator asked.

"Yes, she is—but it's shallow," Layla answered.

"Don't move her. The paramedics will be there momentarily."

Layla noticed a hint of jagged bone protruding through Coco's running pants and the stream of blood that flowed from the gash on her head.

"Coco, can you hear me?" Layla asked, her voice calm. "An ambulance is on its way."

In the distance, the sounds of sirens broke the silence. Layla ended the call. She ripped off her sweater and pressed it to Coco's forehead. "Listen to me, Coco, you must be strong. You need to think of something peaceful. Breathe, *la mia amica*." Coco's head rolled back and she gasped for air, her eyes still closed.

Despite the injured body of her friend before her, Layla remembered the animal that had saved her. She looked at the place where the car had crushed the mountain lion's body. All that remained was a pool of dark blood and a few tufts of fur.

CHAPTER 2

Ventimiglia, Italy.

From a terrace jutting out from an ancient castle high above the coast, Gabriel stared out at the Ligurian Sea. His long coat whipped around his body, as he stood poised and unyielding against the wind. He concentrated on the point where the ocean vanished into the sky. All sound of the waves that pounded the shoreline faded into silence as he focused on Coco in Los Angeles.

Thoughts of protection and vengeance fed his vampire instincts. In an effort to control his desire to kill, he held his arms at his sides and clenched his hands into fists while he willed his magical warlock side forward. The muscles in his neck relaxed and he closed his eyes.

He grabbed a handful of stones from his pocket and tossed them to the wind. The stones, polished and worn, gathered together and hung in mid-air.

"Where is she?" he asked. A blast of unseen energy struck his body, forcing his head to fall back and his arms to open wide. Adrenaline pumped through his body as his mind plunged into another world in which he could remotely experience what was happening to Coco.

Her athletic body glistened with sweat while blood pounded through her veins. Deep in the oak woodland and out of sight, a mountain lion shadowed her.

Gabriel knew well the figure of death as it ran in reckless pursuit of Coco. Her scent of orange blossom mixed with lavender and wild geraniums lingered in his nose and sent a rush of pleasure throughout his body.

Gabriel stared at the ancient Nordic rune that floated in front of him.

It was the symbol Thurisaz.

He felt the omnipotent power of the immortal seer behind him. "The gateway rune. You are being asked to wait," a heavily-accented female voice said. "If you choose to go to her now, then the past twenty-eight years will have been in vain. Make your decision wisely, my son."

"This time you ask too much of me," Gabriel said. "Without my blood, she may die."

"The runes have—"

"Can you promise me that she will live?"

The seer placed her right palm under her chin and blew across it slowly and gently. A tiny crystalline ball rolled across her hand and balanced on the tips of her fingers. Gabriel stared into the sphere and received his answer.

O

Christopher pushed back his chair and stood. His hands gripped the edge of his mahogany desk, causing his knuckles to turn white. He received the vision of Coco running along the pitch-dark trail. He searched for an opening in Coco's consciousness, and when he found it, he gently reached out to her. He sensed confusion flood her psyche and hoped she would recognize his presence. After all, this linking of minds was a game they had played as children. He saw her vividly, as she pushed back the strands of hair that fell across her face. He sensed the rise of panic as it spread throughout her body. At that moment, Christopher identified the threat to her life.

He breathed in deeply, willed himself to let go of his fear, and centered his mind on reason and logic. His eyes focused on the view through the window of his spacious corner office on the sixth floor. The Washington Monument and the Capitol Building acted like anchors and guided him back to his current reality. He turned from the window to face his floor-to-ceiling bookcase. His focus touched upon one book in particular before his cell phone rang. When he answered, he heard the anxiety and distress in Layla's voice.

"I'm with her."

"How bad is it?"

"A car hit her hard. The paramedics are here——"

"Layla! How bad is it?"

"I'm not a medical doctor, Christopher! She's lost a lot of blood. She's unconscious and a bone is protruding from her leg. I need to go. I have to talk to the paramedics."

Layla ended the call.

He stormed out of his office. His secretary, Michelle, glanced up from her computer screen. "I need a car and flight to L.A., pronto," he said. "My sister's been in an accident."

"Of course," Michelle replied. "Is she okay?"

"I don't know."

Michelle dialed a number. "I'll have the driver meet you downstairs immediately." Christopher took off toward the stairwell, bypassing the elevator.

The limousine pulled up to the front of the building and the doorman opened the main door for Christopher. Once inside the limousine, he checked his phone. A text message from Michelle: *Plane will be ready when you arrive at the airport. I've told John the destination is Los Angeles. Driver will be curbside to pick you up.*

Christopher called his grandfather. He listened as the soft-spoken and calming voice of Kishu answered.

"What's happened?" Kishu asked.

"Coco's been hit by a car, Layla's with her."

"Do you know the extent of her injuries?"

"No, but I know she needs you and Gabriel ASAP."

"I'll leave immediately. There was always the chance her identity would be uncovered. We've been lucky for a long time."

Christopher hung up and dialed a programmed number.

Gabriel answered, his Italian accent sounding smooth and controlled. "I've spoken with Layla. This was no accident. It was the work of a master hitman."

Christopher took in a slow breath before answering. He was fighting the impulse to hit something. "Kishu's on his way and I'm en route to the airport."

"Our people found the hitman's car abandoned, but full of scent. They'll watch over it until I arrive. Until then." Gabriel ended the call.

The limo pulled into the gated parking lot and Christopher began walking toward the Allegiance's private Gulfstream G650 jet. When he reached the stairs, the familiar faces of the crew greeted him. Christopher passed them without smiling. Better to be alone if he wanted to try and break through to Coco's mind. He sat on a white leather chair, controlled his breathing, and extended his mind to the quiet place where he hoped to connect with his sister. But he slammed into a lifeless void. His pulse quickened as he fought back the perverse panic that awaited him in the shadows of the darkest side of his ego.

CHAPTER 3

A rapid movement makes Coco's eyes snap open. A flock of egrets soars into the sky. Rays of the sun's life-giving energy suffuse her body. Every particle of her soul feels rejuvenated. She pushes herself up onto one arm and gazes at the sight before her. The dazzling blue sky and the emerald green grass that sways in the breeze with a steady rhythm hypnotizes her.

Coco hears someone calling her name and sits up. She sees a cabin. Stone steps lead up to a porch, where two chairs rest. She squints, creating a deeper depth of field, and detects the outline of a man sitting on one of the chairs. The other chair is empty.

"Coco…"

This time she hears the voice in her head—warm and inviting. Her stomach flutters. She inhales and is immersed in the euphoria. But then the ghost of uncertainty torments her. She wills the euphoria back, and a whisper of love caresses her. She smiles and heads toward the man in the chair.

The closer she gets to the house, the stronger the feelings of serenity and belonging grow within her. She sits in the empty chair and the man turns to face her. As he does, she takes in everything about him: the scent of sandalwood and berries, his untamed elegance, and the unusual golden hue of his eyes, which stare at her profoundly. He hands her a small sketchbook. She turns it over and studies the leather binding. It seems familiar to her somehow, but she can't figure out why. An image of her mother's bloodied face *flashes before her just long enough for her to perceive it. Something about her childhood… something connected to the man before her.*

Flashing lights and a loud siren brought Coco back to her body, which felt like a nest of physical pain. A gloved hand pulled a mask over her mouth and she felt a sting in her arm. For a moment, the agony deserted her but then another wave of pain rose and made her body tremor. Was she going into shock? The upsurge of panic in her blood and the thrashing of her heartbeat in her ears became louder with each passing second.

Breathe… breathe… you need to focus. These words became her mantra. She repeated them over and over again in her mind. Gradually, her sense of hearing became clearer. She heard a man's voice.

"Excuse me, miss. Do you know the patient? Any information regarding her identity would be appreciated."

"Her name is Coco Rhodes," she heard Layla say, "and she lives in Westwood…on Le Conte. I need to stay with her. She's like a sister to me."

"No problem. Come with me."

The flashing red lights fade, and Coco slips in and out of consciousness.

For a while, Coco forgot all about the accident. Her mind rode the morphine drip to past memories. She remembered the finality of the graduation ceremony ten weeks ago, saying goodbye to her students, the hugs and tears, families, and photographs. She saw a photograph of an old boyfriend—Sam, the graduate student in the film department, and a screenwriter. They had dated last year—he was a few years younger than her. She was attracted to his eclectic style—a little grunge, a little beatnik.

"Marry me," he had proposed on their third date.

"It's the idea of marriage that you're in love with, not me." Her answer had caused his film noir moodiness to raise its complicated head and made him withdraw. He had gone back to writing, and she to her paintings.

That relationship was an exception to the norm, as most of them had ended with Christopher interrogating and intimidating her suitors.

Once, while out to dinner with a date, she recognized one of Christopher's bodyguards at a nearby table. When she and her date left the restaurant, she had handed the muscular protector a hundred-dollar bill with a note, asking that he stay behind. Not that it mattered. His car followed them back to her place.

"You paternal prick!" she had yelled at her brother.

"Trust me," Christopher said later. "Our father would not have let half of your dates in the house."

"Fuck you!" Coco had replied, slamming the door behind her.

Whereas art was Coco's love, social justice was Christopher's. When he had suggested that Coco join him on the political path of the Allegiance, she had recoiled. She knew little about her family's association with the clandestine organization and wanted to keep it that way. Coco disliked secrets—they were a reminder of the childhood experiences that had been erased as a result of her parents' tragic death when she was four years old.

Christopher's persona was defined by his physique. His perfectly tailored suits emphasized his sculpted, muscular body, and hid the many scars he'd acquired from protecting the causes he believed in. On the outside, he gave the impression of being all business: the lawyer whistle-blowers call in D.C. when litigation is imminent. But Christopher's heart resided in the pro bono work that he performed for those in need, and for the Allegiance.

A flash of images interrupted her thoughts: red paint splattered on her body, cold hands around her neck, a dog barking.

Coco felt numb. She attempted to hold the images in her mind, but was unable to focus long enough to remember what they meant.

She heard more unfamiliar voices:

"Any allergies?"

"None that we know of…"

The smell of disinfectant drifted into Coco's nose.

"Coco—can you count back from 100?"

Another intense pain gripped her torso, but it ended quickly, and the bright light above her faded to black.

O

Christopher's plane landed in Los Angeles at noon. At 12:01, he had Layla on the line.

"I'm in the car. How's Coco?"

"She's in surgery, but the nurse says she'll be out soon. I'll be glad when you get here."

His breathing calmed. "Layla—"

"This isn't the best time for apologies. We're all on edge—"

"Layla, listen to me… please. I just got off the phone with the guy who runs our security system. It seems that some kind of electrical surge caused the system to crash. I'm sorry for the way I spoke to you. When you ran off after her, I thought I'd lose you too."

"Like I said, we're all on edge. And you and I need each other. See you soon, *mi amore*."

"*Ti amo*," Christopher said.

O

Christopher stared at the traffic lights through the car windows. The secrets he'd kept from Coco and the round-the-clock surveillance did not make for a close sibling relationship. But Layla understood his internal struggles. While his work as an attorney often surrounded him with lunacy, Layla kept him moored to the dock of sanity.

Her family's long association with the Allegiance helped strengthen their connection. Since the U.S. invasion of Iraq, Layla's brothers had worked diligently to help track down the 14,000-plus objects of art stolen from the Iraq Museum. The two families often worked together, and like their ancestors, they fought oppression and suppression in the fields of art and science. But their work remained clandestine, just as it had been in centuries past. Like the Templars, the Allegiance's secrets were many, and their motto—"sine virtute omnia sunt perdita"— without courage, all is lost—formed the basis of everything they did and shaped how they treated those they protected.

The driver pulled the limo up to a stop at the entrance to the Ronald Reagan UCLA Medical Center. Christopher got out and listened past the sounds of sirens and traffic noises around him. He stepped inside the foyer and continued forward. When he found the link to Coco's mind, he clenched his fists as his body felt pulverized with pain. Her pain.

"Be strong, little sister," he said in his mind. "There are too many secrets that I need to share with you. I pray you forgive me." He pressed the button to the fourth floor.

CHAPTER 4

For two hours, Gabriel had stalked Damien. Now he observed him while he sat at the counter of the Gallery Bar at the Biltmore Hotel in downtown L.A. By the look of Damien's attire, he sensed the man had a strong desire to accumulate wealth. He acted bold and impatient, antisocial, and arrogant. But it was his slight limp that made Gabriel wonder if this man had suffered multiple fractures in his youth. A microscopic dip and a delay in his step showed that Damien favored the right side of his body.

Gabriel detected the nervous tremor of Damien's hand, which manifested as a spasm in his thumb every time he lifted his martini glass. The casual onlooker would easily miss this detail, being fooled by the cool front Damien exuded, but not Gabriel.

A statue of a small golden angel rested on the counter facing Damien. Its image was reflected in the glass liquor cabinet behind the bar. Damien's body shivered in response to the vibration of his cell phone. He downed the martini and stared at the caller ID before sliding the power to off. He placed a fifty-dollar bill onto the counter and turned to leave. A large mirror framed in black steel caught his attention, and for a moment he thought he saw the angel behind him stretch its wings. He shook his head and walked toward the exit and the crowded sidewalk.

The hordes of people that congregated in cities gave Damien a sense of anonymity. He watched a group of trendy hipsters from the nearby fashion institute merge onto the sidewalk, mingling with the tourists. When a passerby bumped into him, Damien's hand jerked toward the small revolver nestled under his jacket. Realizing his error, he removed his hand and loosened his tie.

A few more hours and he would board the plane and fly out of the country. He wanted nothing else to do with the cold voice at the other end of his cell. The voice, of course, belonged to one very unhappy client. He remembered the thumping sound when his car had struck Coco and wondered why the Italian wanted her dead. Normally, she wasn't his type, but after seeing her on a daily basis in her tight running clothes, he was beginning to wish that he had fucked her. He'd had his chance many times when she was alone in her loft.

He had watched her from a distance for months, taking meticulous note of her daily routine. Over the past few days, he'd kept near her, remaining unnoticed by the many guards who watched over her. The constant changing of cars, hotels, and false names were a few of the reasons why his services carried a high price.

But where the fuck did that mountain lion come from? What were the odds? I'd timed it perfectly, watched that fitness freak run the trail for six months. And what the fuck kind of woman runs that much anyway? Christ, I even played the part of a war veteran just to get into her dumbass art therapy class.

He looked at his watch, then turned into a nearby parking lot, his pace quickening. *Two more blocks and I'm there. Hopefully my usual hooker will be home and give me some relief before I head for the airport.*

He turned down an alley where broken and boarded-up windows further marred the decrepit buildings. Bits of wrappers and Styrofoam cups lined the curb and stuck into the surrounding chain-link fences. The stench of urine rose from the gutters, and cars puttered by with faded paint and rusted bodies. Across the street an entire wall showed a painting of a small boy, his hands in prayer. Next to this image the words *Jesus Saves* had been spray-painted in vibrant blues and purples.

Damien stopped at a building, and scoffed once again at the mural of the Virgin Mary that covered the front wall. Above the main door an awning hung from its metal frame, indicating that the building had once been a hotel. He stepped inside and hiked up the steps until he stumbled onto the landing on the fifth floor.

"Damn those fuckin' bourgeois martinis!"

His right hand reached down in a futile effort to adjust his erect penis. *Should have shagged the Italian blonde. Maybe the two women together…*

While Gabriel waited behind an arched alcove halfway between the landing and the fire escape, Damien's thoughts slammed into his mind. It was difficult for Gabriel to get past his desire to kill Damien, but he needed answers. He struggled with the possessive feelings he felt for Coco and the fact that he wanted to destroy anyone who was a threat to her. This trait he had gained from his vampire father, and at times he loathed it. Damien stumbled closer to Gabriel. Another step and Gabriel made his move.

Gabriel clasped his hand over the man's mouth while simultaneously kicking him in his kneecap. The sudden impact ripped tendon, bone, and muscle, forcing Damien to slump to the floor. Gabriel dragged him along the dark hallway toward a fire escape. With a wave of his hand, the heavy door flew open. With his other hand, he tossed Damien onto the landing one floor down. The thud that followed was accompanied by the unmistakable sound of bones popping and a sputtering shriek from Damien.

When Damien reached inside his jacket for his gun, it was snatched away by Gabriel who had jumped down from the floor above. Gabriel spoke in a voice that was low and devoid of emotion. "I want the name of the person who hired you to kill the art professor."

Damien's facial expression flooded with a mix of hatred and anger. When Damien spat at Gabriel, he found himself hanging over the stairwell by his feet. A guttural scream escaped from Damien's mouth and bounced off the metal stairs and doors of the fire escape.

"You are just a tool to them, someone to do their dirty work," Gabriel said. With one hand he hauled Damien up and slammed him back onto the cement floor. His head hit one of the metal handrails, causing a trail of blood to run down his face.

"Give me a name!"

Damien turned his bloodied head toward Gabriel. "There's never a name, you fuckin' piece of shit!"

Gabriel's voice remained calm. "When were you contacted?"

"Fuck off!"

"Do you really think I was the only one following you, or that the person who hired you will let you live?"

Damien responded with silence.

"In a few minutes, when you do not emerge from the building, an assassin will find you and see that you endure insufferable pain before killing you."

Damien's body began to shake. He opened his mouth and

his words came slowly through a demented smile. "Who needs another assassin? You're doing a fuckin' fine job."

"If you cooperate, I'll see that no more harm comes to you."

"Fine," Damien said, gritting his teeth. "Get me the hell out of here."

"First prove that you consent to my terms. Give me something."

Damien's head fell back against the brick wall. "A year ago, I got a call. He never gave me a name. He wanted me to get some DNA from a female professor…"

Gabriel's body tensed. "How did you get it?"

"I took her art class one Saturday. Got some of her hair."

Damien began to lose consciousness. Gabriel pulled him up and pinned him to the wall.

"The woman you tried to kill is the only chance we have at bringing some sense to this world. Give me something useful. "

Damien's pants became wet with urine. "His accent was like yours."

The sound of a door slamming downstairs was followed by two sets of footsteps.

At the sound of men approaching, Gabriel listened for the telltale rhythm of a regular heartbeat. Its absence told him all he needed to know. The assassins were vampires.

When the vampires kicked the door open and entered, Gabriel had disappeared. He watched the intruders' reactions when they saw Damien's mangled body and how their nostrils flared when they realized that something very powerful was standing behind them. Gabriel gauged both vampires to be less than a century old. Children. Almost a pity.

He lunged at the larger of the two, dropped him to the ground, and held him securely. The other assassin threw a kick at Gabriel, but his movements were too slow. With his free arm, Gabriel grabbed his adversary by his shin and flung him against the wall, causing bits of plaster to fall from the ceiling a few floors above. The smaller assassin responded quickly, but instead of attempting to fight Gabriel, he dove for Damien, and heaved him over the stairwell.

Gabriel hurled off the larger vampire, who was trying to pin his arms, and leapt toward Damien. But he was too late. He watched as Damien fell headfirst toward the cement, four floors below. A terrified scream was followed by a dull thump, assuring him of Damien's death. Gabriel grabbed the assassin by the neck and kneed him in the groin, while the larger vampire jumped over the metal railing, landed on the ground floor, and sped off into the city.

Gabriel leaned toward the vampire in his grasp. "You share the stench of Kenan. How did he find her?"

"The same way we found out what hospital she's in."

"How?"

When no answer came, Gabriel shoved his other hand through the vampire's ribcage and squeezed his heart. "My death is imminent," the vampire said through gasps. "If you do not kill me, my lord will."

"Then choose to die a noble death or join the Allegiance. I will grant you asylum," Gabriel said.

"That's not possible."

"It's always possible."

"What makes you think that my lord is acting alone?"

The words sent a shudder through Gabriel's body. The assassin lowered his eyes and began praying. "I now commit my body to the ground—earth to earth, ashes to ashes, dust to dust—"

Gabriel knew that an ancient oath of confidentiality bound the vampire to his master, and so further interrogation was pointless. He tore out the vampire's heart, broke his neck, and ripped the head from his cold body. He watched the remains turn to dust. Gabriel then jumped over the metal railing, to the ground floor and retrieved the cell phone and wallet from

Damien's jacket. He took out his own cell and sent a text to Alessandro, his friend and a powerful member of the Allegiance, advising him to follow the assassin who had escaped. Alessandro responded via text immediately:

Frederico and I have him in our sights—did you get any other information?

Gabriel replied:

Only that his employer's accent was like mine. I'm betting it is Kenan, but we need proof.

Gabriel brought up another name on his cell and pressed call.

"We need to bring her home," he said.

The woman on the other end replied with a calming and heavily accented voice. "Dragging her here against her wishes is not what she needs. She must do this in accordance with free will—that is our way. But in order for that to happen, she needs you to heal her."

"There's something else we need to discuss. The vampire assassin's body turned to dust after his death."

"Anything else?"

"He insinuated that Kenan is not acting alone."

He ended the call and stared at the name on the screen: *Mother*.

In one swift movement, Gabriel waved his arms and vanished.

CHAPTER 5

Christopher sat alone on a bench outside the UCLA Medical Center, scrolling through the mountain of emails, texts and missed calls on his iPhone. He decided that all of them could wait. For the first time since he'd started practicing law, he had doubts about everything. In truth, he wanted what his father had once enjoyed—a wife and kids. His argument against that scenario: his own lost childhood.

He and Kishu had decided to be honest with Coco when she asked about her injuries, but to withhold the fact that this had been a deliberate attempt on her life.

From a young age Christopher had sworn to keep the truth about their family from Coco, and the guilt kept him awake at night. But her birthday was near and Gabriel had promised that this event would bring change.

He looked up through bloodshot eyes to see Gabriel approaching.

"How is she?" Gabriel asked.

"Stable, but there's another surgery scheduled," Christopher said. "I have serious doubts that keeping everything hidden from Coco was the correct thing to do. If she knew the truth, maybe she'd have thought twice about going anywhere on her own."

"You know where I stand," Gabriel said. "But Prudence

believes telling Coco would not have been beneficial to her. She'd have felt trapped, and that is not conducive to self-growth. We must trust her judgment on this matter. I need to see Coco now and hospitals are not easy places for me to be."

Christopher looked at him questioningly.

"It's the blood," Gabriel said as they walked toward the elevator. "Fresh and old—it lingers everywhere—telling stories of the sick and the dead. It reminds me of what I am. To be blunt, if Coco were threatened in this building, I'd be like a kid in a candy store. Any blood type would suffice." The elevator opened and they stepped inside. Christopher pressed the button for the fourth floor and Gabriel continued. "The other side of my heritage senses emotion, and in hospitals the echelon of death constantly hovers, softened only by the beings of light that comfort the sick and their families. Me being here takes immeasurable control."

The elevator chimed and the doors opened. "Ask some of those angels to surround Coco," Christopher said. "She's going to need all the help she can get."

As they approached Coco's curtained room Layla stepped into the hallway. Christopher took her hand and they left Gabriel alone with Coco.

O

Gabriel stared at Coco. Her face, a mess of cuts and bruises and dressings was almost unrecognizable. Tubes and drains were inserted into her body. Monitors kept track of her breathing and pulse rate, and beeped in recognition of her life. The realization of her close brush with death hit Gabriel hard.

He settled himself onto the bed beside her, his eyes and mind scanning her injuries. Without his help it could take a year for her to heal completely. He had seen her face this pale and fragile once before. Twice in one lifetime was too much for one so precious.

Healing the injured was a skill Gabriel had learned from his mother and of all the facets of his attributes it was the one he used with the most passion. He had witnessed her connect to the source of life and breathe energy into those at the brink of death by restructuring cells within their bodies. With her gentle manner, she was the kindest creature he had ever known.

His demeanor softened. He gently brushed Coco's cracked lips with his fingertips, and then kissed her hand next to the spot where the IV needle plunged into her vein. He pulled a small mother-of-pearl embellished penknife from his pocket, made a small cut on his wrist, and held the wound just above Coco's mouth.

A few drops would heal her internal injuries. Any more and people would start to ask questions. Gabriel closed his eyes and focused on the miracle taking place in Coco's body. His immortal blood worked quickly. Tiny blood vessels were already healing and the bruising was easing. He felt her body relaxing. The worst was over for her now, at least in some respects.

He looked up when a nurse in dark blue scrubs entered the room. The card clipped to her shirt identified her as Kate Valentine. He watched as she checked Coco's vital signs and inputted notes into a computer in the corner of the room. When she left, he scanned and rechecked every part of Coco's body using his telepathic abilities. He wanted to pick her up in his arms and take her back to his home in Italy, but knew that now was not the time. She needed rest more than anything else.

When his work was complete, he watched the rapid eye movement behind her closed eyelids. She seemed to be searching for something. Then a single word escaped her mouth in a whisper that only one with his acute sense of hearing would have heard.

"Gabriel."

She was dreaming, her subconscious remembering names from her childhood, names that were locked away. He knew that when Coco awoke she would not remember his name, or anything about her time as a child in Italy.

He bent low. "*Ti amo*, Colombina," he whispered, then reluctantly let go of her hand and went to find Christopher and Layla.

He found them in the waiting room. "While I'm in Italy, Stefan and Prudence will monitor her security," Gabriel said.

"I'm not going anywhere," Christopher said. "I'll set up my office in Westwood."

"At some point you will need to return to D.C."

Christopher put an arm around Layla's shoulders. "We'll discuss that when the time comes."

"I've healed her internal injuries," Gabriel said. "Our M.D., Dr. Fiore, will arrive later this evening. Coco's broken bones still need to mend, but her healing time will be considerably shorter thanks to her bloodline."

Christopher nodded. "I've organized Dr. Fiore's visit with our man on the board here at the hospital. I'm glad I'm a Bruin."

The corners of Gabriel's mouth turned up.

Layla handed him an iPod. "This is for you. I thought you might enjoy the playlists," she said. "Coco made them."

Two hours later, Gabriel occupied a luxury seat in his private jet headed for Italy. This was not his normal method of traveling, but he needed the time to think. He took out the iPod and chose a playlist entitled "Coco's Painting Mix," then reclined his chair and closed his eyes. Bach's Prelude No. 1 in C major reminded him of earlier years at *Casa della Pietra*, his parents' villa in Northern Italy.

In an effort to keep Coco alive, he and Prudence had brought her to *Casa della Pietra* when she was four years old. The little girl's joy had gone. She lay in a daze, unable to speak, eat, or sleep.

"It is time," Prudence said. *"My strength is in the future. Your magic holds the past in ways I cannot."*

Gabriel stared at the little girl. "Blocking her memory is a big deal, Mother. She may come to hate me for it."

"But with them she may die and never live to decide if she wants to forgive you or not."

Prudence had been correct. Once he had blocked Coco's mind from the atrocity she'd witnessed, she gained back her strength, but lost a piece of her life. It had disappeared along with her parents on that tragic day. Prudence had waited until the little girl gained her strength before sharing the first of her carefully worded lies about their deaths.

Gabriel remembered overhearing a conversation a few days before that sad day between Coco and his mother. Their voices had drifted up the stairs where he stood.

"I miss my mommy and daddy, and Chwistopher," four-year old Coco said.

Prudence turned to face the little girl. "I do too, Coco, but Christopher will visit us soon and you can show him the animals—I know he will like that."

"Where's Gabwiel?" Coco asked.

"He is in his office, working."

"Why?"

"Because he is needed by many people, so we have to share him." Prudence took hold of Coco's hand. "Come, we have chickens to feed." The tall, ethereal woman held the little girl's hand in hers, and guided her along the far-reaching hallway.*

Gabriel remembered how, as a young boy, the long hallway seemed to extend forever. He had stared at the shiny floorboards that edged the long carpet runner where peacocks, dragons, and other animals were woven into the fabric. The walls were lined with photographs and paintings of people from other times. Some were faded or cracked, but all were edged with ornate gold frames carved with intricate patterns.

Prudence waved a hand, and the heavy front door opened onto a wide courtyard with steps that led to a rose garden and an orchard beyond. Dogs of all shapes and sizes waited for them. A large German Shepherd ran up to Coco and licked her face, making her smile.

"His name is Alexander," Prudence said, "I think he likes you."

Coco put her arms around the dog's neck and buried her face in his fur before looking up at Prudence. "I like it here," she said. "Can Alexander sleep in my room?"

Prudence bent down so that she was at eye level with Coco, "Yes, but it shall be our secret. I do not believe that Gabriel's dog rules include letting them sleep with humans on their beds."

"Then why has he got so many dogs?"

"He cannot stand seeing them locked up, and so he rescues them from shelters and brings them home. Gabriel is a big softy."

"I love Gabwiel," Coco said.

"I know you do, Coco. I love him too."

Keith Richards and the opening bars of "Beast of Burden" brought Gabriel out of his trance. He grinned. *How appropriate*, he thought, as he turned up the volume. Over the next few hours, he assessed the information he had gained. He figured that by the time Coco's injuries healed completely it would be her birthday, and the runes had shown him that shortly after she would return to Italy.

Ignacio twisted the heavy-set gold ring on his middle finger. He was not a lover of Los Angeles—he preferred the familiarity of

London and Paris. L.A. was a young city, a fact he felt was confirmed by the multiple city centers, a mediocre rail system, and the deplorable number of fast food restaurants that catered to oversized customers. A twinge in his belly reminded him that he too had carnal needs to fulfill. His dark Ray-Ban aviators concealed his black eyes, allowing his hunger to go unnoticed. Business first. Then dinner.

Bloody Kenan and his human hitman boy-toys. What a screw-up. Now my task is infinitely more arduous with members of the Allegiance hovering around every freakin' corner.

He slid the gold ring leisurely up and down his finger.

Ignacio's sources had confirmed that Gabriel was headed for the airport, and that meant he would finally be able to get some information about the female professor.

Best way to gather information about a patient is from the primary source. Maybe I'll have a little fun with some of her nurses.

Over the following week Ignacio took note of every nurse that went in and out of the ICU ward. He learned each nurse's name and whether they were married, single, gay, straight, or undecided. He heard them discussing in whispers about a woman who had been involved in a hit-and-run, but seemed to be making a miraculous recovery—a detail he tucked neatly away.

By the sixth day he had narrowed down his list of candidates and chosen his prey: Kate Valentine. A single woman with kinky sexual tendencies, who was dedicated to nursing and loved champagne. He balled his hand into a fist and covered it with his right hand. With a quick jolt he cracked his knuckles.

"Well then, nurse Valentine—let the shenanigans begin!"

CHAPTER 6

Coco's thoughts drifted between the gently swaying green field from her dreams and the soft pink hues of dawn that filtered through the window. She succumbed to the pull of reality and focused on the silhouette of Christopher. He had his back turned to her as he stared out of the window.

Only a whisper escaped her mouth when she spoke her brother's name, but he responded as if she had shouted it.

"Hey sis," he said. "Welcome back." Taking a handkerchief from his pocket, he wiped away the tears that Coco was failing to hold back.

She looked at him with pleading eyes. "What happened?"

"Let's wait until your doctor arrives."

"No—you're my family," Coco said. "I want to hear about it from you."

Christopher's eyes glistened with moisture. He pulled up a chair and placed his hand on hers. "You were hit by a car."

"And…"

She noticed Christopher lower his head and inhale slowly, doing his best to hide his own signs of stress and fatigue. "The right side of your femur has a simple compound fracture, your right shoulder was dislocated, and you have two cracked ribs…"

"What else?"

"Cerebral contusion, bruising of the brain. But it's under control. You're going to be strong again. How do you feel?"

"Like I've been hit by a car."

"Well, it seems the contusion didn't bruise your capacity for sarcastic remarks."

Coco managed a smile.

"Grandpa arrived hours after you were brought here," Christopher said. "Now that you're conscious, he can work his healing magic on you."

Christopher stood and turned to leave.

"Chris?"

"Yes."

"Before the car hit, I heard Layla call my name. Why would she be there when it happened?"

Christopher looked at his shoes. "Like I said, cerebral contusion. From what I understand, a lot of memories get scrambled when that sort of thing happens. But I wouldn't be worried about it."

"So, she wasn't there?"

"No."

"Okay, good. Because if she was, I'd start to think that everything I saw that night was real."

"Why? What else did you see?"

"I thought I saw a mountain lion. Silly, right?"

A woman in a white lab coat entered the room and was followed by Layla, who held a large familiar ball of fluff. She laid the big cat gently on the bed, where the feline limped over to Coco.

"What happened to her?" Coco asked.

"The side gate had been left unlatched—she escaped," Layla said. "I found her on your doorstep two days later. The vet thinks she may have been hit by a car."

"Oh my God," Coco said. "I'm so sorry, you poor little

thing." Thalia snuggled in beside Coco and purred loudly. "You and me both, huh?" Coco added.

"Just make sure she stays in here," the woman in the white coat said, keeping her eyes on Coco's chart. Her non-negotiable dialogue flowed from her rose-colored lips. "Coco, my name is Dr. Fiore, and I am handling your case. Do you have any questions?"

"How long have I been here?" Coco asked.

"Just over a week. You have tough months ahead, but for now you need to rest. That's an order."

A soft knock at the door interrupted the conversation. Coco looked up to see her grandfather enter the room. His thinning white hair framed the smooth skin of his face. And when his lips broke into his trademark smile, her world seemed a little lighter. He crossed the room in a few quick steps and stood beside the bed.

"Little one," Kishu said. "It's good to see your eyes open." He turned to Dr. Fiore. "Do I have your approval to use some natural healing techniques on my granddaughter, doctor?"

"Christopher has already asked for my approval," she said. "Go ahead. My guess is that the staff will be lining up wanting your shiatsu treatments themselves in a matter of days. I will see you later today, Miss Rhodes."

"Thank you, doctor," Coco said.

Dr. Fiore slipped out of the room and Christopher and Layla followed.

Kishu gently laid his hands on Coco's shoulders. After a minute, the tension in her body succumbed to the healing energy that pulsed through his hands. "Let me know if it's too much and I'll pull back," he said.

From the little she knew about the Allegiance, Coco understood that each member had pledged to learn a particular ability. For Kishu, his talent lay in natural healing, specifically a mix of traditional Japanese reiki, shiatsu, and the ancient practice of Chinese qigong. She had no doubt that he would be in charge of her rehabilitation. But while medicine and physical therapy would in time heal her physical injuries, she knew they could not ease her mental trauma.

She remembered how Kishu had encouraged Christopher's and her love of learning. He'd provided them with an education focused on inquiry-based learning and lengthy Socratic discussions around the dinner table. He understood Christopher's pull toward social justice and his inherent desire to help others. At the same time he nurtured and respected her need to paint and run.

"I'm scared, Grandpa," Coco said. "And so tired." Tears brimmed in her eyes.

"What you are feeling is perfectly normal after surgery," Kishu said. "Your body and your mind need to rest."

"Will you tell me a story—like you did when I was a little girl?"

Kishu eased himself onto the chair next to Coco's bed and placed his hands in his lap. "I'll tell you the legend of Astridr. It begins with her mother, Sonja, the great Nordic seer. Do you remember this tale, little one?"

"Just bits and pieces."

Kishu closed his eyes for a moment; when they blinked open they were drenched with the joyous twinkle of a storyteller. "Sonja had been held against her will in the city of Constantinople, by men intent on using her talents to bring them riches."

Coco's head rested against the pillows. "Keep going," she said.

Kishu continued. "Sonja waited patiently, and in the year 860 A.D., an army of Vikings rescued her and then turned their mighty warships back toward their homeland. But what the gods had in mind for Sonja was much greater than the life of a seer.

As the boat headed north, the sky dimmed to a dark indigo and thunderclouds spread across the horizon. The sea roared and raven-colored waves crashed against the boat. Their white tips seized hold of the men and dragged them, one by one, into the depths of the icy cold waters."

Coco's eyes drew heavy. She watched Kishu walk over to the window and run the tip of a finger through condensation that had gathered in the upper corner of the glass. She thought of Sonja, alone and frightened, as Kishu's words became one with her dreams.

○

Coco slept for most of the next day, and when she awoke, her grandfather's familiar smile greeted her. He gently washed her face and hands and encouraged her to sip from a cup of water. But all Coco wanted was for Kishu to tell her more stories.

"I shall tell you about the work your brother does—"

"He's a lawyer," Coco said with a hint of sarcasm.

"A very good lawyer. Just as you are a very talented artist."

"I haven't painted for months," Coco confessed through tears. "I don't know what's happening to me. My creativity is as blank as the canvas that stares back at me from the easel in my studio... I'm empty."

"You will find your creativity again, but perhaps you need a new teacher."

She shook her head. "I used to imagine that I was something special, like Grandma Mimi... the stories that you told me about her and my mother, how their art was something pure."

"Yes, but they were both taught by a great teacher. Have you thought about becoming a student again, not here, but perhaps in Europe?"

"I enjoy learning, you know that. But Europe?" Coco laid

her head back against the heap of pillows and concealed a yawn with her good hand. "I'm not sure I can handle that."

Kishu relaxed back in his chair and closed his eyes. *"sine virtute omnia sunt perdita."*

"Pardon, Grandpa?"

"Without courage, all is lost."

"*sine*...what?"

"*virtute omnia sunt perdita.*"

"That sounds like something Christopher would say." She drifted off to sleep memorizing the phrase.

At night, after the nurses had changed shifts, the hospital corridor harbored strange sounds, and Coco struggled to settle herself. A woman in a room a few doors down whimpered in her sleep. She sounded like a distressed puppy. The hushed whispers of nurses' conversations about husbands and wives, lovers, and stubborn patients all drifted back to her room. Coco had memorized how many steps it took each nurse to get from her bed to the door and back to the nurses' station and if they ran or walked. She had it all down. But the dead silence between these moments filled her head with dread.

Before the accident, she had exhausted herself by running miles every day. The repetitive movement of bringing one foot in front of the other brought order to her life, and the minute she felt her mind drifting toward her childhood, she would take off for a mini marathon run into the Santa Monica Mountains. But now she could not run and that meant facing her demons. And no medications helped calm her thumping heart and frantic mind.

Coco had awakened one evening with the sense that someone was standing next to her. At first she thought it was one of the nurses and was surprised when she opened her eyes and saw that no one was there.

She attributed it to the medications she was on, until it happened again the next night. She was not scared because Thalia seemed calm, and in her mind there was no better intruder alert than her beloved cat. But her intrigue grew when she discovered that on the mornings following her anonymous visits, she would find a few sprigs of lavender on her bedside cupboard. The perfume brought back memories of a garden full of lavender bushes, but the memories extended no further. As the weeks rolled by, the loyal delivery of the sprigs of purple flowers became a constant in Coco's life. For the first time in months, she found herself looking forward to the evenings.

The previous week, Christopher had brought Coco a sketchbook and pencils, and left them on her bedside table. She had ignored them, until one night she awoke from the recurring dream she'd had where the man with the dark eyes had handed her the small sketchbook. She felt compelled to draw him. His face had been the last image she had painted, and the canvas now rested on an easel in her apartment.

Coco reached for the sketchbook and a pencil and began to draw. Gradually the lines and dots took on form until his image appeared on the page. She stared at him for hours before falling asleep. When she awoke, three sprigs of lavender lay on the pillow beside her. She lifted them to her nose, closed her eyes, and breathed in the scent. An image flashed before her: *sprigs of freshly cut lavender... a wooden picture frame...*

Coco pressed the lavender against her chest. The explosion of sweetness and a tiny touch of camphor showered her imagination with colors from her well-used palette. She breathed in the scent as she searched for a color to go with it. "Purple," she said, "It always smells so purple."

CHAPTER 7

Coco's face flushed with anger, but Christopher remained firm. No matter what she said or how hard she begged, there was no hope in hell that her brother would allow her to return to her loft.

"The answer is no, and please don't ask me again," he said on his way out of her room. "Frankly, the idea is ludicrous."

She was well aware, after enduring four weeks of multiple surgeries and treatments, that she had weeks of recuperation ahead of her. But for some reason, Christopher insisted on her staying elsewhere with Layla and Kishu, rather than stay in Westwood. His excuse was that he needed to return to D.C. and couldn't look after her.

Frustrated, Coco turned to the middle-aged nurse who had entered the room moments before Christopher stormed out. "Is there any part of my body that I could use to hit my brother without undergoing surgery again?"

"And take the chance of damaging that gorgeous body and face of his? Sorry sweetie, but for the sake of every nurse in this hospital, I can't be a part of anything that might cause your brother bodily harm." She handed Coco a glass of water and a Dixie cup that seemed to be overflowing with pills. "Bon appétit,

I'll be back in a bit with paperwork for you to sign. Layla is on her way to pick you up."

Coco downed the pills, and handed the empty cup back to the nurse. "I miss my own place."

"And I miss my youth, but hey, that's life. It's going to be a while before you're strong enough to be on your own. Meanwhile, let your family and friends help you. Especially that tall one, with the high cheekbones and come-to-bed eyes."

"I have no idea who that is. I must have been asleep or delirious whenever he came to visit."

"Hey, he's great eye candy, and if I were you he'd be my incentive to heal quickly!"

O

Layla turned the car down the gravel driveway and opened the windows. "The air smells so good," she said.

"Jasmine?" Coco asked.

Layla sniffed the air again. "And the ocean. *Perfetto*."

Something about the tall trees that lined the driveway seemed both familiar and foreboding. Coco closed her eyes and willed the memory forward, but just like the lavender she could not give the scent a home.

Layla interrupted her thoughts. "The young girl that you used to tutor—"

"Arianna," Coco said. "Yes, I need to call her."

"She came by the loft a few days ago. She's worried because she hadn't heard from you in a while."

"Yeah, we were going to get together over the summer break."

"I explained everything to her, and she sends you her love and says to get better. She left a card for you and I put it in your bedroom. She also said she could do with some advice."

"I wonder what that's about—hopefully grad school."

Gabriel had purchased the Malibu property when Christopher began his freshman year in college. The location had proven useful for Allegiance meetings as more and more of the group's youngest flocked to American universities. The house had been designed like a fortress, with one side overlooking the Pacific Ocean and the remaining five acres buffered by high fences and cypress trees. The area closest to the house remained clear of clutter—the equivalent of a castle moat.

Christopher had waited at the front of the house to meet Layla and Coco. He opened the car door and helped Coco into the wheelchair he had procured for her, a little unsure of how to break the ice after their disagreement in the hospital.

"I hate it when you're angry with me," he said.

"I know, it kills me too, but right now it's the only weapon I have," Coco said, staring at the brace around her leg. "I'm a little frustrated, I need to work out."

"I understand," Christopher said. "But physical therapy takes time—"

"I'm guessing you're about to lecture me."

"Me? Never."

Coco rolled her eyes.

"Now that you're here, Layla's going to help Grandpa with your physical therapy," he said. "Please listen to them."

"We promise to take it easy on you for the first few days," Layla said.

"I'll take my physical therapy torture-style if it means I can do the Temescal run on my birthday."

Christopher tipped back the chair and headed to the front door. "We'll see about that, little sister."

Christopher noted that upon entering the house, Coco's disposition changed. The natural beauty of the house immediately seemed to put her at ease. The stark whiteness of the exterior made a striking contrast to the dark wood and high ceilings of the inside. Light filtered in everywhere.

"This place reminds me of the lanai at the house in Hawaii, it's beautiful," Coco said. Christopher made no reply. The sound of running water made Coco urge Christopher to wheel her toward a rock wall, where water trickled down to form an indoor pond. "How come I've never seen this place before?" she asked.

"It belongs to the Allegiance."

Coco turned to face her brother. "You think you can bribe me into joining the Allegiance… with a fancy beachfront house in Malibu, a pool, and an indoor pond?"

"On the contrary. That's why I've never brought you here before."

O

Twenty-five miles away, Ignacio leaned against the wall of the entrance to the UCLA Medical Center. He twisted the ring on his finger and stopped when he sensed the nurse approaching. As she came closer, he turned and gave her one of his suggestive smirks.

"Hey handsome," Kate said. "I thought you were out of town on business."

Ignacio grabbed her by the waist and kissed her hard and deep. He could feel her heartbeat picking up and forcing the blood to the surface of her skin. He broke away and raised an eyebrow at her.

"You have bewitched me, Kate. I needed to see you again."

"Well, aren't I the lucky girl? I'm off duty for the next twelve hours."

"Then it's a good thing that my hotel is just around the corner." He took her hand in his.

Three hours and three bottles of champagne later, Ignacio sat naked on the bed, his legs stretched around hers and his back against the wall. Her perfectly tanned body lodged between his thighs.

He massaged her neck. "Any wacky stuff going on at work? ICU must be bonkers."

"Yeah, it can be. But lately they've mostly been normal cases, nothing too out of the ordinary." She was almost purring at his touch. "That professor I told you about, she finally got to go home. Poor thing, she'd been at the hospital four weeks, and in ICU for a big part of it."

Now we're talkin', luv…

"Sounds like quite a story… more bubbly?" He filled up her glass and kissed her neck. He'd be getting closer to that part of her body a little later, but first he needed her to keep talking.

"She's lucky to be alive. We were all pretty surprised that she pulled through—such a mess when she arrived, some kind of hit-and-run accident." Kate took another sip from her glass. "Can't say we'll miss her brother. So damn demanding. I guess he's some big-time lawyer in D.C. 'Get her this, get her that' but he was gorgeous to look at."

She emptied her glass.

Ignacio refilled it. "Should I be jealous?"

"Hardly. He's not my type," she said. "I like you… and your games."

Ignacio let out a carnal growl and leaned Kate forward

so that he could slide out from behind her. "Well, I'm sure the young lass must have been happy to go home," he said.

"No chance. Apparently they whisked her off to some fancy Malibu mansion for some R&R."

Thank you, luv...

Ignacio walked over to the chair where he had tossed his leather satchel, and placed it on the bedside table. Opening it, he extracted a pair of silk stockings, and in seconds was straddling Kate. "These will do the trick."

"Mmmm... yes, please."

He took the glass from her and placed it on the bedside table, then held a hand out toward her. She stared longingly at him, and placed her hands in his. He took a stocking and wound it around her wrist. Then he tied the other before securing both of her hands to the headboard. He kissed her mouth with wanton hunger.

"Kate, you're not going to remember any of what I'm about to do to you." Her eyes suddenly widened and her body squirmed as Ignacio pulled out another silk stocking and stuffed it into her mouth. He stared into her eyes and used his vampire allure to subdue her.

"I suggest you close your eyes, luv, because you're going on a little trip." She was completely under his control, and in seconds he had a rubber strap around her arm and was releasing the fluid from the syringe into her veins. "Fear and H, my favorite cocktail," Ignacio said. Kate sighed. Ignacio waited until her heart rate slowed and then plunged his fangs into her neck.

Over the next few weeks, Kishu regulated Coco's schedule. He introduced herbs into her diet and administered acupuncture daily. When he felt she was strong enough, he held her body and guided her through a series of slow-moving meditations. Each day concluded with massage and silent meditation. After the third week, Coco was able to stand in the hanmi position on her own to practice. A few months ago this would have been easy, but now this simple act of standing—one foot in front of the other, knees slightly bent—took all of her concentration.

Coco looked to Kishu for encouragement. "You know, I Googled 'simple compound fractures,' and my other injuries and I seem to be healing at an extremely fast pace."

Kishu poured hot water into a small Chinese teapot. "It would be a different story if you had not been as healthy as you were before the accident."

"But I'm about four months ahead of others with similar injuries, doesn't that seem remarkable to you?"

Kishu nodded. "You are a remarkable young lady, so, no—I do not find this in any way strange. Plus, you have a good team working with you."

Coco shrugged. "I guess. But then how do you explain my hair? Is it my imagination or does it seem to be growing faster than before the accident."

"Must be the herbs," Kishu said.

O

Kishu had requested that Layla begin to implement longer strengthening sessions to keep up with Coco's accelerated rehabilitation. Layla knew that the pain Coco endured during these periods must be excruciating, but Coco insisted on pushing her own boundaries.

"Let's take a day off and relax," Layla suggested one morning after completing their morning qigong practice.

Coco shook her head. "I'm going to be thirty-two soon and I

made a promise to myself. Come October thirty-first, I'm doing the Temescal run again, minus the bumper."

Layla's body language revealed nothing, though she felt Christopher would forbid Coco from running that particular trail. "Then we'd better get you strong again."

"It's been ten weeks," Coco said. "Being this dependent on everyone is driving me crazy."

They made their way into the workout room, and Coco began stretching her legs. Layla watched Coco's body undergo a series of muscle spasms.

"Shit! I just tweaked something," Coco said.

Layla walked over to her. "Which part of your leg is in pain?" she asked.

Coco grimaced and the tears flowed. "My leg will be fine, it's my head that's fucked up."

Layla helped Coco over to a chair and perched next to her. "It's good to cry. Let it all out."

"I want to go home, back to work—my friends and my students. I'm sorry, I don't mean to sound ungrateful. It's me that I'm angry with," Coco said through sobs. "I've caused so much disruption to everyone's lives."

There was a soft knock at the door. Kishu entered and went directly to Coco. He placed one hand on her abdomen and the other on her forehead. "I think you need some TLC and a visit to your loft," he said.

Coco stopped crying for a moment and looked at Kishu in disbelief. "Really, I can go home?"

"For a few hours, yes." He helped Coco stand and turned to Layla. "We'll be back for dinner." Layla watched as Kishu and Coco walked along the hallway and out the front door.

She was about to open her mouth to protest, when Christopher appeared behind her in the doorway of the gym, and whispered in her ear, "She needs some space, and Kishu will look after her. Besides, I can empathize with her... it's not easy being away from what makes you happy."

"But is it a good idea?" Layla spoke softly. "Whoever planned the hit and run is still out there."

"Nothing will happen to her, Gabriel's in town. We met earlier to discuss some other matters."

"When did you arrive?" Layla asked. Her body relaxed into Christopher's.

"Two this morning." He turned her around and pulled her into his arms. "I have to return to D.C. in about three hours." He kicked the door closed, locked it, and then Layla felt his mouth on hers.

○

Christopher released the clip that held back Layla's hair, and watched as it cascaded around her face and over her shoulders. "You are so beautiful," he whispered, and kissed her again. He lifted her light blue tank over her arms, and felt Layla's fingers undo the belt on his suit pants, and slowly lower the zipper. He felt her desire for him as it spread throughout her body, and when he found her tender spot she lost control. By the time he entered her she was coming again, wanting more, and he gave it to her before releasing his own desire inside of her.

"I miss you," Christopher whispered, as he held her against his chest.

It had been Layla's eyes that captivated Christopher the day he had been uncharacteristically late and run headlong into her. It had happened when he jumped out of a taxicab on his way to an Allegiance meeting near the corner of St. James's Street and Park Place in London. He raced up to the concierge in the hotel at the precise moment that Layla had turned to leave. He stared into her azure eyes and froze. "Are you a fairy queen?" he asked as his gaze lingered to her Cupid's bow upper lip, and then back to her eyes.

Layla looked at him questioningly. "Do you believe in fairies?"

"I do now," he said, and as quickly as his world had become empty at age seven, it was filled with love and joy for Layla. When the time came for Christopher to return to Los Angeles and law school, Layla relocated there, transferring to UCLA to continue her studies in psychology. Her intelligence and verve matched his, except when it came to cars. Layla's passion for driving fast cars made Christopher somewhat nervous.

Layla rested her head on his shoulder. "I miss you too, *mi amore.*"

Christopher carried her to a set of workout mats and laid her down. He held her perfectly-sculptured back close to his body, finding comfort in running his fingers through her hair. He spoke softly and with sincerity. "Will you marry me, Layla?"

She turned to him, resting her head on her hand. "Yes, *mi amore.*"

Framing her face with his hands, he went to kiss her. But she ducked away and climbed on top of him.

"You know I can read your face," he said. "I know what you're thinking."

Layla placed kisses on his eyelids, nose, and mouth before finding her way to his ears. "And are you okay with what I'm thinking now?" she asked.

"More than okay."

She found his lips again, allowing her tongue to explore his mouth while they made love again, slowly, with sensual desire.

CHAPTER 8

Kishu stayed quiet. He wanted to give Coco the time she needed to regain her composure. He drove up the California Incline and across Ocean to Wilshire Boulevard. He noticed her shoulders relax when she caught sight of her favorite coffee shop, and her first Big Blue Bus sighting brought a smile to her face. As he pulled the car into the driveway of the family lofts in Westwood, Kishu punched in his code and the garage door opened. He killed the engine and walked around to the passenger side, where Coco was struggling to stand up.

Kishu went to hold onto her, but she held up her hands in resistance. "I've got this, thanks, Grandpa." He stepped aside to let her pass. "I didn't mean to sound grumpy. It's just that I want to walk on my own. But please stay with me, I don't want to fall."

"Wait one moment," Kishu said as he opened the door to the back of the car and picked up a walking stick. "This will help." He handed it to Coco.

"Thanks."

They walked to the steps that led to Coco's loft. "I understand what it's like to have your spirit and body broken," Kishu said, with a wistful look in his eyes. "Our bodies have the ability to heal remarkably quickly. But our minds take time. Be kind to yourself."

Coco nodded. "I don't like feeling this angry—it's not who I am, but I don't know how to change it."

"Growth does not know time, little one," Kishu said.

Coco released a sigh of frustration. "I'm definitely going to need help with these damned stairs!"

"I thought you might. Here, hold onto my arm and we'll go nice and slow. I think the more time we give Christopher and Layla alone, the better."

"Don't make me laugh or I'll fall and hurt my ribs." Coco began the slow ascent. "I doubt they made it out of the work-out room."

Kishu grinned.

"My brother would never admit it," Coco said. "But he's so much nicer when Layla's with him."

"To find such love in a lifetime is divine."

They were at the top of the landing, outside the door to Coco's loft, when Kishu handed Coco the key. She unlocked the door, opened it, and stepped over the threshold. Kishu could relax a little, knowing that Gabriel had inspected the loft and surrounding area prior to their arrival. He pulled a worn-out copy of *The Love Poems of Rumi* from his pocket and settled into a chair on the small balcony. From here he had a full view of the kitchen and studio area. "I'm here if you need me, and will prepare lunch shortly."

Coco hobbled over to the balcony. "When did you know that you'd be bringing me here?"

"I understand how it is to recover from injuries. At some point, you have to get away from everyone, to find your auton-omy again." He looked up at her from his book. "You know, in all the excitement, everyone seems to have forgotten about the cause of this fiasco, but not me. You were showing signs of going a little crazy a few days ago, when you got upset because I beat you in Scrabble. My winning is not exactly an anomaly."

"I'm a mess."

"Are you sure?" he asked. "Out of chaos comes creativity."

"Hmm, maybe…" Coco said.

It had been ten weeks since her accident. And yet, after all of the pain Coco had endured, nothing seemed more discomforting than facing the painting she had left covered on her easel. She crossed the room, stood before it, and clenched her jaw. Her breathing accelerated. Another step, and she reached out and pulled the blanket away. It fell, like amber liquid onto the floor. The intense dark eyes that belonged to the man in her dreams stared back at her.

Using the tip of her index finger she traced the man's jawline. When her skin brushed against the paint, the image of a bloodied face flashed before her, accompanied by a rush of energy. She felt as if she'd been stung.

She quickly turned away and calmed her breathing as she headed for the staircase.

"Need help with the stairs?" Kishu asked.

"I'm good, thanks. I can hang onto the handrail." Coco hobbled slowly up the 1960s-styled floating steps that led to her bedroom.

Coco loved her loft—the natural light, the fact that she could walk to work, and the humble exterior made it a perfect home for her. The day she had seen the *For Sale* sign go up on the old building, she had called her brother begging that he loan her the money to buy it. Seeing the investment possibilities of the property, Christopher had made an offer and the two of them bought it together.

They'd hired an architect buddy of Christopher's to redesign the building so that the three large lofts encircled a central courtyard and a community room, which Coco later used to teach painting techniques to war veterans a couple of times a month. Every one of her students had, at one time or another, chosen to volunteer. Three of her graduate students had stayed in Los Angeles and kept the program going while she was recovering.

Coco eased herself onto her bed and scanned the room. Everything was just as she had left it the morning of her accident. On her bedside table lay a pile of books, each waiting to be read. A spiral notebook rested beside her digital clock. Candles decorated the top of an enclosed bookcase that held some of Coco's favorite books on art and artists, including Picasso, Banksy, Daumier, and the Italian romantics from the Age of Enlightenment.

She picked up her notebook and flipped the red plastic cover open. Page after page of her nightly dreams were scribbled down, and every so often she had drawn a portrait of the man in the painting downstairs. *"What a wicked game you play, to make me feel this way,"* Coco softly spoke the lyrics to a song she remembered hearing. *"What a wicked thing to do, to make me dream of you…"*

She looked at the other objects on her bedside table. She picked up a small wooden box decorated with carvings. Her fingers traced the outline of what looked like some kind of wild cat standing beside a woman, and a strange symbol that resembled the flowing form of the infinity sign. Kishu had given this to her when she went to live with him in Hawaii after her parents' deaths. Coco remembered his words when he had handed it to her.

"This special box belonged to your Grandmother and I gave it to your mother when she was a small girl. She let you keep it beside your bed when you were little, so I thought you might like to have it close to you."

Coco opened the lid and removed a creased and torn piece of paper that looked like it had been ripped out of a small sketchbook. On it was an amateur portrait of a young woman. It made her think of Arianna. But, of course, that made no sense. She returned the drawing to the box, grabbed her duffle bag, and tossed in the journal and the box. She set about packing some of her favorite clothes, but couldn't stop thinking about the portrait. For some reason, it reminded her of a painting she had completed five years ago and now wanted to revisit. She sorted through the assortment of canvases that leaned against the windows of her studio and located it at once. She walked over to the easel, placed the portrait in front of the other painting, and stared at it.

She had painted this portrait of Arianna the year the young student entered her senior year of high school. Coco had first seen her early one Sunday morning at the local farmers market and had immediately felt connected to her. Her long hair, mostly held up by clips, framed pensive, light blue eyes. Coco had observed her while she helped an older man carry boxes of produce from a beat-up truck to a table under one of the many covers that shaded the fruit and vegetable displays.

"Let me help you, Uncle," Arianna said.

Coco took a few photos and Arianna looked up. Embarrassed that she had been caught, Coco walked over to the girl. "Forgive me, the artist in me made me do it."

The girl's concerned face softened. "It's a little bit creepy, you know."

"I guess it could seem that way," Coco held out a hand. "Hi, my name's Coco Rhodes."

"I'm Arianna. Why the photographs?"

"What you have seems very precious. I wanted to capture that moment so I can paint it—with your permission, of course."

Arianna shrugged. "Go ahead."

Coco had looked at the load of boxes still to be unloaded from the back of the truck. "Can I help with those?"

"Sure, that would be great."

When Coco had time, she would make sure to stop by Arianna's uncle's booth on Sunday mornings. During these visits, she found out that the girl dreamt of going to college but was struggling in school, not because of bad grades, but because the high school she attended had a student population of around twenty-five hundred and did not offer adequate college counseling.

Coco arranged to meet Arianna at the market during the girl's lunch break and tutor her. She found her to be an extremely bright student, eager to learn and ready to do more than what was expected of her.

The sound of Kishu rummaging through drawers in the kitchen brought Coco out of her daydream.

"Food is on the kitchen counter," Kishu said. "I'm going back outside." He grabbed his book and a plate of food from the polished cement kitchen counter and headed back out to the balcony. Coco walked over, dished herself up some salad and grilled tofu, and joined him.

"In the hospital you told me that Grandma Mimi and my mother had a great art teacher. Is this why my mother relocated to Italy?"

"You know that I'm unable to answer this question without speaking of the Allegiance," Kishu said. "Are you sure you want to hear this?"

Coco shifted in her chair and placed a napkin in her lap.

"Yes. I'm not saying I want to be a part of it, but I do want to find my creativity again, and perhaps I need to be more open about finding a teacher."

"To seek out a great teacher like they had, you may need to travel to Italy."

"Italy?"

"Yes."

"That's a lot to think about."

"Surely 'thinking about things' seems somewhat inconsequential after having an experience such as yours."

Coco stared at her plate of food. "Right after the car hit me, I thought of Grandma Mimi and her strength."

Kishu took a deep breath in, and then exhaled slowly. His eyes had teared up, but he found his composure.

"How did you cope with her death?" Coco asked.

"I had time to prepare. Mimi knew about her cancer, but chose to give birth to your mother rather than risk losing her through rigorous treatment. That was her choice to make."

"But how did you go on... without her?"

"At first it was difficult, but I had a little baby to raise, and believe me, your mother kept me busy. I was so angry about Mimi's death, but I realized that to feel this emotion is healthy— to harbor it is destructive. And so I worked on turning my sorrow into happiness. And Chantal brought me so much joy. Then she brought me Alessandro, and Christopher, and then you.

"Later, with Chantal and your father gone, I felt the darkness seeping into my heart again. But I fought it—because I had two children to look after. Christopher was so angry at everything and everyone, and that's why I thought it best that he go to school on the East Coast, away from all of the sadness.

"But I had you to keep me busy, until you went off to the university that you never left. Now please, eat your food, and then we will head back to Malibu. I will speak to Christopher about allowing you to move back here for your birthday."

"That would be good, thanks."

Kishu sipped from his water glass. "Do what you love, Coco, what your heart craves, that is all any of us have control over— imagine it, if you have to. Do a little every day, and then do something that takes you out of your comfort zone. Promise me this?"

"I promise," Coco said. "I needed this day."

"I know, little one," Kishu said.

From the rooftop of the W Hotel in Westwood, Gabriel watched Kishu and Coco drive away. His mother was correct. He needed to have faith in the members of the Allegiance. He felt secure with Coco's safety, but there was something that troubled him. When he had checked her loft earlier for intruders, he had noticed a trace of magic that lingered around Coco's paintings. It was faint, but it was definitely there.

Arianna stood outside the Armand Hammer Museum on the corner of Westwood and Wilshire Boulevards. She looked up at the cobalt blue sky, strewn with clusters of coconut clouds that cruised across the Southern Californian heavens. The vista reminded her of the first time her mother and father had taken her to the museum. She was two years old, and the exhibition was entitled, "The Invisible Made Visible: Angels of the Vatican." She remembered the faces of angels, their wings, and their golden hair that fell in diaphanous threads over their naked bodies. She stared at the tall, gray building that loomed across the street. The structure housed an adoption agency. Her parents had given her the name and address of the company should she ever want to inquire about her birth mother.

Arianna thought of her father's words to her when he had handed her the note.

"Isabel and I did not enter blindly into the adoption process. We filled out an exorbitant amount of paperwork and endured long intense interviews, and then waited with open hearts. Lucky for us, you found us and we became a family. But we will understand if one day you need to find your birth mother, so keep this information. The people there will help you."

A few months later, her father became ill, and within weeks he had died. Arianna hoped that her mother's sadness and grief would eventually fade, but instead she became very quiet and still. She sat for hours every day in their backyard as if waiting for him to return. Arianna felt trapped between a sense of devotion to her mother, Isabel, and a need to protect her, and her own curiosity about her birth mother and father. She placed the note back in her purse and walked away.

CHAPTER 9

Arianna pulled into the driveway of her home right when her cell phone began to ring. She turned off the engine and answered.

"Hello, my name is Sylvia. I'm a caseworker with a private adoption service in Los Angeles. Am I speaking with Arianna Linden?"

"Yes," Arianna said.

"Are you sitting down?"

Arianna undid her seatbelt. "Yes, I am. What's this about?"

"Prior to your father's death, your parents contacted us."

"Is this regarding my birth mother?" Arianna asked.

"Yes, but also to let you know that you have a sibling."

"What?"

"Your brother has hired an agency on the East Coast to find you, and that's why I'm calling you today. Your birth mother is very ill, and she hopes that you will agree to see her."

Arianna's right hand drummed on the steering wheel. " Ah, I—it's—"

"There's one more piece of information that I need to share with you. Your brother is also your twin."

Silence.

Sylvia continued. "What you are feeling is perfectly normal.

May I suggest that you call me back when you've had a chance to take all of this in, and obviously given the circumstance, your brother hopes that you will agree to a meeting as soon as possible. Your birth mother will pay for all travel expenses. Do you have any questions?"

"I have a brother... and he's my twin?"

"Yes, Arianna," Sylvia said. "Your brother, Jeremy, is your twin."

"Does my mom—my adoptive mom, Isabel, know that you're calling me?"

"You're over eighteen, so we contacted you directly. I'm happy to speak with her, if and when you'd like me to."

"No... it's okay," Arianna said, taking the keys out of the ignition. "This is a lot for me to take in."

Sylvia hesitated for a moment. "Miss Linden, your father, Steven, was a wonderful man, and a respected immigration attorney in the Los Angeles community. His dedication to his clients was unsurpassed and sincere. I promised him personally that when the time came to handle your case, I would support you in any way I could."

"I'll call you tomorrow," Arianna said. "I need to speak with my mother."

"Of course," Sylvia said. "Goodbye, Arianna."

Arianna ended the call. It was then she realized how much her hands were shaking. She placed her cell in her purse and headed inside. The thought of receiving more information without having a discussion with Isabel was out of the question. She stared out at the backyard.

Isabel attended her usual place at this time of the day, under the small gazebo that her husband had built for her before he passed away. Because of Steven's long work hours, it had taken him a few years to finish the project. He'd explained to Isabel that although he couldn't afford to build her the house of her dreams, he hoped that she could sit and dream amongst the fragrant jasmine that bloomed around her.

Arianna opened the screen door and approached her mother. "Why do you sit here, Mama?"

Isabel looked up at Arianna. "It makes me feel close to him."

Arianna planted herself in a nearby chair. "I had a phone call," she said. "From a woman named Sylvia."

Isabel straightened her back. "From the adoption agency?"

Arianna nodded.

"May I ask why she called—"

"My twin brother." Arianna said. "Why didn't you tell me? All this time I've felt so detached—like something was missing in my life—"

"Arianna, I wa—"

"And now, I'm told by a complete stranger that I have a twin," Arianna said. She noticed the tears in her mother's eyes.

"It was not our decision to make," Isabel said. "It was your birth mother's request that we withhold this information until you turned twenty-one, or a dire situation arose. Please—let me explain." She gave Arianna a handkerchief and reached for her daughter's hand. "I've sent a photo of you to your birth mother every year since we adopted you. Her name is Katja. It broke her heart to give you up, but she couldn't afford to keep both you and your brother, and Steven and I were so desperate to have a little girl of our own. We went to New York, to the agency, and found you. It was love at first sight.

"Katja and I have never met face to face. I just sent her the photos. I think that's what I would have needed if the tables had been turned. She sent me photos of Jeremy too. She wanted you both to have something of each other."

"She's dying... my birth mother. That's why Sylvia contacted me today."

Isabel knelt on the ground in front of Arianna. "We don't

always get to plan our lives, Arianna. I cannot gauge your pain, but I know it must feel infinite at this moment. I am here for you and always will be. When you are ready I have the photo albums for you." Isabel patted her daughter's knees and rose.

Arianna pondered the path that lay ahead should she choose to take it. She watched her mother walk across the yard and enter the kitchen. Her dark hair was pinned in a low bun at the base of her slender neck. This is how Isabel had worn it since the day her husband had died. Arianna took note of her mother's elegance and thought of how difficult it must have been for her parents to keep this secret from her.

A little later, Arianna tapped on her mother's open bedroom door. Isabel looked up and motioned for Arianna to sit on the bed beside her. In her hand, Isabel held three photo albums. She passed the first one to Arianna. "This begins a few hours after your birth."

Arianna opened the book. The first photo showed a young woman—she looked younger than Arianna. In her arms, the woman held two tiny babies, each bundled in a blanket. Both babies wore beanies, one pink and one blue. Arianna placed her hand on the photo.

"It's no wonder you are so beautiful," Isabel said. "Your mother was too."

Arianna turned to Isabel. "I love you, Mama."

"I know you do. These books are yours now." Isabel took a handkerchief from her pocket and wiped away the tears that had pooled in her eyes. "I feel like a burden has been lifted from my aching heart. I'll be in the kitchen preparing dinner if you need me."

Arianna pored over the books until late into the evening. Each one filled with photos of her as a baby and continued up until her last birthday. She spent the following morning with

Isabel listening to stories of her childhood. When it came time for Arianna to leave for her appointment with Sylvia, she kissed her mother's cheek and held her hand. "I want you to be there with me—when I meet them."

"If that is what you want, then of course," Isabel said.

When the streetlight turned green, Arianna walked with determination across Wilshire Boulevard toward the building that loomed on the other side of the street. She followed the receptionist into a bright office. Sylvia introduced herself with a strong handshake. Arianna sat on the edge of a chair with her hands in her lap and fought down the butterflies fluttering in her stomach.

Sylvia handed Arianna a large manila envelope. A replica of the photograph of two tiny babies cradled in a woman's arms sat on top of the file. The baby girl's clothing matched the outfit she had worn the day her parents had picked her up from the adoption agency in New York. Arianna had all of the proof that she needed. Arrangements were made for Isabel and Arianna to fly out to New York the following week. It was the first time Isabel had shown interest in anything since Steven's death.

Isabel walked out of her bedroom, pulling her suitcase beside her. She had chosen to wear a dark brown pantsuit with a beige silk shirt and high heels. She hadn't worn heels in years, since she'd closed her dancing school to look after Steven during his illness. Arianna took in a breath when she saw her mother. "You look beautiful, Mama," she said. "Your hair is—wow—it's so long!"

CHAPTER 10

Nestled in the eminence of the Italian Alps, Prudence and Stefan's medieval fortress ascended like a herculean monument. *Casa della Pietra* dominated as the central stronghold for the Allegiance. The castle rested atop its own mountain, and at times seemed to float above the drifting clouds. A rigid rock wall protected a raised walkway wide enough for knights on horseback to patrol and protect the inner edifice. Two watchtowers jutted up from the outer wall, poised en garde like rooks on a chessboard.

The main hall lacked the austerity of the outer façade. Plush sofas and a grand piano luxuriated the hall beneath the warmth of tapestries and paintings by the great masters. Perched above the fireplace a portrait of Prudence graced the wall. It had been painted centuries ago by the early Renaissance painter, Botticelli, but the edges had been damaged by fire.

The thick stone walls in the main bedroom curved upward to form a dome-shaped roof. Paintings of cherubs, gods, and goddesses adorned the ceiling and endowed the room with celestial bliss. Prudence stood at the center of the room with a large black female jaguar at her side. Her evening gown of silver satin trimmed with tiny handmade velvet roses accented her delicate body, and her sleek white hair framed her angelic face and tumbled like long strands of starlight to her waist. Her omnipotence had been captured forever in her mid-thirties. The light that touched her eyes charged the flecks of color that formed the mosaic of her golden irises.

She turned and walked to the end of her large bed and knelt down. She detached a key from a leather cord around her neck and fitted it into the lock of a timeworn wooden chest. It was adorned with an intricate carving of a woman and a jaguar standing side-by-side. She turned the key to the left and waited for the soft clicking sound, which enabled her to push back the lid and gaze upon the precious belongings inside.

The scent of lavender drifted from the chest and into the room, but it was overshadowed by the earthy fragrance of ground amber. Prudence's long fingers traced the hilt of a thin silver knife, upon which was engraved the faded outline of a dragon with its tail coiled around its neck. She closed her eyes and pressed the flat edge of the blade against her heart.

"Stefan, *amore mio*," she whispered. She lifted the knife above her shoulder and playfully jabbed it into Stefan's muscular chest.

His strong hands rested on her shoulders. "It is impossible to sneak up on you," Stefan said, his stance strong and his black eyes that mirrored the night sky shone beautifully.

Prudence rested her cheek upon his hand. "Your scent reached out to me," she said. "I can hear each rare pulse of your heart even when we are thousands of miles apart."

"And I, yours." His gaze lingered over the dragon engraved on the hilt of the knife. "Are you planning your own crusade, my love?"

"I wish for peace," she said. "Not war."

"I am not sure that one is possible without the other," Stefan said.

Prudence spoke endearingly to the large black feline. "Sleep, *gattina*." The jaguar sauntered over to the fireplace. Prudence placed the knife back inside the chest and picked up a garment embroidered with ancient symbols and glyphs, and held it endearingly to her cheek.

She rose with tempered grace and turned to face Stefan. The garment that Prudence held in her hands unrolled and lay gently against the length of her body. A gust of wind flew in through the open door and wrapped the cape around them both. Stefan bent his head and kissed her lips, and when he released her, a drop of his blood had appeared on her lower lip. Prudence licked it.

He picked her up in his arms and laid her across the huge canopied bed, and with profound passion he kissed her again. She dropped the cloak, revealing her breasts and above them, the vein to her witch's heart. "Drink, my love."

Stefan brushed her hair away from her face. With his fingertips he gently turned her chin and kissed her behind her ear before leaving a trail of delicate kisses down her neck to her breasts.

"*Ti amo*," Stefan said, before his sharp teeth found her jugular vein. She moaned in ecstasy while he ripped at her clothes. He entered her and Prudence's breath caught when she felt him release his love deep into her womb. Her body responded in a wave of bliss.

"I give thanks each day that you found me," he whispered.

"It is I who was lost, my love. I believe the gods lifted me from my path of loneliness and planted me on the trail that you rode along that blessed day."

"Then to both gods and fate, I give thanks." Stefan leaned on his elbow and took in her beauty. "You seem troubled. Are you hurting?" He went to bite into his wrist.

Prudence grabbed his arm. "Your vampire blood cannot heal this witch's maternal concerns."

"What troubles you, then?"

Prudence turned her head away from him, but Stefan gently turned her to face him. "That look is the one you wear when you are concerned for our son. After six hundred years I had hoped you would be able to let him find his own way."

"Two assassins attacked him," Prudence said. "He is adamant they are Kenan's men. He destroyed one, but the other assassin killed the mortal hitman and escaped."

Stefan kissed her forehead. "That happened weeks ago, my love, and yet you cannot let it go. Gabriel killed the assassin because he was his enemy. He was not his executioner. In matters of love our son has your patience, *tesoro*, but in matters of protecting those we love he shares my instinctive behavior. And that can be dangerous."

A tear ran down her flawless cheek. He wiped it away.

"How do I stop this feeling of over-protectiveness with our son? It is the most difficult tie that I have ever had to break."

Stefan pulled her to his chest. "It is also difficult for Gabriel. He has an inherent need to please you and protect all that you stand for. But he fights internally with his warrior side. My advice is that you stop trying and let your feelings be."

Prudence rose from the bed and picked up a package from the chest. "It is time for you to deliver Chantal's letter to Colombina." She handed it to him. "Chantal predicted that you would be the one who carried it to her."

Stefan took the small package. "I will be honored."

Prudence found comfort in Stefan's arms.

He kissed the top of Prudence's head and smoothed her hair, then began to dress. She watched as he tied his sword belt around his waist and attached his sword, the crest emblazoned with the rune, Dagaz. Prudence remembered the day that he added the crest. It marked Stefan's life after mortality. She kissed

Stefan one last time before he walked to the balcony and vanished into the dark night.

The jaguar rose from her bed on the floor by the fireplace, and loped over to Prudence, who knelt in the center of the room, the embroidered cape draped around her shoulders and over her body. "I miss him too," she said, as the cat curled up beside her. She waved her hands and the candles flared, while above her the cherubs came to life and flew amongst the clouds of the domed roof. Prudence whispered a silent prayer for her husband's safety, and when her last words were spoken, only one candle remained lit and the cherubs had all returned to their places amongst the clouds.

CHAPTER 11

Stefan walked elegantly along the busy streets of Westwood Village; his long cashmere coat outlined his distinctively tall frame. He knew the place well, having scouted properties for Prudence on behalf of the Allegiance many times. He had ridden a horse over the property when it was owned by a Spanish soldier, and done the same when it had become Wolfskill Farm, but that was over a hundred years ago, before it was developed. Such was the life of a vampire: one became witness to development and growth. As much as he missed the natural beauty of the wilderness, he did enjoy modern-day contraptions such as ballpoint pens and iPhones.

He did not think of the village as a place to visit the night before the ancient festival of Samhain—and Stefan had never understood the American take on this Gaelic celebration. Over the years it had developed into an assortment of festivals, from slaughtering animals for food for the winter, to a celebration of death and renewal. He noticed that the traditional ghouls, ghosts and vampires, had, in recent years been replaced by young women dressed in less clothing than he had seen in some of the windows of De Wallen, Amsterdam. There, prostitution has a name, was an honest profession, but here he couldn't help but wonder if this form of coquetry was hidden under the guise of Halloween—sexy nurse, sexy Wonder Woman, sexy pirate.

He chuckled to himself and wished his beloved were walking next to him. Together they could have brought some fun to the streets of Westwood, when the Celtic New Year began tomorrow evening.

His cold fingers brushed across the small package in his coat pocket. The gift brought with it endless possibilities for the receiver, should she accept the invitation. With a final look at the array of bare skin bursting forth like daffodils in springtime, Stefan turned away from the main street and towards the Rhodes family compound.

A tabby cat crossed his path, reminding him of a past night not far from here, and another feline. He had searched the Santa Monica Mountains for hours until he found the injured mountain lion hidden deep in a canyon amongst the brush and trees. He'd crouched beside her and patted her head. She'd groaned in recognition of his presence and gladly accepted the blood that dripped from his wrist and into her mouth. For hours Stefan had nurtured her. His hands had gently stroked her soft fur while he recited cat prose from T.S. Eliot.

At 2 a.m., Stefan stationed himself on a bench in a nearby church courtyard, a place of silence amongst the cacophony of city life. He thought of Prudence and felt the pull of her love drawing at his heart. He took out his small leather-bound notebook and classic Waterman fountain pen and wrote:

One taste of thou and life's burdens lift,
Sorrows fade into joy and my youth is restored.
Thine breath against my skin and my heart is quiescent.
A tender touch and the withered sinew that
girds my wretched soul is hallowed.
I bethink the wisdom born from this dance of life,
The stillness of death and rebirth,

Fairest nymph,
Beloved rose,
My divine Prudence.

Three hours later, Stefan walked toward Coco's loft. The sound of birds singing began to break up the evening stillness. He felt it, the veil between the worlds becoming thinner. He remembered part of a poem by Edgar Allan Poe:

The spirits of the dead, who stood
In life before thee, are again…

Samhain had arrived. When he reached Coco's letterbox, securely molded into the cement and brick fence, he pushed the package through the slit and listened to it land on what he suspected to be a superfluous quantity of junk mail.

"*Buon Compleanno*," Stefan whispered. "Be virtuous to my son, Colombina, for he is worthy of receiving prodigious and eternal love." He caught the scent of roses and knew that he was not the only supernatural creature who had chosen this night to whisper birthday wishes to the young artist.

He looked up at the sinking moon and recited:

And if she faintly glimmers here,
And paled is her light,
Yet always in her proper sphere
She's mistress of the night

"Ah, dear Henry, I do wish you had let me turn you into an immortal. I miss our nights of exchanging poetry and walking through the woods."

CHAPTER 12

The young vampire assassin that Alessandro and Frederico had followed from L.A. had since based himself in Florence, along with other vampires that were known to belong to Kenan. Gabriel returned to Italy, and his father had stayed in L.A. to guard Coco. There were few who would confront the sword of the legendary vampire, Stefan Lazarevic.

Kishu, Coco, Layla and Christopher had returned to the Rhodes family compound in Westwood the evening before Coco's birthday. Coco had given Kishu her word that she would not go anywhere unattended.

Coco awoke early, unrolled her yoga mat and began to stretch. Thalia sat at her feet and watched every move. The cat followed her into the bathroom while she changed into her running clothes, making a beeline to the front door when she realized her mistress was planning to leave. When her meows became borderline howls, Coco picked her up. "There's no need to worry, my friend. My guess is that Christopher has this joint surrounded. Trust me, I'll be fine." She placed the cat on the floor and left. At the bottom of the stairs Layla ran up to her.

"Happy Birthday!" she said.

"I'm glad you're here," Coco said. "Although, I'm

disappointed. I figured Christopher would have a team of Navy SEALs here, too, on the pretense that it was their normal training session."

"Don't speak too soon," Layla said. "Let's go!"

Coco had trained for this day for months. They headed west on Le Conte Avenue toward Wilshire Boulevard and the beach.

The early morning light filtered between the tall buildings of Westwood and fell upon the white headstones that filled the silent cemetery opposite the Federal Building. Layla and Coco ran under the overpass where the hum from cars along the San Diego Freeway orchestrated the dawn in the city of angels.

Further along Wilshire, workers navigated their cars into parking spaces and dashed into coffee shops for their early morning shots of caffeine. By the time they hit the Third Street Promenade in Santa Monica, the smell of fried potatoes, eggs, and bacon sharpened Coco's senses, waking her up when she hit the bike path leading to the beach.

This morning, the ocean seemed gentle, and the drifting waves reminded Coco that the ebb and flow of her life felt close to normal. The two women ran along the bike path for miles, glad for the time to lose their thoughts to the wind and sea before cutting up Sunset Boulevard to the Temescal Canyon Trailhead.

Two hours after starting out, they arrived back at the foot of Coco's stairs. Layla waited while Coco stopped by the mailbox. "Don't worry," Coco said, "I'm going to pick up my mail, then I promise I'll go directly inside."

"Alright, let's catch up later. *Buon Compleanno!*"

Coco opened the flap to her mailbox and pulled out a package wrapped in faded brown paper and tied with string. She brought it to her nose and breathed in deeply to place its scent. "Mm, lavender... and no return address."

Her cell beeped when she opened the door to her loft, indicating a missed call from Christopher. She contemplated calling him back, but the package intrigued her, and she figured his birthday wishes could wait a few minutes longer.

She took a pair of scissors from a drawer and cut the string. An envelope with the name, *Colombina*, written in exquisite calligraphy, worthy of representation in the Gutenberg Bible, was tied with a piece of gold ribbon around a package wrapped in soft natural muslin. She turned the envelope over. It had been sealed with a wax stamp that read C.L.F.

Once more, she checked that it was her name on the front of the package. "Coco Rhodes..." Sliding the scissors carefully under the top of the envelope to preserve the seal, she pulled the card out. She had expected to see some variation of a birthday greeting, but instead the image on the front of the card revealed a perfectly rendered drawing of her face. Her hand trembled. "Who are Colombina and C.L.F., and what is the connection to me?" She pushed off her running shoes and sat crosslegged on the couch, opened the card, and read:

My Darling Colombina,

My wish for you is that you take this birthday gift from me and follow your heart. I used to be fearful of the secrets that our family has held closely for centuries, and I understand if you are too, but with the acceptance of the part I play in the web of the Allegiance, I found purpose.

I am sad that I won't be there to hold you when you feel lonely, but I will be with you in spirit. You and Christopher will always be close to my heart. We are connected by generations of love, and the blood from your father brings passion and strength to us now, and for eternity.

Alessandro is my sacred love. Now open your gift and I will explain its contents.

Coco took the package and opened it. Inside was an airline ticket from LAX to Florence, a brass key, and a bank card. She continued reading.

The key is to the front door of our home in Tuscany. As of today it will be transferred to your name. The bank card will give you access to my personal account in the village and the ticket is self-explanatory.

Christopher has his own journey, but I'm counting on him to help you on your way, for you will have many questions. Listen to him and take heed of his protectiveness.

I've foreseen that you will have my love for art and your father's fortitude and passion for life. Be brave, my little dove. I'm so sorry that I cannot give you any more advice, but this is your journey, not mine. If there had been a way that I could have stayed in this life with you, I would have done so. Until we meet again…

Your loving mother,

Chantal le Févre

Coco's chest tightened. "Until we meet again…"

She grabbed her cell phone to call Christopher, just as his ringtone dragged her back to reality.

She picked up on the first ring.

"Christopher—who the is hell is Colombina and what's with the le Févre? And Mom died when I was four, so who sent me this package?"

"I'm guessing you received Mother's gift," Christopher said. "I'm walking up the stairs to your loft."

Coco raced over to the front door and unlocked it. Christopher entered. "Is this some kind of Halloween trick?" she asked.

"Are you suggesting that I learned to write and draw like that so I could impersonate Mother in a letter?" Christopher asked. "Because that's classified as fraud."

Coco studied the card again, captivated by the author's exquisite handwriting and the perfect portrayal of her face. Every one of her personal weaknesses and strengths were laid out in front of her, etched by lines. It was daunting. She waved the card at Christopher. "Then what should I call this?"

"Well, seeing how your legal birth name is Colombina, a fact you would have soon discovered if you had shown any interest in your family history, I would call it a wakeup call. You were given the name, Coco Rhodes, to keep you safe."

"Safe from what?" Coco asked.

"From the bastards who wanted Mother dead."

"Our parents both died in a car accident," Coco said.

Christopher took a deep breath and fought a bead of perspiration that had begun to form on his brow. "The car accident was a lie."

Coco's hands trembled at these words. "No! They died in a car accident."

"That was a lie, but a lie told in order to find the truth."

"And what is the truth?" Coco asked.

"I don't know."

Coco sprung up from the sofa. "I don't believe you... and I don't need a freaking Ph.D. in micro expression and whatever damn legal degree you have to know that you're lying to me!"

Christopher remained calm. "It's all I can tell you at this time."

"When is it going to be the right time?"

"It's not up to me."

"Then who is it up to?" Coco asked.

Christopher turned away from her. He stretched out his hands, and then let them drop to his sides.

"Damn it, Christopher! I'm so sick of the bullshit you and Kishu feed me. You think I don't know that you've had me followed for most of my life? Christ... do you know how lonely my life has been? I'm too nervous to get involved with anyone because, God forbid, their pedigree isn't good enough for this family, and now you're telling me that some crazed maniac murdered our parents?"

Christopher placed his hands in the pockets of his suit pants. "You have no idea what I've had to endure to keep the truth about our parents hidden from you. And yes, you've been followed, but those orders don't come from me, they come from someone much higher."

"Let me guess... the Allegiance. I've told you, I don't want to be a part of it."

Christopher turned and walked toward the window that overlooked the courtyard. Coco held up the card. "Did you get one of these when you turned thirty-two?"

"No, I was twenty-one."

"Did Mother draw a portrait of you too?"

"Yes, it was a perfect rendering of who I was at the time."

"How did she know how I'd look as an adult?"

"Mother was intuitive."

"And? That's it? That's all you've got to say? That our mother was intuitive?"

The silence in the room was drenched in Coco's anger and confusion. She looked over the letter again. "We have the farmhouse after all these years?"

"The farmhouse was always Mother's. Father had other properties."

"So you're saying that after all this time the Allegiance still hasn't figured out who killed our parents, and you wonder why the hell I don't want to get involved with them?"

He looked eager to change the direction of the conversation. "How do you feel about Italy?"

"I'm still getting over the fact that my mother knew how I'd look today and that my real name is Colombina le Févre. Where the hell did that name come from?"

"Le Févre is our father's last name," Christopher said. "There's an art school in the village near the house. Mother was a student there and the professor specializes in training intuitive artists—like Mother and you. But until you accept your place in the Allegiance this is all I can say."

"Oh, for fuck's sake, you're my brother. Stop acting like my damn lawyer."

"I *am* your lawyer."

"Am I going to be alone in the house?" Coco asked.

"Layla will travel with you and stay until you settle in. The Allegiance is strong in Italy and they are sworn to protect you."

"Protect me? Am I going to be followed for the rest of my life? I'm an artist and a teacher, not exactly 007. And why is someone out to hurt me?"

By the look on his face she knew Christopher didn't want to go any further with this conversation right now. He moved to put his arm around her but she pushed him away. "Did you get an airline ticket when you were twenty-one, and did you want to go?"

"My circumstances were different," Christopher said.

By the tone of his voice, Coco knew that, for now, this conversation was coming to a close. "What if I don't go?"

He took a deep breath. "You will go, because I can promise you one thing, you will find answers to all of your questions in Italy. When you need me, you know the quickest way to make contact."

Coco shook her head in resistance and held up her palms

to him. "Please... Don't." Tears escaped her eyes and trickled down her cheek.

Christopher made his way to the door.

"Is there any water near the house?" Coco asked.

"There's a river that runs by the house and it forms a small lake on the property. The ocean is forty-five minutes by car."

There was a knock at the door. Christopher checked through the peephole and then opened it. He gently pulled Layla toward him, kissing her lovingly before releasing her.

"*Ciao* again, birthday girl," Layla said. "We'll stay with my family in Florence for a few days, then drive to the farmhouse. But for now I'm here to help you pack."

"Wait—you knew about this, Layla?" Coco asked.

"Christopher just told me that we would be leaving for Italy tomorrow. I don't know any of the details."

"If you hadn't received Mother's letter, then I would insist on you going anyway," Christopher said.

"Look, I understand your protective issues with me," Coco said. "But why do I need to leave tomorrow?"

Christopher ran a hand through his hair and Layla placed a hand on his arm. "This predicament isn't easy for either of you," Layla said as she looked at Coco. "Coco, you feel trapped and are reacting defensively," she turned to Christopher. "And Christopher—you also feel trapped. May I suggest that you come to an agreement?"

"And what might that be?" Christopher asked, as he planted his feet firmly and pulled back his shoulders.

"Give Coco three days to organize things here."

"I'll agree to that. But I'm not leaving Thalia," Coco said. "And what about my job? I had planned to return to the university next quarter."

"I've made arrangements for Thalia to travel with you, and

as of Monday you're on a leave of absence from the university," he said. "Okay, I can agree to three days. I'll change the tickets."

Layla and Christopher both turned to Coco.

"Okay, three days," she said.

Christopher gave Layla another kiss and walked out the door.

"I'm not sure I comprehend what this is all about," Coco said, "but thanks for what you just did."

"It's not always easy standing between a creative brain and a logical brain, but we're family," Layla said as she hugged Coco. "Let's have some breakfast and then I can help you pack."

"I'm nervous," Coco said. "About going back there."

"I understand, and that's normal too. Facing our past when we remember it is difficult enough. But facing the unknown is frightening. I'll be there with you—you have my word."

"I need coffee," Coco said.

"Wait until you have Italian espresso—and Maria's is the best."

"Who's Maria?"

"An old family friend."

CHAPTER 13

Florence, Italy.

Layla's family home rests beside the Arno River above a steep rock wall. The timeworn villa and chapel are colored in faded tones of linen and marmalade. This classic architectural example of the Renaissance era is reflected in the steel water that flows below the large outdoor terrace.

Antonia, Layla's mother, a vibrant woman with a youthful look and a Chanel wardrobe, had fussed over Layla and Coco from the moment they arrived. After enjoying a delicious meal, the two young women now waited patiently at the door of a restaurant tucked away near the Ponte Vecchio, watching Antonia chat to the maître d'.

"Since I moved to California, Mother and I don't get to see each other as often as we'd like, so I let her spoil me whenever I'm here," Layla said. "My four brothers have little interest in dining out and shopping."

Antonia approached and a young attendant dutifully whisked the door open. "Did you enjoy your food, Coco?" Antonia asked.

"Yes," Coco said. "Thank you." She hesitated, contemplating her next thought. "Did you know my parents, Antonia?"

Antonia nodded. "*Sì*, I met Chantal at a meeting with Alessandro here in *Firenze*."

Coco noticed the musical lilt of her father's name when spoken by an Italian—the letter *a* held in the air for a moment before it was gently dropped to rejoin its waiting neighbors. Antonia continued, "I've heard that when they first met, they were enamored with each other. She was beautiful, like you. And Alessandro was exquisitely handsome. There was much love between them."

"Did you see them much after that meeting?" Coco asked.

"No. When Chantal became with child, Alessandro was very concerned about her health."

"I didn't know that my mother had any problems with either of her pregnancies."

Antonia placed a hand on Coco's cheek. "Better to ask your grandfather perhaps… but no more sad words. It's time for our beauty treatments."

"Excuse me?" Coco said turning to Layla. "I thought we were going back to your place to get ready—so we can leave in the morning?"

"We will," Layla said. "But for today, let Mother indulge."

"Yes, let's have some fun," Antonia said, looking at Coco. "When was the last time you visited a salon?"

"Sometime before my accident—maybe five months ago."

Antonia made a clicking noise with her mouth and shook her head in disbelief. "Today I will take care of this," she said. "It's time to get acquainted with your Italian heritage. We shall begin with beauty and style."

"I'm not sure one haircut and a single beauty treatment will make much of a difference."

"*Si vedrà*… you will see," Antonia said as she linked arms

with Coco and Layla. "And afterwards we will need to decide on our costumes for the masquerade tonight."

"The what?" Coco asked.

"The university is holding a masquerade to honor one of our longtime board members… he's retiring," Antonia said. "It will be entertaining."

"But I want to get to the village. Christopher promised me that when I came here I would get the answers to my questions," Coco said. "I'm sorry, but I feel like you're all kind of stalling for time."

"It's just a masquerade, Coco," Layla said. "And we're not stalling, we'll arrive at your home as planned. The event is being held at one of the Medici villas just outside of the city, and the ballroom has frescoes everywhere—you'll love it."

A few hours later, Coco stared at her reflection in a large free-standing mirror. "What the heck did they do to me?"

"I love it," Layla said. "You look sophisticated, very chic!"

"I can't remember the last time I let my hair grow this long, let alone dyed it so dark. Every time I see myself I crave dark chocolate. But I think I like it—is that weird?"

"Not at all, and the deep brown looks so natural, it shows off your sexy eyes… you little fox," Layla said with a smirk. As if in agreement, Thalia meowed and jumped onto the dressing table.

"Hey, if Thalia likes it, then I'm down with it too, not so sure about these manicured nails—I give them a day before they're covered in paint. But I do love this dress—very Marie Antoinette." She slipped her feet into a pair of dainty satin shoes and handed a pair to Layla.

"You know what I love most about these dresses?" Layla said.

"I doubt it's the tight corsets."

"No, it's the sound the fabric makes when I move. The way it rustles and swooshes. *Fantastico!*" Layla picked up two masks.

One resembled a butterfly's wings, painted in deep shades of lapis, sapphire, and arctic blues and trimmed in gold. The other involved intricately woven strands of white and gold filigree that flared slightly above the head, the edges trimmed with soft white feathers.

Layla handed Coco the white and gold mask. "This is the closest design that Mother felt resembled a dove. Put it on and we're ready to go."

They admired themselves in the mirror and tied on their masks. "Hang on—we need a photo," Coco said. "I'll send it to Christopher, maybe it'll encourage him to get his butt over here—preferably sooner rather than later." She captured their reflection in the mirror and sent the image to her brother.

As they were about to walk out the door, Layla's cell phone rang. "It's Christopher," she said, heading for the bathroom. She held up a hand to Coco—an indicator that she needed a few minutes of privacy, then closed the bathroom door.

Coco placed her phone inside the small purse that had been rented along with her costume. Antonia had explained that the correct name for it is *saccoccia*, more like a pocket than a purse. She gazed out the window at the darkened surface of the wide river and was startled when Layla opened the door.

"Christopher said to tell you that he likes your hair. He also wants to know if I can keep the dress... and the mask." She blushed a little and instantly popped open a delicate fan and waved it profusely in front of her face.

Coco held up her hands. "He's my brother, Layla, I don't need to hear the details. Let's go."

O

As they were driven through the forest that surrounded *Villa della Petraia*, Coco listened to Antonia recite historical facts about the property. Originally it had been built as a castle and then owned by Brunelleschi and, more recently, members of the Medici family.

Coco leaned forward and gave the view the respect it deserved. She could feel the rise of emotion building within her, just as it always did when she came close to savoring art. The grounds alone seemed to be infused with something sacred, and she breathed in the creative energy reaching out to her.

The driver pulled up to the drop-off area. A tall man costumed in tights, bloomers and fitted jacket opened the door. Antonia offered him her hand, which he took and kissed.

"*Buona sera*, Antonia," he said.

"Ah, *buona sera*, Frederico," she replied. "What fine legs you have, my dear friend." Coco observed the lingering glimpse Antonia gave Frederico's lower body.

He chuckled, and Coco noted the pale tone to his face. He bowed his head slightly. She took his hand, never noticing the icy fingers beneath his white leather gloves. Layla and Coco followed Frederico and Antonia along a path that led to the main entrance of the villa. The view of the city had become christened with lights as the evening sky blanketed the *Firenze* hills.

Coco conceded that Layla had been correct in regards to the frescoes adorning the walls of the large ballroom. Once an open courtyard, the room was now enclosed with a skylight. She was entranced with the works of Baldassare Franceschini (Il Volterrano). She had admired his drawings, but viewing his frescoes depicting stories from the Medici family's reign—with cherubs, and men dressed in fine robes bearing gold crosses, was awe-inspiring. She now appreciated Layla's insistence on attending the event, and breathed a sigh of gratitude for the weight of the tight bodice and full skirt decorated with fine gold brocade—otherwise she may have floated away. She giggled to herself, giddy with joy from being immersed in so much history and art.

After Antonia had finished introducing her to the entire university board and pertinent professors, Coco's ardent love of art prevailed. She excused herself to take a closer look. As the evening progressed, she felt a presence that seemed vaguely familiar, and wondered if somewhere behind one of the masked faces stood an acquaintance from her childhood.

O

Gabriel and Alessandro had arrived at the villa shortly before Antonia, Layla and Coco. This allowed them enough time to acknowledge members of the board before joining their comrades and losing themselves amongst the colorful crowd. Alessandro had followed the assassin from Los Angeles to Florence, and this gave cause for Gabriel to be concerned for Coco's safety.

When Coco entered the ballroom, Gabriel noted how she stared directly at them before being distracted by Antonia. She peered over her shoulder as if searching for a friend. He was also aware of the looks of interest toward her from many of the men in the crowd.

Keeping his distance, he circled the room and watched as Coco admired the frescoes. Her body looked toned and the color of her hair was how he remembered it as a child.

"She's exquisite," Alessandro said, interrupting his thoughts. "Her beauty pervades even through her mask."

"Keep her in your sights," Gabriel said, and turned toward the courtyard. "It appears you were correct. Our uninvited guest has arrived." Gabriel had caught the scent of the assassin, and saw him standing behind a pillar. "No doubt he knows we're here too. Ignorant fool, he's fallen right into our ruse."

He sent a text to Layla directing her to guide Coco to the back of the villa where a car would be waiting. She complied immediately. He saw the assassin's attention turn to the members of the Allegiance who surrounded Coco, and watched him take out his cell and send a text.

○

As she made her way slowly around the vast ballroom, Coco remained unaware that members of the Allegiance surrounded her. Layla approached and placed her hand against Coco's elbow. "We need to leave," she said as she guided Coco through the ballroom.

"Why, we just arrived?" Coco asked.

"There are people here who were not on the guest list," Layla whispered. "It's best that we leave right now."

"How do you know?"

"You're followed everywhere. Members of the Allegiance are your unseen protectors."

The intensity of Layla's grip on her arm affirmed the seriousness of the situation. Antonia joined them and took up her place at Coco's side. They continued to walk briskly along the long hallway to the rear entrance of the villa.

"It's impossible to recognize anyone in these masks," Coco said, straining to see the people following. "Do you know anyone in the group that's shadowing us?"

"Yes," Layla said.

"Who are—"

"Coco, stay with us," Antonia said. "Is that clear?"

Coco nodded. She felt her adrenaline spike, and heard the pounding of her heart. The three women were now within a few feet of the back door. It opened outward as they approached.

When they stepped over the threshold, everything became a

blur. Coco saw splatters of red spurt into the air in front of her, and watched it hit the ground. Instinct told her to bolt, but Layla yanked on her arm and pulled her between the villa's stone wall and the heavy doors. Antonia and Layla huddled over her.

"Don't look up, Coco," Layla said. "Stay where you are. Do not move!"

O

Alessandro crouched near the steps that led to the waiting car. He knew Frederico and his other comrades were directly behind Layla, Coco, and Antonia, but his acute awareness told him the vampire assassin had brought ten aides with him. All were vampires. All were young. The latter confirmed that none exemplified the strength and skill of the experienced members of the Allegiance. The fight would be over quickly.

When the door opened, he sensed an attacker approaching the steps leading up to the terrace. He vaulted forward and kicked the young vampire into the air. Alessandro met the body on its descent and saw the look of horror flash in the young vampire's eyes at the realization of his imminent death. Alessandro twisted the attacker's head and tossed it aside. Blood gushed forth in torrents and splattered on the ground. A gust of wind gathered around the corpse, eagerly waiting to carry the dust of death across the landscape.

Alessandro bounded to the top of the stairs and raced across the blood-soaked terrace where a grisly battle was being fought. He'd sensed correctly; ten vampires, all young. A glimpse at Coco's terror-stricken face ignited his inner fury. He'd seen that expression once before.

With unbounded rage he entered the fight. No one would take his daughter. He lunged at a vampire intent on killing Frederico, and held him while his friend sliced through the vampire's neck with a silver blade. Before the vampire had turned to dust, Alessandro was back in the fight, ripping heads from anyone intent on attacking Coco.

When nothing but the stench of blood remained, he strode over to where Frederico and his comrades had formed a protective circle around the three women. "Get them back to Antonia's and stay with them," he commanded. "I want that villa surrounded."

He saw Coco falling and Frederico catch her in his arms. "She's fainted, my friend, she was not hurt. Go—you have my word—I will keep her safe."

Alessandro nodded and took off to find Gabriel.

○

Gabriel followed the lead assassin as he slipped away in pursuit of Coco. Being part warlock, Gabriel's greatest abilities were of the magical kind—telepathy, healing, and dimensional travel, but his vampire skills were not nearly as strong as those of a full vampire. He was grateful tonight to have Alessandro alongside him: his immortal skills—strength, agility, and the ability to fly long distances—rivaled those of Gabriel's own vampire father, Stefan.

The assassin moved silently through the villa, slipping out through a side door and racing toward the back garden. Gabriel saw the blur that he knew was Alessandro. His friend leaped out and thrust a blow leaving the assassin defenseless, and dragged him into the forest of trees that bordered one side of the property.

Alessandro had the assassin on his knees with a dagger pointed at his heart. Gabriel reached inside the assassin's jacket and retrieved his cell phone. He quickly scrolled through the recent call list, pocketed the phone, and stared down at the vampire.

"You are bound by blood," Gabriel said. "But before you die I give you the chance to honor the Allegiance."

The assassin lifted his head and snarled. "The whore

Chantal has given the Allegiance all the honor it deserves. My lord Kenan is very pleased."

Gabriel noticed the muscles on Alessandro's neck quiver—his black eyes narrowed as they focused on their target. The assassin's mocking laugh ended abruptly as Alessandro plunged his knife through his heart. He ripped the head from its cold body, before he fell to his knees and wept. The assassin's remains turned to dust.

"*Fanculo*! Where the hell is she, Gabriel? Twenty-eight years we've been searching for her, and found nothing, not a trace," Alessandro said, his voice laced with hatred. "How's he doing this?"

"I don't know. But we need to return to Ventimiglia. We've got work to do...I want to track his calls."

"Christ, we've searched the whole fucking planet and still no sign of that bastard," Alessandro said.

Gabriel took out his cell and sent a text to Layla enquiring about Coco's well-being. Then he grabbed Alessandro by the elbow and pulled him up off the ground. "Prudence believes that once Colombina's in her childhood home her powers will awaken," Gabriel said.

Alessandro's dark eyes glared at Gabriel. "I pray she's correct," he said. "When will you head back to San Gimignano? I'll feel better if one of us is there when Layla and Coco arrive."

"Prudence is with Antonia tonight and intends to stay near Coco once they arrive at your farmhouse," Gabriel said. "I doubt that Kenan has the courage to cross her." The two men walked across the grounds of the villa. "It's been many years since we fought together dressed in this form of attire, my friend."

Alessandro pushed his knife back into its sheath. "True. At least we didn't have to pay for costume rentals."

CHAPTER 14

By midafternoon the following day, Coco and Layla had packed up the car and were ready to leave Florence and drive south to San Gimignano. The traumatic incident the night before had left Coco with a lot of questions. She could not shake the visceral feeling that she knew others, apart from Antonia and Layla, at the masquerade.

She hugged Antonia goodbye and fell into the car and watched as mother and daughter embraced. She heard the two women exchange endearments in Italian and then switch to another language unfamiliar to her. Their tone sounded sad. "Look after one another," Antonia said as she waved goodbye.

Layla, Thalia and Coco sped off in the sporty white Audi over the roads of Tuscany. Security closely monitored their trip, with one car in front and one behind. Curious about the conversation Layla had with her mother, Coco asked her what they had said.

"I asked for protection for all of us," Layla said.

"You started speaking Italian and then I got lost. I heard words from about six different languages—it was very confusing."

"It's the language of the Allegiance, and one that you'll learn, I'm sure." Layla pressed her foot down hard on the accelerator and checked her rearview mirror. "Better make sure that our boys can keep up."

The rolling hills, dotted vineyards, and ancient stone ruins of the Tuscan countryside blurred past. Coco's mind yearned for an ephemeral moment of recognition, only to be disappointed. She felt detached from the beauty surrounding her, and wondered why the disconnection was so strong when she had lived here for the first four years of her life.

Layla's cell phone rang. She pushed a button on the steering wheel and spoke. "*Pronto!*"

Christopher's voice came through on speakerphone, but he spoke in the strange language that Coco didn't understand.

"We're near San Gimignano, *mi amore*," Layla said. "I'll call you once we arrive at the villa."

"*Ti amo e mi manchi,*" Christopher said.

"*Ti amo anch'io,*" Layla ended the call.

"You bring out the best in my brother."

"I see only the good within him, for that is who he is."

"I can't imagine ever saying that about any of the men I've been with."

"You just haven't met the right one," Layla said. "But he will find you soon—I feel it."

"You've been saying that for years."

"Yes, that's true, but the space between you both is closing. If you opened your mind and heart you would feel him too."

"Just spit it out, Layla, I'm not in the mood for your word games."

"There are many things I've learned about myself because of my commitment to the Allegiance," Layla said. "It came from my training."

"I don't want to be involved with the Allegiance. And I'm not ready for everything else that goes with that scenario. Besides, I'm an artist and I love teaching. That's what I do."

"What do you mean by, 'everything else that goes with it'?"

"The Allegiance *is* Christopher's life—his work is tied to the cause, and he doesn't seem to ever have time to himself. It's his entire life!"

"Yes, but their cause is what he believes in. And we were lucky to find each other, which, by the way, was because of the Allegiance."

"If there's a true love for me, then he can find me the good old-fashioned way."

"Then he may get lost, Coco. Think carefully before you ignore a closed door merely because you're too afraid to see what's behind it, that's all I ask."

"Okay, I get what you're saying, but Christopher promised I'd get answers to my questions here in Italy, so I'm taking this one step at a time. And after last night, can you blame me for being a little uptight?"

O

The geometric skyline of San Gimignano shone in the golden glow of the afternoon sun. The fourteen remaining towers that once served as symbols of wealth and power now reach toward the heavens, serving as sentinels to the treasured artwork that resides within the town's weathered stone walls.

Layla drove along the narrow cobblestone streets, stopping outside a row of stone buildings that housed a small café at one end. "I love it here," she said. "It's one of my favorite towns."

"Quite a contrast to L.A.," Coco said as she got out of the car and stretched. "It feels good to be standing, even Thalia's acting like she can't wait to escape the confines of the car."

"Put her in the carrier and bring her with us."

"Into the café?"

"Of course, come on."

Coco placed Thalia back into her carrier and toted her out of the car.

Layla took Coco's hand in hers while they walked. "Let's eat and then buy some groceries to take to the house."

"Will we be there before dark?"

"Yes, it's not far from here."

The double doors leading to the café were in themselves a piece of art. The many layers of paint that had adorned the heavy wooden panels over the years gave them a three-dimensional appearance. Above the two narrow doors, five small windows formed an arch, and behind them hung a piece of intricately woven white lace. The doors and windows were framed with a heavy arch atop of which stood a stone statue of a woman. In her hand she held a rose.

Coco waited momentarily on the worn stone step that led up to the door. She stared in appreciation at the aged architectural artwork that festooned the building. Layla pushed down on the door handle and opened one of the blue doors, ushering her companions inside.

A woman in her early sixties arranged fresh flowers in a vase. She wore a floral dress with an apron that hugged her oversized waistline. As soon as she saw the two women, she made her way around the food counter and squealed with delight. "Layla, *bellissimo angelo*."

Her arms engulfed Layla's petite body. "*E 'cosi bello vederti, Maria*." After what seemed to Coco an overabundance of welcoming side-of-the-face kisses and exaggerated hand gestures, Layla stepped back. "Coco, may I present Maria. She makes the best espresso in the world." Maria embraced her in a bear hug.

Although Coco considered her conversational Italian adequate, the speed at which Maria and Layla conversed made it difficult for her to catch more than a few words. She did notice that when Maria mentioned either Chantal or Alessandro's names, sadness fell into her intonation. The mood lifted once a meow erupted from the cat carrier. Maria opened the carrier and pulled Thalia close to her chest. "*Gattina,* welcome home," she said.

"It's okay," Layla said to Coco, "Maria loves animals and she would never let anything happen to Thalia, she's quite safe in here."

"I remember when Christopher insisted on giving her to you as a gift," Maria said, her English lilted with a pronounced Italian accent.

"Yes," Coco said. "For my twenty-second birthday."

Maria placed Thalia on the ground beside her. "Come, I will fix you a beautiful meal." The feline trotted off to the kitchen, following Maria like she was the Pied Piper of Hamelin.

Coco took in the décor, but the smell of food caused her to remember that they'd bypassed lunch. "I'm hoping Maria caters to humans as well as cats," she said. "Did you happen to order coffee?"

"*Si,* espresso and much more. Here comes Maria now."

Coco turned to see Maria rolling a trolley toward them loaded with goodies both savory and sweet, and small cups of espresso. "*Gustare*—enjoy!" Maria said, handing both women plates.

A broad grin broke across Layla's face as she gazed upon the feast. Picking up a fork, she helped herself to a platter furnished with an assortment of Bruschetta—eggplant and garlic, and tomato garnished with fresh basil, before delving into the insalata Caprese that graced another platter alongside a dish of Ravioli A Tartufo.

"I'll have a waistline the size of a cow if I stay here too long," Coco said, as she served herself some ravioli.

"I miss this," Layla said.

"Me too, and I don't even remember it. I'm tempted to bypass the starters and head directly for the desserts," Coco said, stabbing a ravioli with her fork and placing it in her mouth. She closed her eyes and stifled a moan. "Oh, God... I think I just discovered a substitute for sex."

"Then I'd better have some of that too," Layla said. She pointed to a plate of prosciutto. "You're not going to eat that, are you?"

Coco shook her head.

"Good," Layla said, and brought the plate closer to her.

After promising to call in and see Maria the next day, and armed with enough groceries for a week, they packed up Thalia and continued on their way through the narrowing streets. Coco's eyes lingered over the timeworn cobblestones. She wondered about the stories each stone had to tell, the footsteps of travelers who had walked along these streets for hundreds of years.

Layla slowed the car and pointed out a large stone build-ing. "That's the art school. We'll come back another day and I'll introduce you to *Professore* Benatti."

Coco noticed that the entrance to the school mirrored the entrance to the café, with its thick wooden doors painted blue and the statue of the woman holding a rose above the arch. To the right of the door hung a simple sign carved into the shape of an artist's palette. It read: *Scuola d'Arte*. One of the doors stood open—it revealed a tiled entrance that led to green steps indented from centuries of foot traffic.

A feeling of déjà vu ran over Coco as they passed by the building.

"That place seems familiar to me," she said.

"That's not surprising. I'm sure your mother spent a lot of time there, and I have no doubt that some days you tagged along with her."

"When can I meet the professor?" Coco asked.

"Tomorrow, if you'd like."

Coco remembered her grandfather's words: *To seek out a teacher you may need to travel to Italy.*

"Yes, I'd like that a lot."

She glanced into the exterior mirror on the side of the car and watched the medieval town dissolve into countryside behind her. About five minutes passed before Layla pointed toward a group of stone buildings built on a hilltop. "We're nearly there."

"What town is that?"

"It's a villa, not a town. *Casa della Luna Crescente*, and the people who live there are your closest neighbors."

"The house of the crescent moon."

"Nice translation."

"Too easy."

The car in front of them turned into a driveway on the left, then pulled over to let Layla pass. Coco opened her window. Cypress trees lined the paved lane and resembled church spires.

"What's that smell?" she asked.

"Resin—from the cypress trees," Layla said as she downshifted. "A few of these trees are nearly two thousand years old. Some people believed that the scent could ward off evil spirits and planted the cypress to mark a sacred space."

"And what do you believe?" Coco asked. "I'm sure your Jungian side loves this stuff."

"Of course I enjoy the symbolism of the trees—strength and protecting something sacred. What's not to like about that? Whether you choose to believe it is subjective." Layla turned the Audi left onto a stone lane. Before they turned, Coco noticed a set of heavy wrought iron gates.

"Is that the entrance to the villa?" she asked.

"Yes."

About a quarter of a mile down the road, Coco felt a brush of cool air along her arms and experienced a sense of belonging.

She was home.

The road ended at a stone farmhouse, its windows trimmed with weathered shutters and iron trim. An aged wisteria tree adorned a pergola that led to the front door. Twisted vines, grayed from exposure to wind and rain, showed little of their spring beauty, other than a few bruised blossoms that danced across the ground.

The house consisted of two levels with an attic studio over the garage. This was Coco's family home. She stared at the farmhouse and inhaled deeply before making her way to the entrance. For a moment she expected her parents to open the door and welcome her. Thalia jumped out of Coco's arms and onto the ground, rubbing against her legs before finding her way to the front door.

"You have the key," Layla said.

Coco fumbled around in her purse, placed the key in the lock, and opened the door. The house had a definite fragrance of lavender and rosemary—a scent she remembered from her childhood. Her mother's scent. She walked across the room and opened the windows.

"How can it be so clean after all of these years?"

"The house is cleaned once a month."

"Who cleans it?"

"Maria, she insisted that one day you would return."

Coco stood in the middle of the living room overcome with memories: her mother calling Christopher and her inside for dinner and the two of them racing from the garden into her waiting arms. Her father playing the baby grand piano that still remained in one corner of the living room—something from Debussy, the name was lost to her. But Coco didn't care, because for the first time in twenty-eight years she remembered moments from her childhood. In an effort to discover more, she opened the French doors that led to the garden and looked down at the first weathered step. She recalled herself as a three-year-old—her tiny hands pulling leaves off a plant and arranging them to make the abstract design of a face on the top step, and her mother sketching nearby. "I can see my mother and father... and Christopher and me as kids."

"This is quite normal," Layla said. "It's a natural response from being in your childhood home. Are you okay?"

Coco looked out at the loping trees that marked the river twisting through the landscape of rolling hills. "When we're children, we never seem to appreciate the natural beauty of things—it's just there, along with the daily rhythm of our natural lives."

"Children are multifaceted beings," Layla said. "Sadly as we get older we start to label things as beautiful or ugly."

"The beauty of my childhood here was taken away from me," Coco said. "And every shrink I've seen says that the memory loss was most likely brought on by the sudden death of my parents. Do you know how crazy it is that I can't remember anything of my early childhood? Sometimes I feel so empty—but I guess I've learned to push it away. To keep it buried."

"Perhaps being here, near your family's friends, will give you the strength to confront the pain. I believe that our soul holds a special space for the place of our birth," Layla said. "Give yourself time. Meanwhile, come upstairs so you can decide where you want to sleep."

Coco turned and followed Layla up the stairs where they wandered into the first room, knowing instantly that it had belonged to Christopher. Copies of his favorite childhood books were stacked neatly in a bookshelf and pictures of nebulas were pasted on the walls. Coco walked toward a small photo tinged with greens and blues, taped above the headboard.

"Does that one resonate with you?" Layla asked.

"There's a familiarity about the location—it looks like an Aurora or something, doesn't it?"

"Christopher has a copy of it in his home office in D.C. I don't think his décor has changed much, the only difference is that now he places the images into frames rather than just tearing them out of magazines and sticking them onto walls."

Coco picked up a photo that appeared to have once been stuck on the wall above his bed. It showed her brother as a toddler, sitting astride a large black horse while a tall man with dark hair adjusted the stirrups.

"Who's this, Layla?" Coco asked.

Layla peered at the photo and said with an air of sarcasm, "It's a very large black stallion, I can't recall his name."

"I meant the tall guy fixing the stirrups."

"I can't see his face," said Layla nonchalantly. "You might want to ask Christopher."

Coco took a closer look at the photograph, "He feels familiar."

"Nice arse, don't you think?" Layla said.

"Looks like any other stallion to me," Coco said with a smirk.

She returned the photo to its rightful place and preceded Layla to the hallway. Large windows ran along the opposite wall giving a view of the huge villa and its surrounding buildings. The two women continued along the hallway and entered Coco's childhood bedroom.

Photos of animals and drawings from her childhood adorned the walls. At the foot of her bed sat a large carved wooden chest. She knelt down and traced her fingers over the intricate designs. They reminded her of the little box she had brought with her from L.A. When she stood, she noticed a frame sitting on the window ledge. It was decorated with fragments of bark and faded sprigs of lavender. Coco picked it up—inside the frame sat a family photo. Her father, Alessandro, stood proudly beside her mother—an arm draped around her shoulders, and a young Christopher and Coco posed in front of them, surrounded by numerous dogs and cats. She ran her fingers over the frame and caught a wisp of recognition.

She carried the photo with her while she ventured further along the hallway to her parents' bedroom. The door was ajar. She entered, and felt the coolness of the worn, mottled ceramic tiles beneath her feet. She raised her eyes to the ceiling and saw the white plaster and dark wooden beams. This room reminded her of something divine—a holy place: radiating love, while sadness lingered. A plush mohair blanket of pastel purples and blues lay folded across the bottom of the bed, and throw pillows made from dainty floral prints rested neatly atop overstuffed pillows.

Coco pushed open a window, desperately needing fresh air on her face.

"I'll take Christopher's room," Layla said. "How about you sleep here?"

"How about we run?"

"Sure, but give me time to change," Layla said. "And I need to call Christopher to let him know we've arrived."

Thalia wandered into the bedroom, jumped up onto the window seat, and stared outside. Coco wondered if her cat felt the connection too, that she had returned to her original home. From the day Christopher handed her to Coco, the cat had never wanted to leave her side, and once, unbeknown to Coco, had followed her to campus. By the time Coco spotted Thalia sitting in the corner of the studio, it was too late to take her back home, so the animal stayed with her for the entire day, much to the delight of her students.

Coco stroked Thalia's soft, fluffy coat. "We're both strangers in the land of our birth, Thalia." On cue, the cat meowed, and began the dutiful business of cleaning herself. Coco walked over to a partially open door and peered inside.

The smell of paints drew her into the room. This was her mother's studio. She walked over to a windowed door. Pushing it open, she stepped onto a small patio and looked up toward the villa. She touched the delicate lace curtain that wafted in the afternoon breeze, and then turned to take in the rest of the studio.

A sofa sat against the wall directly across from where Coco stood. Blankets lay folded across the plush pillows, and books on drawing and painting lay scattered on a nearby coffee table. To Coco's left stood a large sink stained with paint marking the halfway point of the studio. Ceramic jars with assorted brushes beckoning to be picked up sat on the bench that bordered the sink. On the floor sat a large tub that held folded towels.

On the studio walls, a gallery of her mother's personal paintings were exhibited. She wandered over to the easel that stood in the center of the room and became overwhelmed when she saw an unfinished painting. It was most likely the last piece that her mother painted before her death. Coco turned and bolted out of the room.

CHAPTER 15

Caprecia stared at her face in the tarnished mirror. She had not aged in twenty-eight years. Her Mediterranean beauty, frozen in time, displayed a stark contrast to the ugliness of betrayal that ate away at her soul. She pulled the black veil over her alabaster face, slid into her black stilettos, and walked away from the bleak bedroom that had been hers for the past two years.

Since the day she had joined Kenan, her life consisted of constant location changes and mental torment. It was far from how she had imagined her immortal life would transpire, but it was a fitting life for a traitor. And a traitor she was, nothing more and nothing less. In her darkest moments she prayed for forgiveness, for death, but she knew that because of what she had done, her death—if it ever came—would be slow and excruciating. It would not be a simple silver blade through her heart and the ripping of her head from her body. Kenan liked to play with his food.

During her time with Kenan, she had learned that his connection to the Roman Catholic Church gave him access to certain means of tracking the Allegiance. His spies, along with his keen vampiric senses, and alliances with those involved in the dark arts, allowed him to keep Chantal and his nest of devotees hidden. Whenever the Allegiance grew too close, Kenan ordered his household to relocate. It had become tiresome. Caprecia was his slave—his to demean sexually, and brutally assault, both physically and mentally, at any time. He confined her to the house, castle, manor, wherever they lived. He could not risk her scent being picked up by anyone tracking Chantal. Her attempts at escaping had only brought her more abuse and tighter restrictions. He sickened her, and she vowed that one day she would make sure he paid for the atrocities he had committed.

The sound of Chantal crying echoed through the oppressive stone manor from the basement. This alerted Caprecia that they would soon leave. She vaguely remembered a story that Chantal had shared with her many years ago, when they were playing with their young children by the lake in Tuscany. It was from Chantal's childhood: she had accidently locked herself in an old shed and waited hours in the dark until her father had found her. She was terrified of confined spaces, which was exactly what Kenan used to transport her. The cement coffin was airtight and so was the retrofitted hearse. As far as Kenan was concerned, this was the perfect way for Caprecia and Chantal to travel.

A male vampire dressed in a sharp black suit knocked on Caprecia's door. He escorted her down the austere passageway, cruddy with dust and dirt, to the rancid basement and waiting car. The long black hearse slowly made its way down the slick mountain road before entering the highway. Its darkened windows and tightly sealed doors denied anything living to enter or exit during transportation. Caprecia allowed her tears to run freely while she mourned for Chantal, who, once full of life, now lay confined in her vampire body in the heavy coffin behind her. The private cargo plane that Kenan owned awaited them on the tarmac.

O

Puget Sound, Washington State.

Kenan scanned the view from the spacious deck of his latest hideaway. The sleek modern architecture indigenous to this part of the Northwest, with its exposed redwood beams and floor-to-ceiling windows, did little to bring warmth to this house. Thick forests bordered three sides of the compound—the rest of the building lay open to a rocky bay. A thick blanket of fog shrouded the surrounding forest that edged the waters of the outgoing tide. This area defined bleak and lonely. It was a forbidden place.

Kenan's slicked back dark hair matched the sheen of his tailored black suit; he placed his hands into the pockets of his dress pants, closed his eyes, and listened. He felt annoyed that Chantal's screaming had lessened after she had been released from her travel compartment. His morose mood warded off the silence of the bay.

Gabriel's men had come a little too close to his past residence, not that it concerned him—in fact, the game of hide-and-seek was a practice that propelled him forward. Knowing that he had outmaneuvered the Allegiance stimulated his elitist sense of self-entitlement.

He allowed his thoughts to drift back to his own pathetic childhood, when the only constants were the perpetual hunger that kept him awake, and the biting cold that gnawed through the holes of his pitiful excuse for shoes. Kenan remembered the day when hope came to him in the form of Girolamo Savonarola. He had yanked the young Florentine boy from the filth of the street and offered him food and shelter in exchange for information. It was a simple task: patrol the streets and report any man or woman who dared show immodest dress, decadent behavior, or took part in acts of sodomy. So began the young boy's personal debauched reformation. The year was 1495.

He had listened in awe to the words of the Italian Dominican friar and preacher, Savonarola, as he painted his picture of hell for any man, woman, or child who offended God and practiced or enjoyed humanistic culture. Those who gambled, wore fine clothes and jewelry, or engaged in Pagan festivals would need to be purged of their sins. Savonarola became exhilarated in the servitude of the bonfire of the vanities.

With abandoned passion, Kenan threw carnival masks and jewelry, literature, and artwork into the fire that flared with retribution in Florence. He stood atop a mound of books and paintings and watched the flames devour the artwork like dispassionate demons from Satan's hell.

Through manic eyes, he gazed at the spectacle before him. As the frenzied blaze grew higher, he watched in awe as two flames parted like the tongue of a serpent, and he saw an angel. He knew instantly that God had rewarded him for what he had done. He had never seen anything as beautiful—with her luminous skin, hair as white as freshly fallen snow, and eyes that glistened gold. For a moment he thought of leaping through the flames to reach her. But, for a reason unknown to him, Savonarola's men approached his angel and drew their swords. She fell to her knees wailing.

A tall man appeared before the angel with his sword drawn. He cut down each man who came near her, and then picked the angel up in his arms and carried her away. As she turned to take one last look at something in the fire, Kenan saw her staring at him. The tall man and the angel disappeared into the dark night.

Kenan ran to where the angel had been kneeling and dragged out the painting that he thought had captivated her. It was a portrait of her—his angel with golden eyes. Kenan had seen enough of the scorned artist's paintings and recognized Botticelli's work and the prize he held in his hands. After he'd doused the flames that outlined the frame, he took one last look at the fire and then turned and ran with the painting under his arm through the streets of Florence in search of his angel. He combed through the city for days, but to no avail.

Later, when the chaos in the city had subsided and the church mocked Savonarola's fanatical words and false prophecies, the twelve-year-old boy watched in horror as the tightened rope brought death to his hero and martyr. Kenan swore to revenge this death and uphold Savonarola's beliefs, but in exchange for his aegis, the boy kept the painting. He chose to ignore the fact that he had given in to three of the seven deadly sins: lust, wrath, and greed.

Following the death of Savonarola, Kenan fled Florence. His survival instincts from his youth prior to meeting his idol kept him alive... that, and his hunger for revenge. He became a master at stealing food and finding shelter, and he thanked his God for every maggot-infested morsel that came his way. And when his body twisted in pain from hunger and cold, he thought of the angel in the painting hidden behind a wall in a small church in Florence.

In the year 1510, Kenan stumbled upon a priest, offering indulgences to peasants, and listened while the man explained that by purchasing an indulgence, the buyer would be guaranteed admittance into heaven. All sins would be forgiven. The thought of purgatory was incentive enough for Kenan. That night he stole money from a drunk, and the next day bought his way into heaven. His belief in hell spurned him forward, and he joined the priest in the pilgrimage to bring salvation to the damned, and rebuild St. Peter's in Rome. Kenan responded to those stubborn souls who questioned the idea of having to buy their way into purgatory with his own ambiguous style of enlightenment, mainly in the form of brutality. These peasants threw their last coins at him and begged for his mercy from God. Kenan thought it best that their tainted coins stayed in his pocket rather than join the hallowed ground of St. Peter's.

But his pocketing of these coins dwindled when a professor of biblical studies, one Martin Luther, spoke out against the idulgences with a document that he nailed to the door of Wittenberg Castle Church. Kenan took this as a personal assault and went in search of the author of such blasphemy. But, once again, his religious beliefs were tested.

On his journey from Italy to Germany, he continued to sell indulgences. One evening, as he approached the northern border of Italy, he happened upon a man whose grimy hands and face and tattered clothing told him that this man worked in the fields for his money. Kenan was extracting the last coin from him—his knife pressed against the peasant's neck—when he felt the point of a sword in his back.

"You would take the last of this man's money—that he has earned through honest work—and tell him lies about buying his way into heaven for sins that he has not committed?" the man asked, his voice heavily accented. "It is your church that is in sin. While your pope and those around him dine on lavish dinners and wear costly clothes, this man and others like him starve. Show me your face, so that I will remember it as the face of greed."

Kenan forgot about the peasant and turned to face the man who dared speak to him with such bold words. He noted the man's height and dark eyes. Recognition dawned on him when his vision drifted to the woman who stood beside him.

It was his angel.

"I know this face," Prudence said. "In Florence, I looked up and saw you throwing books into the fire. So many truths were burned that night, so much art..." Tears fell from her golden eyes like stardust from the heavens.

"I pulled your portrait from the flames... I saved you," Kenan whispered. "You are my angel!"

Prudence took a step forward to be closer to Stefan. "Then as your angel, I request the painting be returned to me. You will not be harmed."

Kenan nodded. Stefan insisted that the criminal give every coin in his possession to the peasant, before they made their way back to Florence.

No shadows glowered in the darkened streets when they arrived at the outskirts of the city, and when they entered the small church, Kenan led them to the painting. He clutched it to his chest, and Prudence approached him with caution. Stefan stood ready with his sword.

When Prudence held out a hand, Kenan grabbed it and dragged her to him, tossing the portrait onto the stone floor. He was unsure of what happened next, but in seconds Stefan had him on the ground and had slashed him across his forehead with his sword, barely missing his eye.

The sharp pain struck him but the agony stung his heart. The physical pain would heal quickly, but the loss of his angel would fester within for eternity.

Stefan stared down at Kenan. "*Since to do her honor is for other men's shoulders, not for yours,*" Stefan said. "You would be wise to hinder the words of Francesco Petrach."

Kenan sneered. "The humanist. Never."

Prudence clutched the portrait in her arms and Stefan loomed over Kenan. "You are up against more than you can understand," he said. "I will not kill you tonight, for you are unarmed, but touch my wife again and you will find that no amount of indulgences will save you from the depths of hell." In the blink of an eye they were gone, and so was the painting.

Kenan lay on the cold stone until the light of dawn filtered through the cracks in the walls of the church. He washed the blood from his face in the baptismal font then used a cloth he found on the altar to slow down the bleeding from the gash in his head.

The painting was not the only item he had hidden in this church, and when he found his strength he pulled a bag of coins from behind a loose stone.

Later that night he found refuge in wine, and as he walked the streets he looked on as two young boys ran down an alley, thinking they had not been seen. Kenan followed, and watched from a hidden alcove while they found pleasure in each other's bodies. The sexual feelings he'd held back for so many years exploded in him and he grabbed one of the boys and threw him against the wall. He lost himself in pleasure in the soul of the other. Hours later, when he came out of his drunken stupor, both boys lay bloodied and dead beside him.

That night, gluttony, sloth, pride and envy were added to his list of deadly sins.

CHAPTER 16

The run was perfect. The air had a crisp bite to it, reminding Coco that it was November in Italy. On their way back to the house, they stopped at a place where the river widened and created a lake before meandering back to a stream that twisted through the surrounding hills. They walked to the water's edge, and strolled along a small jetty that moaned beneath their feet. A rickety wooden ladder awaited them, and below a small rowboat rose and fell gently with the flow of the water.

The two women climbed down the ladder and into the rowboat. Coco untied the rope that bound it to the jetty, and then grabbed the oars and rowed the craft into the middle of the lake. "Have we just stolen someone's property or is this normal behavior in Tuscany?" she asked.

"This is your boat, and this land belongs to you too."

"You're kidding, right?"

"No, I'm not. The farmhouse comes with this land, lake, and the boat. It's all yours."

"What the hell am I supposed to do with it? I'm not my mother," Coco felt her anxiety rising. "My life is based in Los Angeles—her life was different. She met my father and they were in love."

"Your mother knew exactly what she was doing, Coco," Layla clasped her hands and stretched them above her head, and then relaxed. "It will be dark soon. Let's head back."

Coco rowed back toward the jetty. She secured the boat and followed Layla up the ladder and back to the house.

That night, while Coco lay on her parents' bed with Thalia curled up beside her, she desperately searched her memories for more childhood moments in Tuscany, but nothing surfaced. And although the subtle twitch in the back of her neck had lessened since she had arrived in Italy, it still lingered. Finally, accepting exhaustion, she drifted off to sleep.

Coco stands amongst the tall, emerald green grass. She sees a house. Its weatherboard exterior is aged, beaten over time by wind and rain. She approaches the building and walks up the steps to the front door. It opens, and she enters. The entire interior is painted light blue, the color of the ocean.

There's a staircase directly in front of her but she's reluctant to proceed. Cautiously, she places a foot on the first step, and slowly begins to ascend one step after the other. She senses the spirits of the dead around her:

"It's her," a voice whispers.

"Yes—finally, Colombina's here!" says an old lady who drifts by, trailing the scent of roses.

At the top of the staircase are three doors. Coco knows she must open one, but feels apprehensive and frightened even with Thalia beside her. She knows it will be safe to open either the middle door, or the one to the right, but something reminds her that the only way to move forward in her life is to enter the room to her left.

Her hand connects with the round door handle and turns it slowly. A large spiderweb greets her on the other side, and she instantly feels the first sign of nausea quench the gums of her back teeth; she has feared spiders as long as she can remember. A huge spider with burnished black legs and a bulbous abdomen is poised and ready to pounce on her, its jaws extended in readiness to drop its fangs into her flesh. It beckons her with an undeniable deadly potency. She steps forward. Panic and fear take over her body, and as much as she wants to run she is unable to move. She waits for her death.

A movement to her left distracts her, and a beautiful spider, silver and white, appears before her. It deflects the larger arachnid before it can strike. This spider's face is gentle and kind, and it reaches out and touches Coco's face, then her heart. The spider does not speak aloud, but Coco feels comforted and safe.

The moment Coco woke up, she grabbed her sketchbook and pencil and drew a quick sketch of the dream. The size, color and positioning of the spiders were all detailed, and then she remembered the face of the woman. She appeared as a grandmother—no one Coco knew, but she felt connected to her. She opened her laptop and typed up the dream, saving it to her dream file that she'd started fifteen years ago.

Coco understood the meaning behind this nightmare. The evil spider represented her fear of facing unknowns—a confirmation that the only way forward was to take the path she resisted the most. The dark spider in her dream had cast a web, a tapestry of sorts, a trap. She remembered feeling paralyzed with fear, just as she had felt for months whenever she had tried to paint. Through her work with dreams she understood that both spiders represented a part of her. Coco had no doubt that the light spider was female and represented her creativity.

Layla's words echoed in her mind: *Think carefully before you ignore a closed door because you're too afraid to see what is behind it.*

CHAPTER 17

New York City, U.S.A.

Arianna waited alone in the small office. The noise of the city dissipated until the only sound she heard was the irritating click from the clock hanging on the wall. It matched the rhythm of her pulse. Footsteps approached and stopped at the door. She ran the palms of her hands over her jeans and held her shoulders back. She focused, breathed deeply, consciously welcoming her fears and anxiety. Clarity stilled her mind. The door handle turned and in the doorway stood her twin brother.

The woman who had escorted Jeremy in to meet his sister excused herself. "I'll be in the next office if you need me. Take your time," she said, and left. The room was painfully quiet, until the ticking of the clock was joined with the nervous muffled sound of Jeremy's fingers drumming against his jeans.

"I'm Arianna. Your twin sister."

He nodded. "I guessed that. So… do we shake hands? This is pretty weird."

Arianna got up and gave him a hug. "We're twins, I think we can hug." She felt his body flinch and was relieved when he finally returned the gesture. They stepped apart and she cleared her throat. "I'm sorry that our meeting is under such sad circumstances. Are you okay?"

Jeremy cocked his head slightly to one side. "No, but I'd rather not talk about anything here. Maybe later."

"Can I ask you one thing before we leave?"

Jeremy nodded.

"How long have you known about me?" She stared at him, intent on not breaking eye contact.

"Mom told me I had a twin sister a year ago—directly after she found out about the cancer," Jeremy said. "I still don't understand why she didn't tell me a long time ago."

"I wondered about that too."

"What about you? When did you know?"

"A week ago. I'm still digesting everything." She grappled with a new emotion seeping into her heart. "But I want you to know that I love my adoptive mom, Isabel, so much and that will never change. And I feel none of the abandonment stuff I've read about that adopted people often feel." A tear rolled down her cheek.

"You sure about that?"

"Yes—I'm just a little emotional right now."

He gestured to the wall. "Is that Isabel in the next room?"

"Yes."

"Well, let's go. Mom will be worried if we're not back soon." He held the door open for Arianna and they walked into the adjacent room.

Isabel drew herself up. "Hello, Jeremy. I'm Isabel."

"Hi," Jeremy shook her hand. "How was your flight?"

"Fine, thanks," Isabel said. "Are you both ready to leave?"

"Sure," Jeremy picked up Isabel's case and then eyed Arianna's duffle. "Is that yours?"

Arianna nodded. "I can carry it," she said.

She went to pick it up but Jeremy hoisted it over his shoulder. "I got it," he said.

"Thanks. Mom and I are kind of used to carrying our own bags," she held her hand out to Isabel. "Come on."

Jeremy turned to the caseworker. "Thanks, I appreciate what you've done for Mom."

"You're welcome, Jeremy."

○

In the front garden of Katya's home resided a collection of garden gnomes. Some lay on their sides with pipes in their mouths, others seemed to be carrying on deep conversations amongst each other, while others looked to be mesmerized by a couple of ceramic fairies peeking out from potted plants. The gnomes' distinctive red hats were the only consistency among the odd gathering. Jeremy guided Arianna and Isabel up the garden path to the front verandah. "They're Mom's—she's been collecting them for years."

"Garden gnomes?" Arianna asked.

"Garden statuary," he said, with a little sarcasm, while opening the front door. "Mom says they're very popular in Europe. Come on, she's been waiting a long time to see you."

In the living room, the soft tones of Cat Stevens singing "Wild World" greeted them. "I love this song," Arianna said, and hummed along to the chorus.

"Then you and Mom have that in common. I find it depressing."

A woman entered the room wearing a set of pink scrubs. "Hi, Jeremy. Your mom's had her meds and I've bathed her, so your timing's perfect. She's doing fairly well today." Jeremy nodded. The woman turned to Arianna. "You must be Arianna and Isabel, it's great that you came. See you tomorrow."

Jeremy guided Arianna across the passageway to a yellow door with white trim. He knocked gently, then pushed it open and motioned her inside. Leaning against numerous crisp white pillows was Katja, the twins' birth mother. Her skin looked pale, but her eyes were the same light blue as Jeremy's, and an elegant silk scarf painted in swirls of blues and purples covered her head.

Arianna had a tight grip on Isabel's hand as they made their way to Katya's bed. "Hi, Katja," she said. "I'm Arianna." They were all the words she could find.

Katja looked into Arianna's eyes and whispered, "Please forgive me..." A single tear rolled down her face.

Arianna swallowed and breathed deeply. "You did what you had to do to keep us all alive, and I have wonderful parents." She reached for Katja's hand and gave it a squeeze. "How can I be angry with you for that?" Arianna urged Isabel forward. "This is Isabel."

"After all of these years we finally meet in person," Isabel said, wiping the tears from Katja's cheeks. "They look alike, don't you think?"

Katja nodded and smiled, then lifted her hand to Arianna's face. "You are so beautiful, I always knew you would be."

"Thanks, I think I look like my brother." She looked over at Jeremy standing by the door. He placed his hands in his pockets and silently left the room. Isabel excused herself and followed him outside.

Katja picked up a wooden box from her bedside table and rested it above her heart. "This is for you, my beautiful girl," she said, her voice frail and soft. "When you were a few days old, before the social worker took you from me, I cut a tiny piece of your hair. I hoped that in some way, it would keep your essence near me forever. Over the years, when the pain of your absence became too much, I'd write letters to you... a few of them are in here." She patted the box as a tear fell over her cheek and landed on the lid, leaving her sadness imprinted on the wood. "Thank you for coming to me. Seeing you and Jeremy together makes my journey to the next world an easier one."

Arianna took the box and looked at the carved detail. "What do these carvings mean?" She touched the outline of a symbol, and a shiver ran over her. "This resembles the infinity symbol."

"It's a rune and the woman and jaguar carved into the wood are from an old story—'The Legend of Astridr.' It's said that the jaguar drank from Astridr's mother shortly after she gave birth to her daughter. This gave the jaguar magical powers. Astridr's father was a fairy prince."

Arianna opened the lid and took out a faded photo of a tall man with white hair and pale blue eyes. "Who's this?" she asked. "He looks like Jeremy."

"He's your father. My beloved. He died before you and Jeremy were born. He gave me this box. When I'm gone, you and Jeremy can read my diaries... they tell our story. Jeremy knows where they are."

Katja's eyes grew heavy and Arianna kissed her cheek. "I promise to look after Jeremy."

"You and Jeremy are destined for greatness—your father saw this. We will be watching over you." She placed her hand on top of Arianna's. "*Trattiene l'amore nel tuo cuore...*"

Arianna repeated the words in English, thinking how serendipitous it was that she chose to learn Italian in college. "Keep love in your heart."

○

Katja passed away two days later with Arianna and Jeremy on either side of her, each holding one of her hands. Arianna kissed

Katja's hand, and then reached out to Jeremy. "I'll be outside if you need me."

He gripped her hand tightly. "Please… don't leave," he said, his voice tearful. "I don't want to be alone." Arianna walked around to the other side of the bed and embraced him. His body trembled as his tough outer shell crumbled. Arianna held onto him while his tears flowed. "You won't ever be alone."

O

Arianna helped Jeremy carry out the funeral arrangements that Katja had organized prior to her death, and her request for a memorial at her home was honored. Arianna seemed to sense when her brother needed time by himself and when he wanted company, and their initial wariness toward one another melted away.

She looked out of the kitchen window and caught sight of Jeremy and Isabel walking around the front garden. Isabel crouched down beside one of the gnomes and pulled out a weed that blocked its jolly face. Isabel looked up and waved to Arianna, and then walked up the steps and into the kitchen.

"Jeremy gave me a tour of the gnome and fairy garden. They all have names, you know," Isabel said. "That twin of yours is a remarkably loving person. You're lucky to have him as a brother."

"I know," Arianna said as she gave Isabel a kiss on her cheek.

She went outside and found Jeremy sitting on the front steps and scooted in next to him. "Katja said she left her diaries for you and I to read together."

"Yeah, they're in her safe deposit box at the bank. Not sure I can handle that yet."

"Me neither, but I'm curious to know about our father," she said. "Maybe my next visit we can collect them."

"Sure," he said. He rested his elbows on his knees and looked around the garden. "What am I going to do with all of Mum's stuff and the house?"

"For right now, nothing," Arianna said. "You've been through a lot and that's never a good time to make a hasty decision. You know you're welcome to come and stay with us, until law school begins. How does that sound?"

He shrugged. "I don't know—I need to be in D.C. for the next few months. After that I'll figure stuff out. School starts in August."

"*We'll* figure it out," she said and gave him a hug. "Remember, you're not alone."

Jeremy shoved her gently with his shoulder and grinned. "You remind me of my boss at work. He's kind of a control freak."

"There's no 'kinda' with me," she said. "I am a control freak."

○

It was midnight when the taxi pulled into the driveway of their home in L.A. Arianna and Isabel unloaded their belongings and made their way through the house to their bedrooms. When Arianna had checked her cell phone while waiting at the luggage carousel at the airport, she'd been excited to see that Jeremy had already left her a text.

Thanks for everything… you're missed.

She'd replied immediately.

Miss you too—I'll call you soon. xo

Arianna placed the wooden box next to her bed, lay down, and stared at the rune carved into the wood. She made a mental note to research the symbol, but for now she needed sleep. She set her alarm for 4:30 a.m. and fell to sleep immediately. When the alarm went off a few hours later, she showered and then went in to check on Isabel. She found her busy in the kitchen.

"I was about to come and wake you up with some coffee." Isabel handed her daughter a large mug. "Is it okay if I come to work with you today? I was thinking that with the holiday season coming up that you and Tio could use the extra help."

Arianna was taken aback. "Of course, Mama... that'd be great." She pushed a strand of hair back behind her ears.

"I'll just get my purse," Isabel said.

Arianna followed her. "Mom, are you okay?"

"Yes, I'm fine," Isabel said as she smoothed down her long hair.

"But it's time, Arianna. Steven would have wanted me to get on with my life."

CHAPTER 18

San Gimignano, Italy.

Professor Eduardo Benatti was a tall man with graying hair and eyes to match. His style emulated early Monet: upturned white shirt collars, hand-tied bow ties, tweed vest and pants. Elegant hands and slender fingers revealed a faded mark on his ring finger, perhaps the semblance of a wedding band. The Professor's stern deportment took a softer turn on seeing Coco, and when he spoke, his perfect English melded with his Italian accent.

"You are Chantal and Alessandro's daughter," he said. "There's no mistaking the amethyst hue of your eyes." He put his hands on her shoulders and kissed her cheeks.

"It's good to meet you, Professor," Coco said.

"Come, let me show you around the studio and gallery. I hear you are also a teacher."

"Yes, and I miss my students."

Layla stepped toward the stairs. "I have errands to run, *professore.*"

He waved his right hand toward her. "Take your time."

Layla turned to Coco. "Text me when you're ready to be

picked up—I won't be far away." She gave Coco a quick wave then darted down the steps. The Professor guided Coco away from the staircase and into the studio. The mere act of stepping into the room, with its easels and familiar smell of paints eased Coco's tension. The brushes that rested in jars beside sinks, or lay on tables in wait of an artist's creativity, and the palettes with their myriad colors reflected the temperament of their owners.

"I have some of your mother's paintings here, Coco. Would you like to see them?"

"Of course," she answered, feeling a touch of anxiety at the mention of her mother. "I'd like that a lot."

The Professor led Coco to a small room off the gallery, where he opened a cupboard and pulled out a large leather portfolio. He carried the portfolio out into the main room where natural light flooded through extensive windows, and proceeded to display her mother's paintings on easels around the room. One painting immediately stood out to Coco. It was a portrait of a little girl with dark brown hair, big lavender eyes, and pale skin.

"She painted me."

"Yes, many times, and Christopher too. You two were her favorite models, of course."

Coco picked up another portrait of her brother. "Christopher hasn't changed—I bet he was a wild child."

"No, he was a gentle little boy. You were the wild one, you never sat still—you were perpetually moving."

"My brother, a gentle little boy? That's not what I expected."

Coco noticed that most of the other paintings were of the garden at the farmhouse, the lake, and a large willow tree.

"What can you tell me about my father, Professor, were you two friends?"

"Yes, and I was with your mother on the day they met. Chantal and I were at a meeting—at the villa above where you live. We were discussing a recent painting she had completed when our host suddenly ran outside. We heard a raucous noise erupt from the courtyard. Moments later our host returned with his arm around the shoulders of a man who equaled his stature, and his eyes were also flecked with amethyst."

"My father. And the man with him—he owned the villa?"

"Yes, they were the best of friends. But the moment Alessandro saw your mother it was as if no one else existed. So much so that we suggested the two of them go for a walk together." The Professor held up a hand as if holding a small glass. "This is how it is when two souls find each other after years of searching for their beloved."

"Do you really believe in that concept?" Coco asked.

The Professor looked at Coco. "Yes, my dear, I believe it can happen."

Coco sat pensively in an antique armchair, its velvety dark green cushions reminded her of the long grass that swayed in her dreams. "Sometimes it's difficult to remember Mother's face," she confessed.

The Professor opened another door that one might assume to be a cupboard. Inside, revealed a large room drenched in light that beamed in through skylights. He motioned for her to follow. The studio was an extension of the Professor's private office.

He waved an arm to the opposite end of the room where the wall was taken up with multiple portraits of a woman who Coco knew could only be her mother. "Before I began teaching here," he said. "Chantal and I were students together—we shared the same teacher. Your mother was my favorite model. Choose a painting and take it home. Chantal would have wanted that."

Feeling overwhelmed, Coco rested on a nearby chair.

"Take your time, I hear my students arriving." The professor walked over to the sink and poured a glass of water from a crystal jug and handed it to her. "When you turn around you'll see a painting of Alessandro—they asked that I hang their portraits across from each other so they could always look into each other's souls."

Coco turned and saw the striking image of her father. She was immediately awed by the color and intensity of his eyes. There was no doubt where her enthusiasm for life derived. All of the gentleness that she faintly remembered of him was there, but she couldn't help wonder why this image reminded her of something else. She saw the passion and strength that emanated from her father's stare. He looked fearless.

Sometime in the late afternoon Layla returned. While they drove home, Coco drank in the fall colors of the countryside. The fruits of the pomegranate and persimmon trees brought warmth to the browns of the November Tuscan palette, and she felt the urge to pick up her brushes and begin painting again.

"So... what did you think?" Layla asked.

"He's a fascinating man. I'm going to help him in the studio in exchange for private lessons. I can't wait to get back there tomorrow," Coco said. "How was your day?"

"Interesting. I met with a friend who I've known for years, we attended university together. She also studied analysis, and recently settled down with her longtime boyfriend. They live in Siena. She's invited me to help her with a support group she's starting. So, if it's okay with you, I'm going to stay in Italy a little longer. Hopefully, that will encourage Christopher to join us. He needs a break."

"That'd be great. Besides, those answers he promised me? Well, I have even more questions after the other night and today."

"He's obsessed with a case right now, so perhaps we both need to be patient. Plus he's stressed about our safety."

"Christopher's always stressed. It's part of his makeup."

With each passing day, Coco understood why her mother had loved Tuscany. Professor Benatti was one of a handful of professors who taught painting in the area, and Coco's days were spent at the studio. He encouraged her to return to the basics of observational drawing, detailing the intricate lines of her hand, followed by the curves and shadows of a rose.

He hired models for the life drawing classes, and, like most, he had a favorite. Louisa was aloof, smart and sassy, and often showed all three attributes in the space of a minute. But there was no doubting that she was the best model Coco had ever witnessed. She never moved during sittings, not a twitch or a scratch, and there was no denying that Louisa was a true classic Italian beauty. Coco noticed the scent of marjoram that always wafted around Louisa, and it reminded her of the overgrown herb garden at the farmhouse.

Professor Benatti seemed protective over his favorite model, and, at times, when Coco noticed the sideways glances between the two, she wondered if they had been lovers. Louisa never spoke of her own family, but once, when she followed Coco into the Professor's studio, Coco noticed tears on her face. Louisa's gaze focused on a small watercolor painting on a shelf behind an easel.

The subject of the piece was a naked woman. She walked away from the observer, her lustrous dark hair danced in the wind, and the soft curves of her body bled into the heavy paper as if being washed away by the rain. It emoted a raw quality, like a caged animal that had finally been set free.

"Do you know her?" Coco asked.

"I did once…" Louisa turned and walked back out to the main studio. They never spoke of the painting, or the woman, again.

CHAPTER 19

Ignacio extended the kickstand and planted the Ducati on a road near the outskirts of San Gimignano. Seconds later, he had established himself up on the roof of the building across from the *Scuola d'Arte*. He found himself in this part of Tuscany whenever Kenan needed someone to do his dirty work—and mostly his requests involved the corruption not of the Allegiance members, but of those closest to them.

The DNA sample that Damien Smith had procured proved that Chantal and Coco were mother and daughter, but one question still bothered him: why had the Allegiance waited twenty-eight years to bring Coco back to Tuscany? Chances were she was a Creative, but she'd showed no signs that she was involved with, or in any way interested in, the work of the Allegiance.

He hoped to figure out why she had been brought to Tuscany and if she could be of use to Kenan. Unfortunately, the grounds where she was living were heavily guarded, as were any buildings adorned with the statue of the lady and the rose, so he'd have to find a way to get close to her here in town. With Gabriel away, Ignacio only had a small window of time to complete his task before the powerful leader returned to Tuscany.

He watched as the professor unlocked the door to the school and disappeared up the steps. He almost felt sorry for the guy—he'd die instantly if he knew what his precious wife was up to with Kenan. An Audi pulled up a little ways down the street. Coco and Layla climbed out and walked in the direction of the school.

Ignacio turned to leave, but the alluring scent of wild marjoram in the air distracted him. He closed his eyes and his nostrils flared. He swung around to where the smell lingered and felt struck by a yearning sensation. A soft breeze gathered up the scent and it whirled in a torment around him, warm and sweet. The woman had dark hair that billowed past her waist, pale skin, and lips stained a deep red. She stood perhaps six feet if you counted her high-heeled shoes. They were reminiscent of those worn by women in the 1930s. The cardigan draped over her shoulders allowed Ignacio a perfect view of her bare neck.

He breathed in deeply as the marjoram wafted over him. The scent taunted his bloodlust, but it was another aroma that lured him: a slight trace of heroin lingered in her blood. Ignacio remained on the rooftop wrestling between his predatory instinct and the work he'd been sent to do. In the end he tracked the woman's trail back to her apartment and became familiar with his prey. Kenan could wait.

Ignacio had always prided himself on his timing—it was impeccable. This, combined with his Machiavellian tendencies in the area of flirting with his prey, made him a deadly vampire to the fairer sex. With his head in a newspaper, he turned the corner of the narrow cobblestone street and ran into the woman. The moment her eyes connected with his he knew she was putty in his hands.

"My apologies, I wasn't watching where I was going," Ignacio said. "Forgive me."

"I accept your apology," the woman said. He watched as her

gaze shifted from his eyes to the rest of his body and back to his eyes before she smiled. "I like your boots."

"So do I."

He allowed the silence between them to stretch out, just long enough to make her feel uneasy before he spoke. "I'm on my way for a drink. Care to join me?"

The woman showed a shimmer of hesitation, and for a moment Ignacio wondered if she would decline his invitation.

"Are you attempting to woo me?" she asked.

"It's that obvious?"

"Yes, but a drink would be nice."

O

Louisa had known the second she laid eyes on Ignacio that they were destined to be together. When he touched her hand a jolt of energy shot up from her toes to her fingertips. She didn't need anyone else to instill in her that his presence meant danger, or that his background most likely harbored acts of violence. And yet his childlike sense of fun and witty sense of humor enticed her. Their initial drink ran into dinner, and then regular dates. When she asked what kind of work he did, he replied that he did research for a travel company. She didn't believe him for a second.

At first he was the perfect gentleman, taking her to Siena for dinner, arriving at her apartment with flowers, and caring for her sexually in ways that she had never imagined. But he quickly became demanding of her time, insisting that she return to her apartment immediately after work. When Louisa spoke to him about feeling trapped, he backed off, saying that he'd leave town for a while to give her some space.

But Louisa knew in the back of her mind that she had fallen for the handsome Englishman, with his common accent and dangerous habits. They were more alike than each cared to admit. What she needed was some time alone to understand the deep emotions she had for the dark-haired gypsy-like vampire. She knew what he was—she'd met his kind before, but had never been attracted to them the way she was to Ignacio. She needed time to think this through.

Ignacio let her believe that he had left the village, but Louisa was his weakness, and to leave her would have driven him insane. Instead, he chose to secretly stalk her. His attraction to her was magnetic, but he was not blind to the fact that her life was in danger whenever they were together. He had never felt for another, human or immortal, the way he felt about Louisa. In essence, he knew they were addicted to each other, and worse— at least for her—they had fallen in love.

He watched as she opened the door and walked up the steps to the art school. He sent a text to Kenan:

Consider this my letter of resignation.

The response was immediate.

A decision you will come to regret.

Ignacio dropped his cell into the pocket of his leather jacket, looked down at the ring on his finger, and cracked his knuckles.

CHAPTER 20

At the end of each weekday, when the students had left the building, Coco spent time painting on her own. Being a student again had freed up the creative roadblock that had haunted her in L.A. After concentrating on her observational drawing skills, the Professor had suggested to Coco that she paint using only one primary color plus black and white. This brought the emphasis back to shading and tonal skills. Gradually, he encouraged her to introduce other colors to her palette and now she found it difficult to tear herself away from painting—she felt great being back in the groove of creativity.

The studio reminded her of her own students, and from time to time she checked in with them via email. She repeatedly turned down Louisa's invitations to join her for drinks. She didn't know how long she would be in Tuscany and the thought of becoming attached to friends in faraway places did not appeal to her.

Her continued excuse of being busy worked for a few weeks, until one evening Louisa planted herself on a chair in the studio and wouldn't take no for an answer.

"Coco—come on—it's just for one drink," Louisa said,

while she watched Coco clean brushes. "You're in Italy and it's nearly Christmas. You need to have some fun. *Vivere!*"

Coco dried her hands on a nearby towel, took out her cell phone and called Layla. "Hi, is it okay if I go and have a drink with Louisa? Maybe you can join us."

"Sure, sounds okay to me," Layla said. "I'll there in about an hour. Text me the address."

"Really?" Coco said with wide eyes. "Great, I promise to text you as soon as I know where we're going."

Coco ended the call and picked up her purse and turned to Louisa. "Let's go have some fun—Tuscan style!"

Louisa grabbed Coco and dragged her down the stairs. "*Presto!*" she said. "Before you change your mind."

Arm in arm, the two women walked through the maze of streets until Louisa guided Coco into a bar. The arched walls inside were completely covered in posters that depicted art shows, music events, and films. The barman leaned across the bar and kissed Louisa on both cheeks.

"*Ciao, bella!*" he said. "*Come stai?*"

"*Cosi cosi, Carlos, e tu?*" Louisa said.

"*Va-bene, va-bene,*" Carlos said, shrugging his shoulders and lifting his hands in the air.

"Tonight you will practice your English," Louisa said. "This is my friend, Coco."

Carlos looked Coco up and down, reminiscent of a drill sergeant in an inspection lineup. "*Una bellezza!*" He picked up a bottle of wine and poured two glasses, and handed one each to Louisa and Coco. "Enjoy, Coco," he said in stilted English.

"*Grazie,*" Coco said.

Carlos winked. "You are welcome."

Coco sent a text to Layla as promised, and after her second glass of wine she began to unwind. It had been months since she'd gone out with friends, and she felt grateful that Louisa had encouraged her to do so.

○

Coco enjoyed meeting the colorful inhabitants of the village, and Louisa and her quickly became good friends. On weekdays they met for lunch at Maria's café. Louisa would play one of Maria's Italian gypsy CDs and dance with Maria and a few willing customers. On days when Louisa seemed melancholy, she changed the music to Portuguese Fado—songs full of heartache and loss. She would stand by the window and stare at the bricked street and pedestrians walking by. When Coco tried to comfort her, Louisa would shrug and smile, choosing instead to keep her emotions to herself.

One night when they were about to leave the studio, Louisa's cell rang. Coco noticed that Louisa seemed hesitant to take the call, but after the third ring she answered. Coco saw the tension creep over Louisa's body and the muscles in her jaw clench. She nodded when Louisa motioned that she needed a moment, and watched her walk toward the back of the studio.

When Louisa finished the call she approached Coco. "A friend of mine is in town," she said. "I need to see him. Are you okay going on without me tonight?"

"That's fine—a night at home won't hurt me," Coco said. "Everything okay?"

Louisa picked up her purse and threw her cardigan over her shoulders as she walked toward the stairs. "Of course—I'll see you tomorrow night."

But the next night and each night the following week, Louisa had the same excuse. Her friend was still in town and she needed to be with him.

At UCLA, Coco had often held dinner parties for her students. She enjoyed their discussions and campus gossip, but more importantly, she loved surrounding herself with like-minded creative people—members of her tribe. December at UCLA seemed crammed with exams and social gatherings, and Coco missed the rituals of the holiday season that she had come to know and love. And so when a few of the students at the studio approached her, suggesting that she join them for dinner, Coco accepted. She felt homesick and needed company.

The small restaurant felt quaint. The interior stone walls entertained the grotto style that Coco had become accustomed to in the small town. She savored the conversations, which ranged from current films to the Professor's unusual attire, and she found herself even enjoying the flirting that seemed to run rampant no matter where she went. After dinner, she walked outside to her car and spotted Louisa approaching, accompanied by a man.

"Louisa," Coco said. "I've missed you."

Louisa lifted her head. "*Ciao*," she said and snuggled in closer to her friend and looked up into his eyes. "This is my friend, Coco."

He turned his gaze to her. "I've heard a lot about you," he said. "I'm Ignacio."

Coco nodded, gave him a half-hearted smile, and held her hand out toward him. When his hand touched hers, she shivered. The night was cold, but his skin felt icy. She couldn't help noticing that something about Louisa seemed a little off—her lack of eye contact and joie de vivre were amiss. Coco stepped forward and noticed Ignacio's grip on Louisa tighten.

"I haven't seen you in a while," Coco said. " Have you been ill?"

She felt Ignacio's cold stare and looked at him. His gray

eyes edged with black onyx made her feel vulnerable, and at the same time the compulsion to flee entered her mind. Instead, she did her best to hide the fear that had begun to rise in her belly.

"She's fine," Ignacio said. His body seemed to move in rhythm with his Cockney accent. "Just a bit of a cold—right, Lu? Nothin' to concern yourself with, Coco."

Louisa nodded and kissed him.

For some reason, a line from *Oliver Twist* popped into Coco's head: *Of all the horrors that rose with an ill scent upon the morning air, that was the foulest and most cruel.*

This man with his arm around her friend was a replica of Dickens' Bill Sikes. His dark demeanor, hidden behind a modern façade of black jeans and a collared shirt that hung from his lanky muscular body, caused Coco's muscles to tighten. She pulled her gaze away from him and focused on Louisa.

"*Buonanotte, bella,*" Louisa said, as they walked off down the dark street.

A chill ran up Coco's spine, and she noticed a low fog creeping along the cobblestone road. Her heart pounded and her hands shook. She dropped her car keys and she trembled as she picked them up, unlocked the car and drove quickly home.

Coco began seeing Louisa and Ignacio out on the streets and in restaurants regularly after that first meeting. Whenever Louisa left to use the ladies room, Coco observed Ignacio watching her like a hawk hunting its prey. She loathed that any man could make her feel afraid, and when she tried to speak to Louisa about Ignacio her friend became protective and defensive. His borderline-insane possessiveness of her made it difficult for Coco to speak with her friend, until one evening at a restaurant, Coco confronted Louisa in the ladies room.

"Louisa, I miss our time together. It seems serious between you and Ignacio—are you happy?"

Louisa stared at Coco's reflection in the mirror. "Yes, I'm very happy." She checked her watch. "Let's talk soon. I need to go." She kissed Coco's cheeks and walked out of the room.

Coco's distaste for Ignacio deepened one afternoon when she walked into the small dressing room and found Louisa dabbing makeup onto her arm, covering marks resembling small bruises. Louisa jumped when she heard Coco enter.

"What's going on?" Coco asked, staring at Louisa's arm and holding it firmly in her hand.

Louisa bent her head and turned away. "This is not something new for me, Coco," she said quietly. "This is a part of who I am."

"Oh, Louisa," Coco said.

Louisa's lip trembled.

Coco took the sponge from Louisa's hand. "Is this Ignacio's doing? Why do you stay with him?"

Louisa looked up at Coco. "You know nothing of Ignacio. He's a good man—and I stay because I am in love with him."

Coco grabbed the bottle of liquid makeup, tipped it upside-down onto the sponge, and did her best to cover up the marks. "I'm here for you. I can get you some help. Whatever you need..."

"Thank you," Louisa whispered. "But I'm fine."

At the end of the drawing class Louisa excused herself to get dressed. She gathered her belongings and ran down the steps. Coco noticed the professor staring out the window as the rumble of Ignacio's motorbike filled the air.

CHAPTER 21

San Gimignano, Italy.

Thunder rolled across the raven-colored sky and bolts of fierce lightning illuminated the sheeting rain as it deluged the countryside. The streets of the town were deserted. Streetlights hovered. No human dared step out into the dismal night.

Baylor followed his quarry along the empty streets. In his hand he held a cane, a prop he had carried prior to his vampire life. As a child, a piece of glass embedded in his cornea had left his right eye blind and clouded over. The cane, originally given to him for guidance, had since become a deadly weapon.

It had been decades since Baylor had been face to face with the English vampire and he was well aware of his dexterous ingenuity, having seen him in action many times. He watched him dart across the Piazza Duomo, and up the steps that led to the Church of Collegiata, then slip inside the 11th century sanctuary of the arts and faith.

Baylor followed.

The interior of the church brought shelter from the harsh

storm. But a sudden strike across Baylor's face and chest caused him to drop to his knees, his neck caught in a strangle hold.

"Evenin' Baylor," Ignacio purred in his ear. "What brings you to these parts, you murderin' li'l shit?"

Baylor spat blood onto the sacred stone floor. "I need your head on a silver platter," he said. His good eye searched the floor for his cane. It lay just out of his reach. "Kenan's got a bounty out for you and your lady friend." His words caused the Englishman's body to twitch. "Never thought I'd see the day you'd fall for one piece of pussy." He slammed his elbow into Ignacio's gut and reached for his cane just as his accomplice, a young vampire, entered the church.

O

Ignacio rebounded from Baylor's hit and landed a silver knife into the heart of his new adversary. The young vampire staggered for a few moments before Ignacio knocked him down with a kick and twisted off his head. Out of the corner of his eye he saw Baylor charging at him, his cane held out like a sword. Ignacio knew that Baylor's aim was on his heart but in his haste he miscalculated Ignacio's swiftness, and missed. The silver-tipped point struck his shoulder. Ignacio grabbed the cane and vaulted into the air. He landed behind Baylor and rested the tip of the cane against his neck before thrusting it into Baylor's heart. For a moment, Baylor's screams echoed above the raging storm.

Ignacio broke the cane in two pieces and threw them across the room. A moment later Baylor's head fell with a thud to the stone floor. Just before turning to dust, the head rolled over and Baylor's cloudy eye stared up at Taddeo di Bartolo's fresco, *The Last Judgement*.

Ignacio felt Stefan's presence as he came forth from the

Cappella de Santa Fina, the small chapel on the right side of the basilica. He turned to face him.

"So," Stefan said. "You are in love with her."

"Yes," Ignacio said. "And now Kenan has a bounty on our heads." He picked up his silver knife, wiped the blade on his black jeans, and returned it to its sheath. "I only ask that you leave us be."

"Louisa is one of ours and therefore under our protection," Stefan said. "You know that."

"I will not live without her."

"That may be," Stefan said. "But it is no secret that over the centuries Kenan has paid you well for your talents. Most recently in Los Angeles, you watched Colombina, and even here—"

"I'm done with all that! Nothing matters to me now but Louisa. I thought you of all people would understand. I'll give you the last location I have for Kenan—although I'm sure he's moved by now."

Stefan inhaled deeply and cast his eyes over the horned creatures torturing the humans cast to Hell in the frescoes before him. "Knowing that Kenan has a bounty on Louisa, means we will not leave her unprotected."

"I was hoping you'd say that—and I'd be grateful for her added protection. I only ask that you speak with Prudence and Gabriel."

Stefan pulled a notebook and pen from his coat and handed them to Ignacio. "The location."

Ignacio wrote down the information. "I will never hurt her," he said.

Stefan looked down at the notepad. "I know." He returned the notebook and pen to his coat pocket and strode out of the basilica leaving the door ajar.

Ignacio watched as a gust of wind gripped the ashes of death that lay on the floor and gathered them into a dust devil.

Higher and higher it rose until all that remained was a wisp of cold air.

He walked to the door. The wind roared. He gazed around the piazza, wary for signs of Kenan's men. He pulled the heavy doors closed and fled into the night, home to the warmth of Louisa's embrace.

○

On Christmas Eve, Coco and Layla joined the festivities in the town square. A bonfire burned and families admired the display of *presepi*—nativity scenes made by the town's best carpenters. A large outdoor market had been set up, and locals strolled along the main street, stopping at stands, tasting treats, and purchasing goods made by local artisans.

After spending most of her vacations in Hawaii, D.C., or Los Angeles, Coco enjoyed the local celebration. She did not miss the over-commercialization that the holiday season accrued in the United States. She pulled her hat down over her ears and navigated her way through the throng of people to Maria's booth.

As they approached, Maria waved. "*Buon Natale!*"

"*Buon Natale*, Maria," Coco said as she looked over the vast array of food that Maria presented. "Everything looks delicious."

"Then you must have one of everything," Maria said as she handed Coco and Layla each a bowl of soup. "But first taste my minestrone, *buon appetito*."

Maria pointed to a table where a family gathered—they motioned for the two women to join them.

"*Buon Natale, signorinas*," the father said.

"*Buon Natale*," Coco and Layla said in unison.

The landline started ringing the moment Coco and Layla walked into the house. Coco slammed the front door closed to keep out the cold night air and raced into the living room.

"Hello."

"*Buon Natale*, sis," Christopher said. "How are you?"

"I was beginning to think you'd fallen off the face of the earth," Coco said. "Where have you been?"

"Either in court or at the office."

"That doesn't sound like much fun."

"It is to me," he said. "And we won the case—so that's good."

"I miss you."

"You miss me? My little sister misses me?" Christopher said. "I'm flattered—I figured you were still angry with me because I haven't answered all of your questions. "

"When can you come and visit?"

"I'll be there soon, I promise. Can you put Layla on?"

"Sure, here she is."

Coco handed the phone to Layla and went upstairs to give them their privacy. For the first time in many years she felt lonely.

○

Christmas and New Year came and went, and Coco's life fell into a routine that consisted of running, working, and painting. She would often eat with Maria at her café and listen to stories about her parents, and her life as a child. According to Maria, Alessandro had been a highly respected member of the community, and when he fell in love with Chantal, the village celebrated their love with them.

"When Chantal went into labor with Christopher, Alessandro was inconsolable with worry," Maria said. "He did not leave her side. He could not bear to see her in pain."

"Antonia mentioned the same thing," Coco said. "What concerned him?"

"I can't remember," Maria said with an air of nonchalance. "It happened a long time ago. Chantal had seen you before you were conceived. She knew the importance of your birth."

"What do you mean?" Coco asked.

The small bell that hung above the door to the café chimed, alerting Maria to customers. She excused herself, leaving Coco's questions unanswered.

CHAPTER 22

Gabriel felt the calling to Tuscany even before he had received the call from his mother asking him to return. He'd spent weeks following up on the information Ignacio had given Stefan.

He drove up the familiar driveway and parked the car at the front of the villa. The heavy doors opened and a pack of dogs quickly surrounded him. He clicked his fingers and pointed to the ground. They all sat down immediately, wagging their tales in anticipation of his attention. He patted each one, and walked up the stone steps to the front door where Maria greeted him.

"I think they have a better sense of smell than you—they've been scratching at the door for the past hour," she said. "Welcome home, Gabriel. It's good to have you back."

Gabriel kissed Maria's cheeks, and then went through to his office. "How are you?" he asked.

"*Bene, grazie,*" Maria said as she followed him. Tall bookcases lined two sides of the room and classical paintings enhanced the soft, mandarin-tinted plastered walls. In an alcove behind Gabriel's desk stood a small statue of a woman holding a rose.

"Eduardo called," Maria said. Gabriel looked at her questioningly. "He'll be at the studio for the rest of the afternoon."

Gabriel turned his gaze to a large window and looked at

the farmhouse in the distance. "Does she seem happy here?" he asked.

"Yes, but I suggest you not linger. Every young male in the town has been vying for her attention. They're behaving like a pack of frisky stallions!"

Gabriel's shoulders tensed.

"However," Maria continued, "Coco seems completely oblivious—and Eduardo says she's a dedicated artist."

As he drove his Porsche Panamera S E-Hybrid away from the villa he heard Maria chuckle and whisper. "*L'amore comincia…*"

O

The Professor glanced at his fob watch, which hung from a chain on his waistcoat. His normally composed posture seemed rigid. He looked up and beckoned for Coco to join him in his office. "She's late," he said. "We need to cancel the class, and reschedule at another time."

Coco glanced past the door to the class full of students. "I'll take Louisa's place today," she said. " There's no need to cancel."

"I've made my decision. Please ask the students to come back next week."

Coco ignored him and walked to the dressing room. A few minutes later she made her way to the raised platform in the center of the studio dressed in nothing but Louisa's silk robe.

The Professor approached her. "Why are you doing this?"

"Because it will be interesting being on the other side of the stage," Coco said. "Maybe I'll learn something—although I doubt I can keep as still as Louisa."

The Professor removed the silk robe slowly.

Coco quickly glanced at the students who seemed oblivious

to her unease. She closed her eyes and took long measured breaths in and out.

She felt vulnerable, completely stripped of all her armor. The Professor placed the robe back over her body. "I'll be okay," she said. "It's another first in my life—that's all." She pushed the robe back from her shoulders and it fell around her. Once over the initial shock of being naked in front of a class full of students, she focused on a spot on the ground and found that she had left her modesty in Los Angeles. A bell rang in the foyer indicating a visitor to the gallery.

"*Mi scusi per un momento*," the Professor said to the students and walked to the gallery.

Coco became acutely aware of a change in the atmosphere, an undercurrent had abruptly surfaced along with the scent of something sweet—like freshly picked berries with a touch of sandalwood. The scent heightened her sensuality but simultaneously made her feel uneasy. Concerned that she would get distracted and move from the pose, she continued to focus on the spot on the floor—it had become the center of her universe. She heard the Professor in conversation with another male somewhere near the back of the studio. The stranger's voice triggered a memory. She'd heard the voice before—something about it calmed her. Coco listened for words that might tell her what language the two men were speaking. She caught words here and there—*pinturas,* being one, and remembered where she'd heard the dialect before. Christopher and Layla—the language of the Allegiance.

Good grief, they're everywhere…

The more she listened to the visitor's voice, the more Coco felt herself being drawn toward the man speaking. Every cell in her body felt alive and suddenly over-stimulated. She found it difficult to keep still. Her heartbeat quickened. She yearned to lift her head to see this man's face. His velvety deep voice was like chocolate melting against her skin—thick and sweet. She wanted to lick his words as they flowed from his mouth. The dot on the floor had become a little fuzzy.

O

Gabriel detected Coco's scent the second he arrived at the *Scuola d'Arte*. Her close proximity gave him the chance to listen to her thoughts, and he made a mental note to keep the kitchen stocked with chocolate. He gathered his focus back to the Professor, who ushered him toward a painting on an easel at the back of the main studio. Gabriel knew immediately that Coco had painted the image—the paint practically danced off the canvas with magic. He recognized the location. The pomegranate tree had grown for years at the corner of Chantal and Alessandro's farmhouse. He ran his fingers over the paint and felt the pigments of color breathe as if awakening. The two men continued toward the front of the studio where the students focused on the model. They focused on Coco.

When Gabriel saw her posed naked, the muscles in his neck tightened and his protective instincts awakened. This reaction caused a surge of his quintessence to rush over Coco. He felt her heart flutter in reaction, evoking a sudden excitement in her blood.

As he circled behind her, Gabriel's gaze lingered over the curve of her spine. He admired how the shadows of light touched her flawless skin and brushed the dips and rises of her muscles and shoulder blades. With profound effort, he swallowed a low moan and abruptly turned away. "Enquire if the painting is for sale, Eduardo," he said. "You understand its value."

Coco strained to listen to the Professor's footsteps as he guided the visitor past the students and into the gallery. She felt the stranger hesitate for a moment and a wave of warmth caressed her body. She wondered if he sensed the sexuality he had aroused in her.

"*Dove è Louisa?*" She heard him ask. The Professor replied quickly but she couldn't translate his words. Their footsteps faded. Gradually her breathing slowed and the blood that flowed to and from her heart returned to its normal ebb and flow.

Splashes of water and idle chatter amongst the students alerted her that the class had ended. She looked up, frustrated to find that the stranger had gone. A hand with long fingernails draped the robe over her shoulders. "My client has inquired about your painting," the Professor said. "He's willing to pay a substantial amount."

Coco slipped her arms through the sleeves of the robe and covered her body. She turned to her teacher. "None of my paintings are in the gallery. You must have my work confused with someone else's."

Professor Benatti walked back toward his office and she followed. "I'm not referring to the gallery paintings," he said. "It's your painting in the studio that interests him."

"That's not even finished."

The Professor turned to her. "Then I suggest you complete it."

"Who is this man?"

"A collector, a friend, and a good man."

"Any word from Louisa?" she asked.

The Professor shook his head.

"I'll call her," Coco said, "she probably overslept." She

146

slipped into the dressing room, put on her clothes, and dialed Louisa's cell. It went directly to voicemail. Coco pushed her phone into the pocket of her faded jeans and returned to the studio to help the Professor clean up. She noticed him checking and rechecking the time on his fob watch. He looked up as she walked toward him. His face was lined with apprehension.

"She didn't pick up," Coco said. "I'll go by her place and check on her."

The Professor's cell phone vibrated in his hand. "*Pronto!*" he said. Coco heard a voice speaking rapidly in Italian. The Professor drew his left hand into a tight fist and when he released it Coco saw droplets of blood on his palm.

He ended the call and gazed out the studio window. He seemed to be staring at nothing in particular, lost in a distant memory. He walked to his desk, opened a drawer, and grabbed a set of keys. "It's Louisa…" he said. His eyes brimmed with tears.

"What's happened?" Coco asked.

The Professor's lips trembled. He turned away, shaking his head. His tall body appeared to shrink in stature with every step.

Coco ran after him. "Professor—please—tell me what's going on!" He placed a hand on her face, shook his head and then turned and dashed down the stairs.

Coco ran into the dressing room, tugged on her shoes, and bounded after him. She caught a glimpse of the Professor as he fled along the street and followed him through the twists and turns of narrowing alleys. While Coco ran, she remembered Louisa's voice the last time they had spoken. She'd reiterated how happy she and Ignacio were together. Coco ran faster.

CHAPTER 23

The buildings in this part of town lacked the cared-for look that Coco had become used to seeing in the area closer to the studio. Potted plants and lace curtains were absent from the apartments that lined the alley, and as the streets became narrower the buildings loomed over her, blocking out what was left of the dwindling light of day. For a moment, Christopher entered her mind, but she pushed the thought of him away and continued in her pursuit.

Up ahead she saw a police car parked on the sidewalk. The Professor was nowhere in sight. She waited and listened. She heard faint footsteps to her left. Two policemen walked out of the doorway of one of the stone buildings at the end of the street. The older of the two spoke into a cell phone. "*Il professore sta qui*," he said.

Coco waited until they left in the police car and then slipped through the entrance and up the stairs to the first landing. Another officer stood with a notepad in hand and questioned tenants. They were answered by silence and shaking heads. Water stains adorned the walls and the prickly stench of mildew lingered.

The door to an apartment had been roped off, but was slightly ajar. Coco strained her head to see through the small crack and her body instantly stiffened. The Professor sat on the edge of a chair beside a bed. His head hung and his elbows rested on his knees. He lovingly caressed a woman's pale, lifeless hand. Coco's gaze moved slowly from the hand to the woman's naked body. Louisa's wild hair flowed across the pillows, and Coco watched as the Professor gently pushed back a stray lock that had fallen over her closed eyes. Coco's eyes flickered to the bedside table where an empty syringe lay in a clear evidence bag.

"*Lo sapevate figlia del professore?*" a policeman asked Coco.

Coco jumped. "His daughter?"

"*Sì,*" he said. "Louisa is *Professore* Benatti's only child."

Coco found it difficult to tear herself away from the image in front of her. As she turned to leave, she glimpsed a few drops of blood on the floor beside Louisa's bed. She turned and stumbled down the stairs and ran back toward the studio. She felt embarrassed that she had not known of the relationship between her two friends—that every sideways glance she'd seen the Professor give Louisa indicated love and concern for his only child.

Gabriel had shadowed Coco through the village streets to Louisa's apartment. When she ran up the stairs, he already waited in Louisa's bedroom hidden from her view. From where Coco stood she could not have seen the bloodstained sheet or the two tiny puncture wounds strategically placed beside Louisa's heart.

Before he arrived, he perceived what the Professor would find. He had smelled the stench of heroin and death from the streets surrounding the building. Fury ran through his mind.

"I warned her," the Professor said, his voice weak and full of sorrow. "Louisa knew the dangers that came with being associated with Ignacio."

Gabriel tossed a handful of runes into the air. Before they stopped spinning he had the information he needed. He snatched them out of the air and threw them back in his pocket. "Ignacio did not kill her. Another vampire has been here," Gabriel said. He walked over to the plastic evidence bag, opened it and inhaled. He returned the bag to the bedside table. "He was not the last vampire to inject her. Another injected her with a lethal dose."

"Who?"

"I'm not familiar with his scent, but I have no doubt that Ignacio has already killed him." Gabriel held his head in his hands and evaluated the situation. "I am so sorry, Eduardo."

The Professor shook his head and silent tears fell from his eyes. "Ignacio was as addicted to her as she was to heroin. He wanted to change her to an immortal, but honored her decision when she said no." The Professor wiped his eyes. "Ignacio and Louisa fell in love. Nothing else mattered to him. At least my girl died knowing how it is to be truly loved."

Gabriel clenched his hands in a desperate effort to control his anger. A large mirror that hung above the mantel shattered and fell to the floor in a waterfall of broken images. He stormed out of the room to find Coco.

O

Ignacio had woken up and found Louisa dead in his arms. He kissed her as his merlot-colored tears fell over her naked body. The scent of another vampire still clung in the air, and when he realized what had happened he dragged on his clothes and went in pursuit of Louisa's killer.

He found him on the outskirts of town, talking on his cell

phone. Ignacio stalked him slowly—this murderer would pay for what he had done. When the young vampire had finished his call, Ignacio held a silver blade to his neck.

"You will die a slow, excruciating death for killing my Louisa."

"Fuck you!" the young vampire said. He went to kick Ignacio but instead found himself on the ground with multiple deep slashes on his body.

Ignacio placed the tip of his knife on the young vampire's neck and slowly sliced down his torso to his abdomen. The young vampire screamed. Ignacio felt rage rising in his own blood. He shoved the knife into the young vampire's heart and stabbed him repeatedly. He looked at the young face that had begun to decay.

"Rot in hell!" Ignacio said, as he tore the young vampire's head from its body. He walked back to his Ducati and rode toward the forest.

Ignacio hurled the bike into the bushes at the side of the road and staggered into the trees. He heard water falling over rocks and stumbled to the side of the creek, throwing icy water onto his face while he retched. The reality of Louisa's death exploded beneath his tough façade. He collapsed onto the icy rocks and released a pain-filled scream.

Eventually darkness cradled him. It brought up memories of another time when he lay in pain, praying for death. He remembered the metallic taste of the blood that had run from his face and into his mouth. And how the pain of defeat throbbed throughout his body. But that night death had not answered his call, and instead an immortal had taken away his physical pain. That gory scene still haunted him, and now he had another death to add to that list.

In an effort to get their addiction under control, Ignacio had begun to cut back on the heroin. But this time they were both caught up in the lust of the high and had passed out. Hours later, when he awoke and caught the scent of another vampire in the room, he clung to Louisa's cold lifeless body.

Kenan had taken his revenge.

Louisa's body had been drained of all life. This time his addiction had proven fatal. The only woman he had ever loved would never drink his blood. His beautiful Louisa...

CHAPTER 24

The empty gallery felt lifeless. Coco picked up Louisa's robe from the floor of the dressing room and draped it over the bench where her friend had once posed. Tears spilled down her cheeks, and her breathing came in sporadic gasps. She gathered up her belongings and ran out of the building.

Her loneliness intensified when she remembered that Layla had gone to Florence to visit family. She drove aimlessly, numb with sadness.

When Coco arrived home, she went directly to her mother's studio and dropped onto the chair by the picture window. She stared at her mother's unfinished painting. Gradually, the scent of lavender purged the stench of death and mildew.

A cool breeze stirred the lace curtains that hung across the glass door that led to the patio. The night air carried with it an owl's evening song while darkness crept into the room. Coco switched on the lamp beside her. She pushed up the sleeves of her shirt and walked to the easel, picked up a depleted tube of Cobalt Blue and smeared some onto a crusted pallet. Burnt Sienna, Burnt Umber, Cadmium Yellow, Cerulean Blue, Mars Black, Titanium White, and her favorite Alizarin Crimson followed. Her mother's brushes felt familiar—as if they had been waiting for her all these years. The paint wove its way effortlessly onto her mother's unfinished canvas, and Coco shifted into a deep creative zone that she had not felt for months.

○

Gabriel stood on the patio, hidden by the lace curtains and a veil of magic. He watched Coco paint. The lynx that lingered in the darkness, ready to risk its life to protect the woman behind the half-open door, approached him.

"You were a mountain lion when we last met, my friend," Gabriel said. "I'm in your debt." The feline curved her body around his legs.

Gabriel noted the ease at which Coco painted and how it mirrored the talent of her mother. He remembered the many times he had visited this house when it was a happy place— before that fateful day when death denounced this part of his life. He tossed his runes into the air and contemplated the past.

He sat with Alessandro and seven-year-old Christopher in the back seat of the Mercedes while Eduardo drove. They were en route to Christopher's first Allegiance meeting. Chantal's screams echoed around them. Eduardo slammed on the brakes. Alessandro and Gabriel opened the car doors and disappeared.

Alessandro stared at the splatters of blood on the green grass beneath the ancient tree. Colombina lay unconscious on the ground.

Prudence made the decision to separate the children in the hopes of keeping them safe. Lies were created, and in an effort to keep them alive, a family was torn apart.

Gabriel sat on a chair beside Colombina's bed at Casa della Pietra. Her precocious spirit and unbridled courage had been daunted by fear. He placed his left hand gently on her forehead and trailed it down her face, finally bringing sleep to her manic mind. He gathered her hands together and then placed his right hand just beneath her hairline and breathed in deeply. For a quick second his body tensed as Coco's eyes sprung open. Seconds later her eyelids closed over her lavender eyes and Gabriel slowly let out his breath. He watched, as a pink glow returned to her face and her breathing calmed.

The runes fell back into Gabriel's pocket. He stared at Coco. A soft glow emanated around her entire body while she painted—she was entranced. For eight hours, both Gabriel and the feline silently watched her. Birds beckoned each other with dawn trills. When daylight approached, the paintbrush fell from Coco's hand.

Sometime during the night she'd kicked off her shoes and taken off her jeans. Paint had splattered her legs and arms. She removed the rest of her clothes.

Gabriel noticed an aura of magic a few centimeters above Coco's left breast. The outline of the rune, *Dagaz*, quivered below her pale skin. It pulsed in rhythm with the beating of her heart—like a baby bird waiting to escape the confines of its shell. Within days Coco's world would change forever. Gabriel prayed that when that time came she would find the strength to accept her new life and its challenges.

He watched as she filled a shallow dish with water, placed it on the floor, and stepped in. She washed her legs and arms with a paint-stained cloth. Gabriel observed the water mix with the paint from her skin as it fell into the dish, drop by drop. The draw to her had magnified since he had healed her in the hospital so many months ago. He lusted for her. It coursed through his body like water gushing through an open floodgate. He stumbled back in an effort to gain control of his cravings.

His gaze followed her as she wrapped herself in a blanket and sank into the down pillows of the sofa. Sleep was instantaneous. Gabriel slipped through the door and entered the studio.

As he pulled another blanket over her body he detected the rise and fall of her breath. Was she aware of her mystical talents? There were times when he had secretly visited her apartment in L.A. that he had felt strands of untamed magic waiting to be used. He had searched through her paintings and found nothing. But tonight, as he witnessed her talents, he wondered if there was something he'd missed. Her innate gift had emerged without coercion.

Magic seeped into the air.

He turned around and reached toward the Tuscan landscape. As his hand moved closer to the canvas, the landscape began to shift. Small particles of color lifted from the surface and hovered at his fingertips. Underneath the façade of Coco's peaceful painting a gruesome scene emerged. One that Gabriel had only imagined for twenty-eight years, and the identity of Chantal's attacker was finally confirmed.

In the painting, Chantal's long blonde hair is tinged with blood, her body limp and pale. The man who holds her slowly raises his bloodied and scarred face toward four-year-old Coco. The little girl flees while a large black wolf runs alongside her. Chantal's words echo: "Run, Colombina! Don't look back, run…"

The man with the bloodied face laughs as he wipes blood from his mouth with his forearm. He tosses Chantal to the ground and breaks out after Coco. The wolf jumps toward the man's throat but he swipes the animal away. When his cold hands grab Coco by her neck, she screams. He dangles her in front of his distorted face. "Your imprudent mother is delicious." Chantal's blood drips from his mouth. He cocks his head and listens, and throws Coco to the ground with such force that she is knocked unconscious. Alessandro and Gabriel arrive, but they are too late. The attacker is gone. So is Chantal.

The particles of color dissipated from Gabriel's fingertips, and the canvas returned to the landscape façade that Coco had painted. Gabriel stared at her, his eyes glistening with moisture. The large feline made her way across the room and jumped onto the sofa beside Coco. Gabriel lifted his hand and stroked her. "You have protected her well, Thalia," he said. The cat purred. Gabriel pulled out his phone and sent a text message to his mother:

It has begun.

CHAPTER 25

Coco had slept on the sofa in her mother's studio until late in the afternoon. She awoke to a familiar sensation, like wet sandpaper drawing against her skin. Thalia was licking her cheek. No sooner had she opened her eyes when the dark cloud of death swept over her again, bringing images of the Professor holding Louisa's limp hand—her lifeless body, and the syringe in the evidence bag. Louisa was dead. She raced into the bathroom, vomited, and turned on the water in the shower. Kneeling on the tiled floor, she let the water wash away her tears.

The house felt cold, and Coco knew that without company, she would fall into the abyss of depression. She drove to the café and found comfort in Maria's embrace. The soulful melody of a woman's voice singing one of Louisa's favorite *Fado* melodies, floated through the air.

Maria's café had quickly become a second home to Coco. She loved the smell of baking and coffee that beckoned to her each time she entered. Vases of fresh flowers always graced the wooden tables, each one different from the other—just like the pieces of crockery and furniture that Maria had used to decorate. The café served as a refuge for mismatched objects.

An extension of Maria's personality, it mirrored the motherly essence that flowed within and around her.

Maria settled Coco at a table and went to make coffee for them both. Coco rubbed the back of her neck, rolled her head, and then straightened her back as she sensed a shift in the energy around her. She sat poised in readiness and kept her gaze focused on the tabletop.

The door opened and a gust of cold air rushed over her. His essence caressed her. She dared not move. His scent of sandalwood and berries permeated the room. Her heart thumped and she shifted slightly in her chair. She knew without a doubt that the man who stood before her now, and the man she had sensed while posing in the nude yesterday, were one and the same. Very slowly she lifted her gaze, wanting to stretch this moment between them. She gasped. He stared directly into her eyes and she felt his empathy encase her fragile emotions.

Coco was entranced. She drank in everything about him— his dark hair, roughly parted on the side, falling over his eyes— light eyes flecked with gold. An air of sophistication, balanced with an element of hip was reflected in his stylish clothing. The tailored jacket, slightly untucked white shirt, and fine, dark-gray cashmere sweater, drawn together with a pair of well-worn 501s. Coco thought of the countless times she had drawn this man, and how often he'd appeared in her nightly dreams. She knew him well, and had often peeled off his layers of clothing and sketched his muscular naked body.

The man cleared his throat and she snapped out of her daydream. She held out a hand, which he took and brought to his lips. She felt him inhale, as if tasting her scent before he kissed her skin. Her entire body felt electrified, and she found it increasingly difficult to keep herself together. She lowered her hand.

"May I call you 'Colombina'?" he asked.

The image of liquid chocolate jumped into Coco's mind. His demeanor made him seem slightly older than what he appeared, which she guessed hovered between his middle to late thirties.

She remembered that the man standing in front of her had seen her naked. She swallowed. "Colombina is fine," she said, fluffing her bangs and shifting her pose. "I know you. Have we met before?"

"Yes, many years ago," he said. "I'm Gabriel. And while I visited the Professor yesterday, I enquired about one of your paintings. Have you considered my offer to purchase it?"

Coco looked down at her hands. "I'm sorry, but that painting isn't for sale."

Gabriel rested his hand on the chair opposite her. "May I?" Coco nodded.

Maria entered and placed an espresso in front of her. "I take it you two have already introduced yourselves," she said.

"Yes," Gabriel said, looking up at Maria. "The funeral will be held tomorrow, at four in the afternoon." His words brought Coco back to the reality of Louisa's death. She stared at the flowers in the vase. Gabriel took her hand in his, and immediately she sensed his empathy, but it did not stop the sudden surge of tears that poured from her eyes. "Maria," he said. "Some of your tea."

Maria returned a few minutes later with a mug and placed it in front of Coco. Steam drifted up from the rose and chamomile-scented liquid. Gabriel released her hand while she lifted the cup to her mouth and sipped.

"I'll take some tea to the Professor," Maria said. "He's not come out of his studio since yesterday. I won't be long." She removed her apron, picked up a large ceramic pitcher from the kitchen, and turned the small sign on the door to *closed* before leaving.

A faint numbness permeated Coco's body. It cleared her

mind and allowed her to think and speak clearly. "I didn't know they were father and daughter," she said. "Why didn't they tell me?"

"Louisa and her father had a close, but strained relationship," Gabriel said. "It is difficult to protect one who does not wish to be protected." His words sent a shiver down Coco's spine. She wondered if they were directed at her.

"I wanted her to stay with me... but she couldn't say no to Ignacio." Coco sensed a sudden shift in the air around Gabriel.

"What do you know of Ignacio?" he asked.

"We met when I was out one night," Coco said. "He made me feel... uncomfortable. And then, when I saw the small bruises on Louisa's arms, I questioned her. She told me about their shared addiction and that she loved him."

Gabriel got up and walked over to the window. Coco saw him staring back at her through the reflection in the glass.

"Were you and I childhood friends?" she asked.

"Sort of," Gabriel said. "Do you remember?"

"No. I don't remember much of my childhood here." Coco pushed back her chair and walked quickly toward the door. "The tea was perfect, thank you."

Gabriel turned away from the window to face her. "You had a beautiful childhood, Colombina. It was full of love."

Coco did not look back. The draw toward Gabriel was magnetic, but she felt emotionally drained and needed fresh air. She fled the café and opened the door to her car where she sat quietly.

The narrow street was wet from the mist that had gathered over the small town, and the darkness of night was upon her. Coco pictured Louisa and her—arm in arm, and tipsy from too many glasses of Chianti. Her friend had always made sure Coco arrived home safely—she had treated her with kindness and made her feel welcome in the small town. Coco's body trembled.

Whether from sadness or the dire need to have family near, Coco remembered Christopher's words to her: *If you need me, you know the quickest way to contact me.*

Coco needed to feel her brother's love: she needed the security of family. She closed her eyes and did something she hadn't done since she was a child. Breathing deeply she found herself effortlessly drifting to a place of light, and into her brother's subconscious mind.

Christopher's ringtone dragged her back to reality. She picked up her cell.

"Chris... it's Louisa... she's dead."

"I know. I'm on my way," he said.

"Layla's in Florence... I need you."

"Remember when I said that we have many friends in Italy?" Christopher asked.

"Yes," her body relaxed a little at the sound of his voice.

"Gabriel's like family to us. You will stay with him until I arrive. Is that understood?"

"I understand," she said. "Wait, am I in danger again?"

"Go with Gabriel," he said. "I'll be there in the morning. We can talk then."

"But I don't remember him—"

"This isn't open for discussion. Go with Gabriel." Christopher ended the call.

She remained there for a few moments and looked up when she saw the blue doors to the café open and Gabriel step outside. He was speaking on his cell, way too fast for her to comprehend, except for his last words: "*Arrivederci*, Christopher." He dropped his cell phone into his coat pocket and walked over to her car.

He opened the door and offered her his hand. Coco accepted. Maria had returned from the studio. "Call me if you need anything," she said. "I'll leave here in an hour or two and drive directly to the villa."

Gabriel nodded as he guided Coco toward his car and helped her into the passenger seat. He waited until Maria was safely inside the café before driving away.

"Why can't I drive myself home?" Coco asked. "What's going on?"

"It's not Christopher asking that you stay with me," he said. "It is my insistence. The stress of Louisa's death has taken its toll on you."

Coco stared down at her hands fidgeting with her purse. "Christopher promised that I would get answers when I came here. Instead, I feel like I'm being kept in the dark."

"Ignacio has a few very dangerous enemies," he said. "And Christopher needs to know that you are safe."

Coco lifted her head and turned to Gabriel. "So... I'm in danger?"

"Yes."

"Why?"

"Because of what you are," Gabriel said.

"That makes no fucking sense!" Coco screamed. "Please— what the hell's going on?"

"We'll talk tomorrow, on this you have my word," he said. "You're safe with me, no one can harm you."

She felt her bottom lip tremble.

"If you're concerned, I suggest you either call Kishu or decide to start trusting me now."

Coco dialed Kishu's cell.

He answered on the first ring. "Are you alright?"

"I don't know—that's why I'm calling you. Christopher told me to go home with Gabriel, and Gabriel suggested I call you." Coco stole a glance at Gabriel's face. His eyes were focused on the road.

"There's no one safer for you to be with, little one," Kishu said. "Gabriel, although a little different, will keep you safe."

He ended the call, and Coco decided that this was one of the times in her life where she would do best to give in to the Allegiance.

"Breathe, Colombina," Gabriel whispered through the darkness.

"The last time I was told to breathe I was lying in a heap on Sunset Boulevard, my body tangled in a bloody mess." The memory brought a shiver to her body.

The crystal clear notes of Chopin's Nocturne in E Flat Major crescendoed as Gabriel drove by the edge of the town, past the meadows and cottages that nestled the roadside—their lights glowing through the layer of low cloud that permeated the valley. A soft rain began to fall. She watched the water bounce off the front of the car—the headlights lit each drop and then sent them off into the darkness.

For a moment, Coco thought she saw Louisa's beautiful face through the fogged-up window beside her. She placed a hand to the glass but the image faded, leaving only the rain and her tears. She slumped back into the seat. It was then that she realized Gabriel had turned off the main highway and onto the road toward her house.

Coco took a moment to study him. His strong jaw gave him an air of distinction—he could have been sitting in a Viennese court watching Chopin himself play the wistful nocturne. He seemed ageless. Once again she became conscious of the fact that she was staring at him. She turned and looked directly ahead while Gabriel continued driving toward *Casa della Luna Crescente*.

The iron gates opened automatically at their approach. They continued along the road lined with a canopy of ancient trees that offered refuge from the rain. The road ended in a circular driveway to reveal a massive stone villa.

Gabriel parked the car and then walked around and opened Coco's door for her. "Layla is arriving tomorrow with Christopher," Gabriel said. "Her family members have been with the Allegiance for many years."

"You know Layla?"

"Yes."

"But she never told me—"

"Tomorrow, I'll explain," he said, as he placed his hand gently on the small of her back, and guided her up a row of ancient stone steps and through the set of heavy carved wooden doors that opened up to the foyer.

Gabriel's pack of dogs hurtled toward him but came to a halt at his feet, and waited in readiness for affection. Coco bent down to the motley bunch, which ranged from a wire-haired dachshund mix to an enormous Irish Deerhound. She patted the dogs while they kept their eyes poised on Gabriel.

Coco stood up and stared, wide-eyed, at the vision before her. The vast foyer was entirely lit with candles, and ornately carved pillars reached from the stone floor to the high ceiling above her. The cold floor, accented by rich earth-toned embroidered rugs, added an ambience of warmth. Surrounding the outer area of the foyer were archways that opened up to hallways. Coco felt like she had walked into the pages of an Etruscan fairy tale.

"This is your home?" she asked, "It's so beautiful—like an enchanted castle."

Gabriel nodded. "I've been away for some time," he said. "It's easy to forget how magical the villa must seem to new eyes."

Coco walked to the center of the spacious entrance. "If I lived here," she said, "I don't think I would ever want to leave."

A slight breeze fluttered past Coco. She saw the corners of Gabriel's mouth lift slightly at her words.

He turned and walked toward the staircase, followed closely by the pack. "I shall remind you of your words when the snow begins to fall and these steps—of which there are many—are cold upon your feet," he said. "However, the view from the top of the turret is quite rewarding."

"There's a turret?" Coco asked, "May I see it?"

"Not tonight. But yes, I promise to take you there."

They walked up two flights of stairs and Gabriel motioned Coco forward to an open door at the end of a short hallway. Only one dog followed. A dark-faced German Shepherd that fell into step beside Gabriel.

A sizeable candle sat on the mantle above the fireplace, its flame flickered when she entered, causing shadows to dance on the eggshell-colored walls. Exquisite rugs in muted hues accented the dark polished floorboards that lay before her. A familiar meow brought Coco's focus to a large carved four-poster bed, where Thalia stared at her. The cat strutted across the thick white covers and toward Coco's waiting arms.

Gabriel stepped into the room. He clicked his fingers and the German Shepherd entered and sat beside him. "Colombina, this is Max. Think of him as your constant companion while you're here." Thalia meowed in resistance and Gabriel raised his eyebrows at the cat.

"You have a way with animals," she said.

"Sometimes."

In the car, his eyes had looked dark, but now, in the candle-light, they seemed lighter and flecked with gold again. She felt herself being drawn to the intensity of his stare.

He walked over to a set of glass doors that led to a large patio, and stepped outside. Coco followed. They stood together, sheltered by the rain. She extended her gaze and saw the outline of the trees surrounding her parents' home. Dark, velvety shadows crept up the exterior of the old building, and the light outside the front glowed like a beacon.

"Your family home awaits your return, on this, you have my word," he said. "You're not a captive here. You're my guest." He walked back inside and motioned to the table in front of the fireplace, where a crackling fire brought warmth to the room. "There's a bowl of hot soup and bread, and a glass of brandy too. I thought it might help you sleep. Your clothes and bags are in the wardrobe and the bathroom has all of the essentials." He walked toward the door and turned to her. "An easel, painting tools, and supplies are set up in the studio. Is there anything else I can do for you?"

"There's a studio?" Coco asked.

Gabriel retraced his steps and she trailed behind him. At one end of the spacious patio a huge fireplace occupied the entire wall. Opposite, stood a door that opened to reveal a room with a sink and everything Coco needed to paint. "I hoped this would help you feel a little less homesick," he said and turned to leave.

Coco raised a hand. "Excuse me, but how did this all happen?"

Gabriel shrugged his shoulders. "As Christopher explained to you, we spoke earlier and arranged accordingly," he walked to the door. "Goodnight, Colombina. I'll leave you to get settled." He closed the door.

"Wait." She ran over and flung open the door but he had vanished.

"Thank you," she said.

She closed the door, sank into the plush sofa, and stared into the flames. A growl from her stomach reminded her that she had not eaten all day. She devoured the food he'd left for her, picked up the brandy, and headed for the bathroom. She ran a hot bath and drank the contents of the large goblet while she lay in the bathtub immersed by bubbles.

Later, she snuggled into the large bed with Thalia beside her and Max stationed on the floor at the foot of the bed, and fell into a deep sleep. Visions of her past seeped into her mind.

Sometime in the early morning, the haunting melody of the second movement of Beethoven's Pathétique sonata drifted through the villa. The delicate sounds of the piano lulled her back to sleep.

○

When Coco opened her eyes, she was looking at the back of a dark furry head. Max had maneuvered himself so that he was parallel to her body. The back of his head rested on the pillow beside her. His heavy panting had woken her. Coco took inventory and remembered where she was. "I don't think this is exactly what Gabriel had in mind when he told you to guard me." The large dog whined, lifted his head then laid it back down on the pillow. Thalia sat perched on the back of an armchair, observing the view across the grounds toward the farmhouse. She meowed and leapt onto the bed beside Coco, snuggling into the covers and ignoring Max.

Coco shifted to a sitting position when she heard a soft knock at the door. "I'm awake," she said. The door opened to reveal Layla carrying a tray laden with coffee and eggs and toast.

"*Ciao, bella*," Layla said.

Max bolted to the door and attacked Layla with licks and friendly cries. She placed the tray on the table and then turned her attention to Max.

Coco pushed back the bed covers. "I hope you two know each other, because if that's his way of protecting me, it's a little pathetic," Coco said. "Although I should let him do whatever he wants. Why did you keep the identity of the mystery man in my paintings and dreams hidden? How could you do that do me?"

"First things first. Max and I are old friends," Layla said. "He won't hurt me. And don't be bluffed about this show of affection. His bite—I assure you—can be fatal." The canine's ears shot up when he heard Gabriel call his name. Max turned toward Coco. "He needs your permission to leave," Layla said.

"Seriously?"

"Gabriel told him to stay with you," Layla said. "He needs your permission to leave."

Coco pointed toward the door. "Go, Max!" He raced through the door.

"Okay," Layla said. "I couldn't tell you about Gabriel because you needed to find out for yourself."

"How could I do that in L.A.?"

"Exactly—you just answered your own question. You needed to open a door."

Coco walked over to Layla and the two embraced. "I'm glad you're back," she said. "Even if you do dance around my questions, but I have plenty more for Christopher."

"Good—he's downstairs."

"He's here?" Coco asked.

Layla nodded and handed Coco a cup of coffee. "Have a shower and get dressed—we need to leave soon for Louisa's funeral."

"What time is it?"

"2:30 p.m.," Layla said. "You slept well."

"I guess…"

A wave of sadness crashed over Coco. She dropped her head, walked quickly into the bathroom and closed the door. When she turned on the shower, she noticed paint splattered on her hands. She had no recollection of painting last night and it was unusual for her to go to bed without washing the pigments from her skin.

This had happened a few times before at her Westwood loft. That was when she had discovered the self-portrait with the shadow of the man standing in front of her—and the other painting, a landscape of steep mountains and an expansive stone fortress. She had taken the self-portrait to her office at UCLA and brought it home the day before her accident. The other painting she kept in the bedroom closet.

Coco stepped into the shower. The hot water brought her comfort, and an image of Gabriel appeared in her mind. She wasn't used to being attracted to any particular man—relationships for her always seemed too complicated, and after the grad student, there had only been a few other casual dates. Liaisons never lasted more than a few weeks—no commitments, no heartache, and no complications. But there was no denying her attraction to Gabriel. She got out of the shower and dressed.

CHAPTER 26

Overgrown grass and rock walls flanked the road leading up to the ancient chapel. The weather wavered between a light rain and a thick mist, making the timeworn stone church look cold and lonely. Coco had come to accept that no matter the size of the building in Italy, the doors were always heavy and large. She wondered if this was to keep evil out or goodness in. Or perhaps it was simply to keep the weather from intruding. If she'd seen this place from a distance, Coco would have thought it abandoned—a relic from a time when the doors remained open daily and voices singing holy songs beckoned followers to enter.

The church was located a few miles outside the village. Once a month the surrounding stone courtyard became a palette of colors and fragrances as local farmers sold vegetables, flowers, olive oil, and other goods. But today showed no trace of joy or laughter, and the only scent in the air stemmed from incense burning inside the chapel.

Coco, Christopher, Layla, Gabriel, and Maria entered the church and took their places near the Professor in the first few rows. The church was filled with students from the art school and the many friends connected to Louisa and her father. Gabriel commanded Max to remain on guard at the back of the church.

Coco looked across at the Professor and noticed, for the first time, his resemblance to Louisa: the long eyelashes, strong nose, and perfect poise. He turned toward her and a sense of deep sadness washed over Coco. His pain felt infinite.

After the secular service, everyone gathered at the Professor's home. A stone wall extended around the property, and tall Italian cypress trees lined the driveway and lay long shadows across the road which climbed to the villa. The outer walls of the two-storied home mirrored the color of bisque red clay, and aged vines crept up the outer walls toward the terracotta curved roof tiles.

Coco stood underneath a covered patio and gazed out at the picture perfect view of the Tuscan hills.

Christopher approached and put an arm around her shoulders. "Did Louisa and I know each other as children?" she asked.

"Louisa was my age. We went to school together until you and I left this place. She was fearless—always up to mischief. Climbing trees that our parents had marked as off-limits and catching snakes. We were buddies."

"Did you keep in touch with her?"

"Yes—well, I tried. I encouraged her to apply to colleges in the states, but she wanted to stay here. She loved everything about this place and assured me that she was happy." Coco noticed that Christopher's eyes appeared red and his voice lacked its normal command. He stared out at the eclectic group of friends who had gathered. It seemed that most of the population of San Gimignano had come to support the Professor in celebration of Louisa's life. Carlos and his co-workers from the bar that Louisa often frequented along with the art students had pinned soft pink roses to their jackets in recognition of their friendship with her.

"She was loved by so many people," Coco said. "How could this happen to her?"

"The police are looking at suspects," Christopher said. "But Ignacio didn't kill her."

"Then where is he?" Coco asked. "I would have thought if he loved her he would be here."

"He's most likely searching for whoever did this to her," Christopher said. "And I do not doubt that he loved her."

Gabriel approached with the Professor, who carried a ceramic container embedded with a repeated intricate pattern that looked like a small upside-down arrow. The gritty texture of the clay and simple glaze seemed Japanese in origin.

"I'd like to place Louisa's ashes over the water on the lake," the Professor said. "Chantal, Alessandro, and… myself would take the three of you there for picnics and to play." His grip tightened around the urn. "This is where Louisa would want to rest. Can we do this now, please—before the darkness arrives? She was always so afraid of the dark."

Christopher nodded in agreement and Coco felt his arm tighten around her shoulder. He guided her across the court-yard, followed by the Professor, Gabriel and Max. Layla and Maria offered to stay with the guests.

Gabriel drove the small group to the farmhouse in silence. He parked the car, and they solemnly walked along the path that sloped toward the lake. The rain had eased and a soft mist dampened the air, infusing the area with the sweet scent of lavender and rosemary.

"Mother's favorite scent," Coco whispered.

"Yes," the Professor said. "Chantal insisted that Alessandro plant them everywhere. She said the aroma radiated love."

When they arrived at the edge of the lake, the Professor stared out across the water. No words needed to be said. No songs sung. Gabriel laid a hand on his shoulder.

The somber moment was broken by a long howl from Max. "Get her to the boat," Gabriel said. Coco saw him dash back up the path. When she looked back at the Professor, she saw him nod to Christopher. With the urn clutched tightly to his chest, he began running from the shoreline to the jetty.

Christopher grabbed Coco's hand, and they followed the professor along the rickety wooden boards to the end of the pier. He helped her down the ladder, and she settled herself in the boat opposite him. Christopher hoisted himself next to Coco. He grabbed the oars, and plunged them into the water and rowed to the center of the lake.

Coco jerked her head around to Christopher. "What's going—"

Christopher let go of one of the oars and covered her mouth with his hand. He glared at her and spoke with his mind.

Be silent. We're safe here.

Where's Gabriel? And who the hell is that? Coco looked past her brother's head to the end of the jetty, where a tall woman had appeared.

I'll explain later. You must trust us. Coco nodded and Christopher removed his hand, but her gaze did not leave the woman. She held her hands toward the sky and a sudden gust of wind whisked her long white hair around her face. White light exploded around her, and shot into the air like well-orchestrated fireworks. When the light began its descent, it emanated out across the water and over the small dinghy, stopping at the edge of the lake.

Coco's body trembled with fear. Instinct told her to turn her gaze to the shore. Through the light and mist, the shadow of another female emerged at the edge of the lake. The scent of rosemary and lavender permeated the damp air and Coco felt undeniably that the female shape standing on the shore was her mother. While the rational part of her brain reminded her that this was impossible, the image of Chantal at the water's edge beckoned to her.

"Mother…" Coco said.

She shoved Christopher's hand away, threw herself into the cold water, and began swimming toward the bank. The icy water lapped at her body, and the light around the lake became a dense fog. The tendons stood out on Coco's neck as the panic in her body surrendered to the sudden rush of adrenaline. Christopher's voice screamed out to her telepathically, but she kept her lips tightly shut. Something else infinitely stronger tugged at her mind—pulling her down, deeper into the cold, dark water. She dared not move.

Christopher's voice faded and a peaceful silence embraced her. All the while, Coco felt herself sinking further below the water's surface. An image came into focus. The woman she had seen at the edge of the jetty. Her white hair floated around her body, which was covered in a long silver satin gown. The image brought back memories of fairies that her mother used to paint for her, and this made Coco smile. The woman's skin glowed like polished alabaster, and her eyes sparkled with golden specks of glitter—similar to the glitter she'd used as a child.

"Accept what you are, Colombina," the woman's words echoed. "You cannot help your mother until you receive what is intended for you." The woman opened her hand and revealed an amethyst stone. She reached out and placed it firmly against Coco's heart. A blast of light burst forth from Coco. It caused her body to arch, and for a few moments she floated in the water. This made her wonder if she had drowned. But when she straightened out her body, the ethereal being stared directly at her.

"Colombina—this is your moment. You may choose to cross the threshold and own your fears, or continue with your life as it is," the woman said. "Your gifts have been awakened. There is no turning back. Listen…" This last word rippled through the water.

Listen…

"Who are you?" Coco asked.

"I am the safe-keeper of the Creatives," the woman said. And as quickly as the silence had entered it was lost. Icy water poured into Coco's mouth and her arms clawed at the abyss around her as the woman pushed her toward the surface.

○

Gabriel wrapped his arms around Coco and carried her to the shore. She clutched at the wet sand beneath her. "Where's Mother?" she spluttered through gasps. "Let me go! She needs me." Coco kicked and punched at him until exhaustion and the elements overtook her.

In seconds he had her back at his villa and in her shower. Hot water streamed over her shivering body. "You can open your eyes now. You are safe, Colombina."

He looked up when Layla ran into the bathroom. She stopped quickly when she saw him in the shower with Coco.

"Is she alright?" Layla asked. "And Christopher—where is he?"

Gabriel noticed Layla's bloodshot eyes and wide-eyed look. "Christopher and Eduardo are fine. They will be here momentarily." He turned off the water and moved Coco onto a chair as Layla wrapped towels around her.

"I can take over from here," Layla said. "I'm sorry, I thought that something had happened to Christopher—"

"It's alright." Gabriel tilted his head and listened. "He's downstairs and I need to speak with him. Take care of Colombina. We'll meet in the living room shortly." Gabriel turned to leave but stopped mid-step. "Your scent has changed," his face softened, "Have you told Christopher?"

Layla's cheeks flushed. "Not yet, there's been too much going on."

"This is good news," Gabriel said. He grabbed a towel from a basket and dried his hair as he walked out of the bathroom.

Layla peeled the wet clothes from Coco, dried her, and fetched a glass of brandy. She held it to Coco's lips but Coco pushed it away.

"I saw my Mother…" Coco said, her voice sounded distant. "And then she vanished."

"The others are waiting for us downstairs," Layla said. "We can discuss this with them."

"I saw Mother—"

"Coco!" Layla held Coco's shaking body close to hers. "Listen to me. You're in shock and need to get warm—please, have a sip of the brandy."

"I'm scared," Coco said. "Christopher and you… I don't think I can ever be as strong as either of you. I have nothing to offer the Allegiance. What the hell am I doing here?"

Layla cupped Coco's chin with her hands and looked directly into her eyes. "I didn't feel strong when I ran in here tonight. The thought of life without Christopher is terrifying to me, and for a while, I didn't know what had happened to either of you." She picked up a towel and dried Coco's hair. "We all have moments of fear. But in truth the fear reminds us of what we have to lose, and what we have to live for.

"Life is not the fairy tale we hoped it would be… it's only the moments of love woven through our path that make our lives exceptional. The Allegiance is about enabling those moments for everyone, giving us all the opportunity to find happiness and balance in our lives. It shouldn't be as difficult as it is, but people find it easier to feed traits like power, greed, and hate rather than accepting love and equality. To love is not always easy." She tossed the towel in the sink. "Our society has it all backwards. We can't lecture or force love. It must be given and shared freely in order for it to grow. You've been doing the work of the Allegiance all your life. Your paintings bring joy to others."

Coco shrugged. "This is so freaking confusing. Up until a few months ago my life seemed so calm."

"True, but you were asleep and now you're awake." She tossed Coco some clothes. "You have to admit that Gabriel's pretty damn hot!"

"I hadn't noticed…" Coco said.

Layla shook her head. "You're so full of shit!"

Coco tossed the wet towel at Layla and drank down the brandy.

CHAPTER 27

When Coco entered the living room, she was reminded of the level of anxiety that pulses through an examination room during finals week at the university. Everyone carried their personal concerns but were drawn together by one goal. The Professor held his fob watch in one hand and circled his thumb over it, as if it were a talisman. Gabriel sat on the edge of a well-worn leather armchair and stared at the antique rug beneath his feet.

She remembered how perfectly her body had fit into his while he had held her in the shower. He lifted his head, and when their eyes met she wondered if he knew what she was thinking.

"Would you prefer to ask questions, Colombina?" Gabriel asked. "Or rather me explain what I can?"

"I think that both are needed, but for starters I'd like to know this: why is it that since the car hit me, I've been followed—never left alone? And I'm pretty damn certain that was my mother standing by the side of the lake tonight before she was suddenly whipped off into the sky. And please don't tell me it was nothing—because Max was barking like crazy and I trust his instincts. And that fairy-like woman—with the purple stone—"

Coco's body trembled and she reached for Christopher's hand.

Gabriel rose from his chair and stood by the fireplace. "What do you remember of your parents?" he asked.

In a useless effort to hold off more tears, Coco closed her eyes. "Not much at all. Just quick flashes of imagery: the four of us together, Mother painting, playing with Christopher in the garden. I think we were happy."

"Did you know that your parents were both members of the Allegiance?" Gabriel asked.

Coco reached for a strand of her hair and twisted it around her finger. "My mother came here to study painting. She fell in love with my father and gave birth to Christopher and me. Then they both died… in a car accident. That's what Kishu has always told me."

"Chantal did relocate here to study with a teacher," Gabriel said. "And yes—she fell in love with Alessandro. But the truth is that your mother was a very important part of the Allegiance, and we thought she would be safe here, in this valley, to do her work."

"What are you talking about?" Coco asked. "What kind of work? "

"She painted truths within paintings, secrets only visible to a few. Chantal met Alessandro right here in this room and they were together until…" Gabriel looked down at his shoes. "Alessandro is my good friend… you must understand that."

"I think you mean, *was*. My father is dead," she said. "Besides, you were a child yourself and too young to know any of this."

The room fell silent. Coco looked up at Christopher, but he was staring at the floor.

"I'm older than you think," Gabriel said.

Coco turned to Gabriel. "How much older?" She was momentarily lost in his gaze before she realized that he was kneeling before her. She jumped.

"It's easier to show you," he said.

"How?"

Gabriel reached for Coco's hand but she leaned back. "You have no reason to fear me," he said.

Coco kept her eyes focused on Gabriel but reached out to Christopher with her mind.

"Is this safe, Christopher?"

"Yes—and our story is less complicated when seen. I'll be here the whole time—I promise."

Coco nodded and eased forward. "What do you need me to do?"

Gabriel held his hands toward her. "Place your hands in mine."

Very slowly she lifted her hands toward him. Right before they fell into his grasp she felt a tingling sensation pulsing from Gabriel's hands. In a flash, her mind tumbled into a vision.

Alessandro and Coco stand in Chantal's studio at the farmhouse watching her paint. Alessandro takes Coco's hand and guides her behind Chantal so they can see what she is painting. It's the unfinished painting that Coco completed a few nights ago.

Chantal turns to Coco, her eyes are glazed over with tears. She steps aside and allows Alessandro and Coco full access to the painting. Alessandro takes a step and encourages Coco to do the same.

"Is this like that scene in Mary Poppins*?" Coco asks. "Where they step into the painting?"*

"A little," Alessandro says. "But more complicated, and without the penguins."

Together they step forward and Coco expects to hit the canvas. She's surprised when she finds they have been transported to the garden behind their farmhouse. Alessandro guides Coco to the grassy area directly outside the door to the living room.

Gabriel walks down the steps and onto the grass as seven-year-old Christopher races across the yard and tackles him to the ground. But Gabriel isn't a child—he's the age he is now. Coco gives Alessandro a questioning look, but he takes her hand and jumps up into the air. They land in the garden at the front of the farmhouse. Coco watches from the pergola.

Alessandro kisses Chantal tenderly—they break apart and Chantal leans down and hugs Christopher. Alessandro and Christopher walk toward an elegant 1940s Mercedes-Benz. Christopher scoots into the back seat between Gabriel and Alessandro. A young Eduardo drives the car down the driveway.

Four-year-old Coco holds her mother's hand. Chantal kneels down on the grass so her eyes are level with Coco's. "Please don't be angry with Gabriel for blocking these memories from you, Colombina. Above all else, the Allegiance must protect you and Christopher so that you can both continue our line as Creative, and legal council." Chantal stands and Coco notices the splattering of paint on her mother's hands.

The image dissipates, and Coco finds herself standing in a field near the farmhouse. She sees her mother, and herself as a four-year-old, dancing together in the meadow and laughing at the large canine running in circles around them. Mother and daughter fall to the ground and look at the clouds gathering in the sky. Chantal's black wolf barks furiously—his hackles rise and he snarls as a dark figure walks briskly toward them.

Chantal jumps up and grabs Coco. She holds her so that her face is directly in front of hers. "You must leave me now, little one," Chantal says. "Run with Clio back to the house! Don't stop—Daddy and Gabriel will be here soon—I promise we will find each other again."

"No, Mommy," Coco says through sobs. "I don't want to leave you with him." Coco points to the dark figure striding toward them. Chantal screams, "Run, Colombina, don't look back, run…" She pushes Coco away and the wolf runs around the little girl, herding her away from Chantal. Coco turns her head and witnesses the dark figure strike her mother with such force that her body flies through the air and into the old willow tree.

Young Coco is terrified. She runs, but the man rushes after her. The wolf lunges at the man's throat, but he tosses it to the ground as if the huge animal is a piece of paper. He grabs Coco around her neck and dangles her in the air. Blood runs from his mouth. The man slowly licks his lips.

"Your imprudent mother was delicious," he says. "Creative blood is something divine."

Coco waits to die—to be near her mother, but the man throws her to the ground beside the dying wolf. Coco reaches for the wolf and lays her hand on his body. Alessandro's screams erupt into the still air. Strong arms lift Coco up from the ground. "You are safe now. Hush, Colombina." Gabriel holds on to her.

Coco opened her eyes and pulled her hands away from Gabriel. She turned to Christopher. "Are you a part of this secret too? How could you hide Mother's murder from me?" Christopher reached out but she pushed him away.

"You need to listen to everything. We had to protect you," Christopher said.

She stood up. "Protect me? You've all lied to me. My whole life has been a lie!" Her heart pounded as she glared at Gabriel. "And you… what the fuck did you do to my head?"

She ran out of the room and up the stairs to her bedroom. Max waited outside in the hallway and howled until she opened the door. One glimpse at the dog's sad eyes and Coco pulled him into the room. She leaned against the wall, slid onto the floor, and let her sadness and anger pour out through sobs. Thalia jumped into her lap and Max lay down and rested his large front paws on her thighs.

She felt violently ill from reliving her mother's gruesome attack—and angry with everyone. Tomorrow she would confront her demons and get answers to her questions.

In the living room, Christopher looked defeated. "Christ, she hates me," he said. "I always feared that telling her the truth would play out this way."

"She's been overloaded with new information," Gabriel

said. "I have no doubt that she'll have a long list of questions for all of us once her pain has subsided. For now she needs solitude and the unconditional love of one cat and a gentle shepherd—they'll comfort her through the next few hours."

"I can sense her pain... she feels betrayed," Christopher said. "Will you speak with her?"

"Through my observations, it is best to let your sister's temper settle before attempting to reason with her," Gabriel said. "We have Alessandro to thank for that gene—he reacts similarly in moments of anger." He clicked his fingers and the pack of dogs followed him outside into the dark night. Coco was not the only member of the household who required solitude and the comfort of animals.

○

Coco sat on the floor, overwhelmed by the sudden influx of information. She had questions that needed answers. But in order to gain information, she would have to delve into her mother and father's past. And after what she had witnessed, that meant learning about the Allegiance. She thought of everything that had transpired over the past few days. And then she remembered something the strange woman at the lake had said to her.

Listen...

Coco got up, opened the door, and stormed down the steps.

When she entered the living room, her heart pounded. "Where's Gabriel?"

Christopher looked up. "Out walking. Most likely he's gone to the farmhouse."

Coco walked out the front door, followed closely by Max and Thalia. The rain had ceased, leaving a clear night in its wake. Coco did not feel the frigid air. Her internal temperature had increased and continued to do so with every determined step she took along the road to the farmhouse.

CHAPTER 28

C oco approached the heavy iron gates. They groaned and creaked as they opened. She continued on and listened to the ominous clang as they closed behind her. The yellow glow of the moon lit her way along the road. She wondered how Gabriel had blocked her memories.

Maybe he has hypnotic skills…

When the farmhouse appeared, Coco noticed the glow of candlelight flickering through the windows. Pachelbel's Canon in D drifted through the darkness as if beckoning her inside. She took a deep breath, opened the door, and entered the house, Max and Thalia right behind her.

Flames from the candles reached out across the room, drawn, like Coco, to the man playing the piano. The pack of dogs lifted their heads but went back to sleep when they saw her. Gabriel's back faced the door, allowing her to quietly slip inside the room and ease herself onto a nearby sofa. This wasn't the entrance she had imagined, but the music soothed her. Her two companions jumped up beside her.

The warm ambience of the room relaxed her. She stretched out and listened as Gabriel finished one piece and began another. When he was halfway through playing a piece by Debussy, Coco became aware that all of the pieces he played replicated one of her playlists. One that she played whenever she painted. This particular piece had always evoked something from her childhood and she remembered that her father had played it for her. She was begging the name of the piece to come to her memory when the music suddenly stopped.

"Max really shouldn't be up on the furniture," Gabriel said.

"I thought you gave him to me. I have a feeling your animal rules and mine are quite different. And this is my home, so my rules. I want answers… now!"

Gabriel pushed back the piano seat and turned to face her. "Would you like a drink?"

"Of my own wine?" Coco asked. "Sure—why not? In fact, bring the whole damn bottle. It might help me talk to you."

"Do you find it that difficult to converse with me?" He grabbed two wine glasses and opened a bottle of wine.

"Under the current circumstances, I'm finding it difficult to speak to anyone. It comes under the heading of trust."

Gabriel sat on the armchair opposite Coco and poured the wine. "No child should have seen what you saw," he said, passing her a glass. "Alessandro and I did what we felt needed to be done. We thought we would lose you as well as Chantal."

"I don't understand. What did you do, exactly?"

Gabriel stared into his glass of wine.

"And what type of man was that who killed my mother?" she asked.

He inhaled deeply. "A very dangerous one, and not a good example of the species."

"You're not making any sense." Her chest felt restricted. She did her best to steady her breath, but the underlying shadow of fear did not dissipate.

Listen…

Gabriel rose from the chair and extended his hand to her. "Please, come walk with me, I want to show you something."

"You don't like to sit still for long do you?" She refused his hand, but rose from the sofa. "Where are we going?"

"Upstairs," he said. "To your mother's studio."

Coco nodded, took a large gulp of wine, and followed him across the room. She glimpsed quickly at the seductive man in front of her, confused at why she was so attracted to him when he had somehow messed with her head. She felt a flush of warmth in the lower part of her torso and had the urge to fluff her hair.

He stopped suddenly and she ran into him. He turned his head and peered at her. "Are you alright?"

"Of course, I'm alright. You stopped for no reason and I ran into you. That's all," she said, mortified with the fact that her cheeks were most likely scarlet.

He continued on to the stairs. "After you," Gabriel said and stepped aside.

He placed a hand on her back and urged her forward. Once again, Coco was taken with the energy that pulsed through his hand and into her body. It was not uncomfortable, but calming, and extremely sensual.

They walked through her parents' bedroom and into the studio. A wave of nostalgia came over Coco. "It's only been a few days since I've been gone, but I miss this house." She walked over to the window and looked up at the moon. "It's starting to feel more like home than my loft in L.A."

"That's probably a good thing," Gabriel said, under his breath.

"Why are we here?" Coco demanded.

"I'll tell you, but I ask one thing."

"What?"

"That you hear me out, no running or slamming doors. Can you agree to that?"

She settled down on the sofa. "I can't promise you anything.

I'm not open to deals where my mother is concerned. But I need to know what happened to her."

Gabriel sat beside her. "Then I believe it's time for you to know the truth."

Max and Thalia were standing by the door. Gabriel pointed to the ground by his feet, and Max trotted over and lay on the floor beside him. He turned his attention to the cat. "Thalia, show this beautiful lady what you can do, although I can't guarantee that you will be welcome on her bed once she knows the real you."

Thalia walked to the center of the room. She shook her head and then the rest of her body followed suit. The cat's fur changed to a mottled gray, and her body grew larger. She gave her body a final shake and turned her head to Coco.

Coco shot back into the sofa and she grabbed Gabriel's arm. Thalia had transformed into a large lynx. She shook her furry head and the tufts of hair below her chin fell into place. She tilted her head toward Gabriel. He nodded at her, and Thalia morphed into a black jaguar. "She's really quite beautiful." Gabriel said.

Coco's anxiety level was rising quickly.

Listen...

The black jaguar rubbed her body against Coco's legs. Coco couldn't resist placing her hand on the animal's velvety coat.

"Thalia is your animal guardian," Gabriel said.

"My cat turned into two other animals, can you at least acknowledge that first?"

The jaguar placed her head on Coco's lap and looked into her eyes. Reflected in them was the image of Coco as a little girl clutching onto the neck of a large black wolf, blood seeping from a gash in its body. Coco gasped.

"I wish I had the courage and tenacity of Clio, Colombina," Gabriel said. His voice was gentle. "She died protecting you."

"Are you saying that Thalia was also my mother's wolf?"

"Yes."

They remained silent for a few moments.

"But you said she died."

"Yes, she did," Gabriel said. "The Allegiance has always protected Creatives—we believe they are the key to a balanced civilization. Your mother had many protectors, but her animal guardian was Clio. She could become many adaptations of a canine, but preferred the wolf. When her time came to pass, she became Thalia, choosing the feline persuasion. It's a perfect choice for you, in your own way you are mysterious, like a cat."

"Why the name Thalia?" Coco asked.

"Thalia was also a muse, like Clio, and I thought the name suited her when she changed to become your guardian."

Coco stroked the soft coat of the enigmatic feline. "It was Thalia I saw before the accident, wasn't it?" To confirm her question the jaguar shook her body and her color changed to sand. Her deliberate stare and long tail defined her appearance. Thalia had transformed into a mountain lion. "But she wasn't with me when the car hit."

"Actually, she was. The car hit her first."

"But Thalia didn't die?" Coco asked.

"My father searched the mountains and found her in time. He was able to heal her."

"Your father?"

"Yes, and I will speak of him later. But first, I need you to understand that the car hitting you was no accident. It was an attempt to kill you, and you can thank Thalia for alerting us, otherwise we would not be having this conversation. I would like to show you something more."

"You said you'd tell me about yourself, Gabriel."

He stood up and offered her his hand. She took it and followed him toward one of her mother's paintings. "I will, but do not let go of my hand," he said. "This is one of Chantal's favorite paintings." Gabriel extended his left arm toward the canvas—his long delicate fingers stopped a few inches before the paint. Coco noticed that his breathing had slowed, his face held perfectly still, and a soft light radiated around the frame that bordered the painting. Particles of paint lifted slowly from the canvas and gathered at the tips of Gabriel's fingers…

Alessandro and Gabriel are fighting a group of men, and all are armed with swords and knives. They are dressed in dark leather pants tucked into long leather boots, dark shirts worn under leather vests, and long coats. When their attackers are all dead on the ground, Alessandro and Gabriel open a heavy wooden door and enter a small room. On the walls hang paintings by Botticelli. They quickly gather up the artwork and wrap the pieces in their coats.

They leap up to a high window, fling it open, and leave. They're standing on the roof of a villa clutching the paintings and watching the smoke from the Bonfire of the Vanities drift through the city of Florence. Seconds later, Stefan is beside them holding a woman with long white hair to his chest. She is sobbing hysterically…

Chantal and Alessandro stand together in the Piazza de Duomo, San Gimignano—Chantal is dressed in a white wedding dress of antique lace, and Alessandro wears a dark suit with a long dress coat. Gabriel stands beside him. Kishu and the fairy-like woman with the long white hair stand beside Chantal…

Alessandro is holding Chantal's hand and wiping her forehead with a white towel. A baby screams and Alessandro leans down and kisses Chantal's lips. Both of them have tears in their eyes. The woman with the long white hair wraps the baby in a blanket and places him in Chantal's arms—it's Christopher. The doctor walks over and Alessandro hugs her.

Gabriel is speaking with a group of people: two graduate students from Coco's advanced painting class, a fellow professor of Coco's, the gardener who works at the sculpture garden, along with a prominent member of the UCLA board of directors…

Coco lies in bed asleep in ICU at the hospital after the accident: Gabriel is standing beside her bed speaking with Alessandro. As Gabriel leaves, Coco's doctor comes in and speaks to him—she's the same doctor that delivered Christopher—Dr. Fiore.

The picture faded and the paint from Gabriel's fingertips returned to the painting.

"Are you… like Dumbledore, or something equally as weird?" Coco stumbled back toward the door. "How was that possible? And my doctor in L.A.—at Christopher's birth—what the fuck is this about? How do you know the people I work with?" She crossed her arms.

"They're all part of the Allegiance, Colombina. And unlike Dumbledore, I am not a fictitious character. To understand what I am, I need to tell you a little about my mother. She is able to do many things, but primarily she's what you might call a witch… an ancient and powerful witch."

Coco poked him in the chest. "Did you drop some kind of psychedelic mushrooms into my wine? That's it—I'm hallucinating—my cat is a freaking leopard—"

"I don't believe I've ever seen Thalia as a leopard."

"Shut up! Answer my fucking questions!"

"I can only do one or the other," Gabriel said. "Which will it be? Stay silent or answer your questions?"

Coco ignored him. "You're making paintings seem real. Am I tripping? Shit—I've never smoked anything but weed. Damn you fucking Italians! Your mother's a witch? You wish! If I were a witch and your mother, I'd turn you into a common housefly and swat you. That's what I'd do!"

"Thank God you are not my mother. And for the record, I would never put any kind of hallucinogen in anyone's wine. By the way, you are half Italian. And to say that this is something that Italians do is ridiculous. I find it offensive."

"Yeah—it's right up there with 'my mother's a witch'!'"

"Am I to understand that after seeing your cat transform into other feline forms, stepping into other realities via paintings, and witnessing a few of my... abilities, that you find the word, *witch* offensive?"

Coco took a long, slow, deep breath and calmed herself. She remembered the voice telling her to listen. "Go on, I'm listening."

"You will understand why your father and I have not aged if you listen to my explanation." Gabriel inhaled deeply. "My father is a vampire—an extremely strong vampire. He belonged to a powerful order."

Coco slowly began backing away from him.

"I've told you before, Colombina, I will never hurt you, and you said you would consider not making a run for the door. Besides, I promise that I am faster than you."

"The only word I heard in your previous sentence was vampire, and there is no way in hell I'm staying in this room with you a moment longer—you're either as nutty as a pecan pie or indeed a vampire-witch-hybrid-whatever. Either way, I need to get the fuck out of this house and away from you—you're insane."

CHAPTER 29

Coco bolted down the stairs, flung open the front door, and sprinted through the darkness toward the lake. She slid to a halt at the end of the jetty and climbed down the ladder.

Where the hell am I going?

She stepped down into the boat and jumped at the sight of a figure sitting there. The woman wore a long cloak covered in embroidered symbols with an attached hood that fell around her face.

"What is the matter?" the woman asked, her voice heavily accented.

"I have to get away from here," Coco said, trying to catch her breath. *I need to get back to L.A.*

"Then sit," the woman said.

Coco sat on the wooden seat opposite. The woman picked up the oars and rowed to the middle of the lake. Coco's gaze drifted to where Gabriel stood at the water's edge. She turned to the woman. "Please, I'm scared and I have no one else to turn to."

The woman looked across the water and spoke to Gabriel. "Well, you handled that well. The young woman is scared out of her wits."

"What? You know him?" Coco grabbed the oars from the woman and desperately began rowing.

"Where are you going, dear? This is a lake," the woman said. "He may not be able to walk on water, but wherever you try to go, he will reach the other side before you." She stretched her arms toward the oars and they leapt instantly back into her hands. "We are going to sit here and have a discussion."

Coco's eyes darted around, searching for a means of escape.

"I am gathering, by your accelerated heartbeat, that Gabriel told you of his heritage. Have you ever been fearful of him before he told you this?" Coco shook her head. The woman continued, "What frightens you more—the warlock in his blood or the vam*pir*?"

The way in which the woman pronounced the word vam-*pir* intrigued Coco. She broke it down into two syllables, and stretched out the final part of the word so that it fell to the ground like an autumn leaf. It sounded romantic. Almost.

"The latter," Coco said.

"Did you love your father, Alessandro?"

"Of course," Coco said. "I adored him."

"What if I told you that he was also a vam*pir*, and was when he married your dear mother."

"Vampires are fictional," Coco said, fighting back panic. "Like Dracula."

"Be careful what you say about *Dracul*," the woman said in hushed tones. "It is time to open your mind and your heart."

Coco looked down at her hands. "But if my father was a vampire then that makes Christopher and I half—"

"Vam*pir*. Yes. Christopher's ability to read others, and the fact that you can speak to each other telepathically are not considered normal human traits." She pushed back the hood from her head and revealed her golden eyes and long white hair.

Coco gasped. "You're the woman in the lake... with the amethyst stone."

The woman nodded. "You and Christopher are quite unique—you are both half vam*pir* and Creative. But unlike your brother, you have been asleep for most of your life."

"What?"

"When I placed the amethyst stone into your heart, it awakened you," she said. "My apologies for being so abrupt—but with Chantal's sudden appearance I had no choice."

"So that did happen?"

"Of course." The woman inhaled. "Tell me, Colombina, why do you teach art?"

"Why do I teach art?" Coco thought about her answer. "Because I believe that every child deserves a humanistic education... when the arts are taken away we lose the ability to communicate." She looked up at the stars. "Creativity is like any other muscle—if it's not used, it becomes weak. But used daily, it becomes strong and can support one's body and mind. Art is a form of communication."

"Your words give me hope," the woman said. "And it is good to hear you speak with such passion. So many people refuse to understand the profound significance of a balanced education. The fifteenth century Florentines, like Lorenzo, had it right—they did not divide their learning into school years. They understood that learning never stops. A degree is not the only thing that can show an individual's intelligence. I yearn for another Renaissance."

"Me too," Coco looked nervously at her hands. "If you'd brought me here earlier, could I have helped find my parents?"

"Looking back will not help this situation."

Coco's gaze shifted to Gabriel. He stared back at her. She felt something shift and her heart opened to him.

"That is better, my dear," the woman whispered. "He is as

gentle as a lamb." She turned toward Gabriel. "Bring wine, my son, the night is young and we have much to discuss."

"Gabriel... is your son? But he said you were ancient. You look more like his sister."

The woman's golden eyes lit up. "He called me *ancient*?" she tutted. "Yes, Gabriel is my one and only and I apologize for the scare he gave you this evening. He has waited a long time for your return, and patience can be somewhat difficult for the men of my family. But I promise you this—he will never hurt you, and he will destroy anyone who even thinks about bringing harm to you. Vam*pirs* are extremely protective of those they love."

Coco shuddered. "What can you tell me about my father... what happened to him after my mother died?"

"Your mother did not die. That scum who took Chantal *turned* her. A crime within the Allegiance—especially for our Creatives."

"He made her... like him?"

"Your mother has been a vam*pir* for the past twenty-eight years, concealed in captivity."

The silence between the two women stretched into the darkness. Coco's eyes brimmed with tears again, but she wiped them away. She held back her shoulders and found her composure.

The woman looked out at the edge of the lake where Coco had seen the image of her mother. "We have been searching for Chantal since that sad day she was taken," she said. "That was not her you saw earlier this evening."

"You're speaking in riddles," Coco said. "Are you saying that my mother is alive but is being held against her will by the vampire that I saw kill her? And that my father is also alive?"

"Yes, that is what I am saying."

Coco gripped the wooden seat. "I understand that when it first happened I was a sick little girl, but surely, more recently I could have helped somehow."

"If we had taken you away any earlier from your familiar community at the university you may have lost your sense of purpose. And our sense of purpose is what gives us our moral compass. Of course, there have been many, many times when I thought about bringing you here earlier. But you see—you are not the only part to this puzzle."

Coco noticed that the oars were silently propelling them in the direction of the jetty without any help from the woman. "I should be happy," she said. "But instead I'm more confused and quite frankly—pretty pissed off. My life has been full of lies, and my own father deserted my brother and I when we needed him most. I'm not sure I can forgive him for that."

"You may live to regret your words when you see Alessandro. He is a broken man. And a broken-hearted vam*pir* is an exceedingly sad being. He did what he needed to do at that time. His anger drove him mad for quite a while. You were in a severe state of shock. You could not talk, eat, or sleep. I asked Gabriel to block your memories rather than the alternative, which would have meant your death… not an acceptable consideration.

"Thankfully, Christopher did not witness the brutality that you saw, but because of your connection with each other, he became withdrawn. We said nothing to others to insinuate that you were alive—rather, we hoped they would believe you had died that day. Gabriel and I took you to *Casa della Pietra*—it is protected, and its location is a closely guarded secret. We changed your name to Coco, and gave you and Christopher the last name, Rhodes."

The woman dipped her pale hand into the water and let it fall through her fingers.

"Christopher went to live with Kishu, and Gabriel brought him to visit you once you were stronger. But you were not the same person that your brother remembered. Your laughter had been replaced with sadness and that broke his heart. Christopher was seven when the tragedy happened," she looked out toward the shadowed hills. "Such a fragile age for children—it is the age when they discover that there is a real, and an imaginary, world. The day of your mother's abduction marked the end of Christopher's childhood. And when he saw you at *Casa della Pietra* his heart broke once more. Gabriel took him back to Hawaii when he saw the boy lose his spirit."

"But how did Christopher move forward with all of this weight on his shoulders? And how the hell has he put up with me?" Coco said. "I feel terrible—he's given up so much for me."

"Talk with your brother—he will tell you his story. He remained quite the rebel for many years."

"With good reason."

"Yes, and Gabriel took the brunt of it. He explained to Christopher that it would be best if you were told your parents were killed in a car accident. He swore an oath to Christopher that on your thirty-second birthday he would tell you the truth."

"You had a little boy tell a lie—one that he kept for over twenty-eight years?"

"You must understand, Colombina, your mind had closed down. We could not connect with you. We had to keep you safe. Once you gained strength, we took you to Hawaii to be with Kishu—you were protected there—and before we left, Gabriel made sure you would not remember either of us. It broke his heart.

"Christopher did not see you again until he returned to Hawaii during his early university years, and by that time, you did not resemble the little girl from his youth. For some strange reason the shock of what you saw took all of the color from your hair. But I have noticed that it has changed back to its natural hue. It must be magic."

"It's called dye—Antonia talked me into it."

"Ah yes, beautiful Antonia, such a fashionista."

"Please, continue with my story," Coco urged.

"Of course," the woman said. "You begged constantly to be allowed to apply to the same university that Christopher attended. We knew that once you turned eighteen you could leave on your own accord, and in Los Angeles the Allegiance watched over you. However, your safety has always been in jeopardy—and we could not keep you tucked away from the real world forever. We have noticed that you do not do well when you feel confined in any way."

The rowboat had reached the jetty. They got out and walked up the path to the farmhouse. Coco opened the front door to find the room still aglow with candlelight and Gabriel waiting patiently by the fireplace. He handed the woman a glass of wine and another to Coco. She felt a tingle of energy as his fingers brushed against hers.

"I apologize for frightening you, Colombina," he said. "Our lives are complicated, to say the least."

Coco sat and took a large gulp of wine. Although she felt confused and wary about his vampire attributes, she could not deny the chemistry between them. "I guess I'm more flight than fight," she said.

"Your reaction tonight was not unexpected," he said. "And it's good to know that you have the stamina to run and row a boat when you need to."

Coco sat quietly and did her best to come to terms with the world of creatures that, up until now, she thought belonged in mythology. If her mother had fallen in love with, and accepted, Alessandro, then for today, she needed to accept this life too. "I'm doing my best to comprehend everything," she said. "But there are a few more answers I'd like before I go to sleep."

"What are your questions?" Gabriel asked.

Coco looked across at the graceful woman sipping wine. Her fingers were folded daintily around a crystal glass. Flickers of candlelight bounced off her long white hair and golden eyes, making her look even more celestial than she had on the lake.

"What's your name?" she asked.

The woman smoothed the fabric of her long satin dress. "I have had many names. But for centuries I have been known as Prudence."

"Prudence, where is my father?"

"At Gabriel's home in Ventimiglia. He will be here in a few days. He is working on a lead we have on Chantal's whereabouts and wants to wait until you are ready to see him," Prudence gazed across at Gabriel and then to Coco. "Christopher promised you answers when you arrived here in Italy, and I appreciate your patience. Sometimes matters are not ours to control. But tonight I will tell you the truth about your life. You may not like all of it—and what you do with this information is your choice to make.

"When you were four, your mother was taken by an immortal. His name is Kenan. He wanted to possess Chantal's power as a seer and her creativity. But he separated mother from child—the worst sin, and a foolish thing to do, because Chantal became weak without her children.

"My guess is that he withheld elements of life from her: sunlight, fresh air, trees, all things that we take for granted. Without these gifts, Chantal would wilt like a dying flower. Creatives need growth and new life to sustain their ability to enact artistic changes upon the world. I believe this is why we have been unable to find her. And yet, she appeared to you by the lake. No doubt she will share that story upon her return.

"Now, I shall speak of the miracle of our lives. It begins with numbers, for they have a great significance in your personal story. Imagine all of the cells that divide to become the embryo—they contain everything in the world. We can call this swirling mass of cells, creative chaos: good, evil, creativity and destruction, they are all contained here. This is the number *one*—everything in potential.

"But there exists a powerful force within this number. The energy splits and *one* becomes *two*. The opposites. Are you with me so far?"

Coco nodded.

"Good. Now we have *two*—two polarized opposites: night and day, light and dark. It is like this when two people first fall in love—the union of opposites—everything feels whole again. This is their 'you complete me' moment. But the realities of life set in and the lovers do not understand the meaning behind their union. It can manifest as frustration and petty arguments, or they may choose to separate, or stay together and work through their challenges.

"In a healthy relationship the two people come together and yet remain distinct. They continue to grow and this is the number *three*. *Three* wants to bring these opposites together again. But remember, by bringing the *two* together, existence can become unstable.

"With *three* we often crave the passion of our youth and this can emerge as infidelity, sadness, or perhaps… we are unable to let go of our children." Prudence paused for a moment and glanced at Gabriel. Her eyes glistened. She took a sip of her wine. "Conflict arises until *three* breaks into *four*—the *quaternity*. Opposites, and they equal the original attraction, *two*. This is what we all crave, the agreement to be authentic and together— the strength in true love.

"After *four*, the quintessence arrives—*five*. And after *five* we go back to one again. *Five* is how we feel when everything in our life is going well, and then we turn another corner and something challenging happens in our lives. We are forced to begin the journey again. You see, the healthier the psyche the more it wants to live. It constantly upends us. This is how we learn our lessons in life."

"But what does this have to do with my mother?" Coco asked. "Why did you wait until now to bring me here?"

Prudence placed her glass on the table. "How old were you when Kenan stole Chantal?"

"I was four."

"The quaternity—you were ready to break off and expand your life."

"No! I was a little girl whose mother was ripped away from her and then half eaten by some evil maniac in front of her. He killed my mother's wolf, threw me on the ground, and took my mother away from me!" Coco broke down, crying. Prudence sat beside Coco and comforted her.

"Colombina, you were born under the sign of Scorpio. You are extremely powerful, intensely passionate, and want to get to the point of everything quickly. So please listen. You must trust that I am getting to the heart of the matter. Do you remember how old your mother was when she was taken from us?"

Coco nodded and answered through her tears. "She was thirty-two."

"Yes, and if we add those two numbers, two and three— they equal five. That day was Chantal's quintessence. It was time for her to become one again. Time for her to learn new lessons—and Chantal loved to learn."

"You're suggesting that she chose what happened to her?"

"No, but she is a seer. She had seen what would transpire that day and planned accordingly. Understand that being a seer is both a gift and a curse. Your mother's heightened selflessness and compassion allowed her to see that she needed to give up her own human life in order for both of you to move forward. Unfortunately, she did not see who would betray the Allegiance and let Kenan in, but she saw everything else. She wrote the letters to Christopher and you many years ago and gave them to me… she asked that I made sure you both received them at the ages she requested."

"But why that age? Why thirty-two?"

"She wanted to wait until you were thirty-two because she knew that by then your psyche would be ready for this journey. It is interesting that it has been twenty-eight years since Chantal was taken. Added together and they become one. So, do you see now? Life is never black and white. Sometimes it is the gray that holds the truth, and the truth is gold."

She took Coco's hand in hers. "Colombina—you are an artist. You are already doing the work—the proper tests that your psyche gives you. I ask that you do not give up, but rather you keep moving forward and growing. This is your quintessential moment. Take the good with the bad, the light with the dark— we need both, in balance. Now, it has been a long night and you need rest. Perhaps you will allow my son to walk with you."

"I'm fine—it's just up the stairs."

"Not here," Prudence said. "In Gabriel's villa, where you will be safe."

Coco pleaded with Prudence. "Please, can I stay here tonight?"

"No, not tonight," Prudence said.

Coco stood up. "I have more questions."

"I would be surprised if you didn't. We can talk again tomorrow." Prudence squeezed Coco's hands, and released her.

Coco walked over to the door and turned in time to see Gabriel embrace Prudence. She listened as they spoke in the language of the Allegiance, before Gabriel turned and walked in her direction.

"Everything alright?" Coco asked.

"Mother will take care of your house tonight." He opened the front door and they stepped outside, followed by Thalia and Max.

Coco shivered, and Gabriel placed his jacket around her shoulders. "Thanks," she said, as they walked along the tree-canopied driveway. "May I ask you some questions?"

"You may ask me anything."

"Can vampires be in the daylight?"

Gabriel smiled. "Yes, the daylight myth originated from fear of our kind. Sunlight can burn them as sure as any mortal, but it would have to be a very bad sunburn to kill."

"While we're on the myths," she said. "What about mirrors? Do vampires have reflections?"

"Of course. But remember, Colombina, I am half-vampire, half-warlock, so I am an exception to these sorts of things."

"Can they procreate?"

"Some of them, yes. Vampires who mate with Creatives can reproduce, and those who are half vampire—it's complex."

"I'm half-vampire, but I don't feel any different than when I didn't know any better."

"Most people do not run marathons every week. You seem to know exactly what to say to your students, and you are empathic, like Christopher, only he has developed his skill to a higher level than yours." His golden-flecked eyes stared directly into hers. "Not only do you have stamina, but your running speed from the farmhouse to the lake was impressive."

"Fear has a tendency to enhance my speed."

"Another vampire trait." Gabriel read her expression. "Go on, ask me."

"Do you drink—I mean, should I be concerned that my blood is something you might crave?"

"You are half vampire. Do you feel an urge to tear out my throat and consume my lifeblood?"

Coco frowned.

"No? Well, there's your answer. But blood *can* be a power-ful tool at times, when used properly. And, for the record, your blood smells like mornings spent lazily in bed, orange blossoms, and snowflakes."

"So I healed quickly because I'm half—"

"Vampire. Yes, but you had a little help too."

"What do you mean? Did you or Prudence spin a little magic over me?"

"I gave you a few drops of my blood, to stop the internal bleeding."

"Oh, God." Coco's hand flew to her mouth and she began to heave. Gabriel had her lean over. He placed a hand on her neck and Coco's nausea dissipated immediately.

"Oh shit, yes, I remember, you showed me the image of you with Dr. Fiore at the ICU unit at the hospital. That piece of information may send me over the edge. I'm vegetarian, for God's sake!"

They continued walking.

"I don't want to hear any more tonight. I need sleep, I haven't had much lately." She could feel the pull to succumb to slumber. "Maybe tomorrow…"

Gabriel whispered close to her ear. "The name of the piece that I played tonight is 'Doctor Gradus ad Parnassum' from Debussy's *The Children's Corner.*"

"Yes—my father played it to me when I was a little girl."

They had arrived at the villa. Gabriel opened the door to her bedroom, helped her onto the bed and pulled the quilt around her. He placed a hand on her forehead and she fell into a deep sleep.

CHAPTER 30

Coco stretched and focused on the alarm clock that read 4 p.m. She habitually patted Thalia, and then the cat's shape-shifting abilities roused her conscious mind, along with the profusion of information she had learned about her family and members of the Allegiance. Her anxiety accelerated. "Vampires and witches... my parents are alive..."

She flung back the covers and noticed fresh paint splatters on her hands. She ran into the studio. On the easel sat a freshly completed landscape painting. It was of the view from the window of the studio: a stone-paved road, the farmhouse and a pomegranate tree laden with dark red fruit.

That explains the paint on my hands and my extended sleeping hours.

Coco recalled her mother's paintings from the night before. She showered, dressed, and went in search of Gabriel. Thalia happily morphed into a lynx and kept stride with Max. The library door was slightly ajar and Coco heard Gabriel's modulated voice in conversation. He paused his speech.

"Colombina," he said. "Please, come in."

Coco eased the door open and stepped inside. When her gaze met his, she felt a flush of heat flare below her belly. The pull of Gabriel's seductive charm enticed her, and she noted his slightly open lips. A shiver of pleasure ran over her. She crossed her arms in front of her body and tore her gaze away from his.

Gabriel spoke into his cell phone. "I'll call you back." He placed the phone into a pocket of his faded jeans.

The tickling sensation seeped over Coco.

"What is it?" Gabriel asked as he walked toward her. "I trust you slept well?"

His mouth curled up into a suggestive smirk that left her lightheaded. She clutched the doorknob for support.

"I noticed paint on my hands when I woke up." Her words came out too fast. She inhaled deeply to calm her heart rate as she guided him up the stairs. "This has happened before but I've dismissed it, thinking that I've done a lousy clean-up job. But this time there seemed more paint than usual." They entered the studio. "I came in here to see if I'd painted anything—not that I have any memory of it." She held her hand out toward the painting on the easel and waved it around. "Can you do that magic thingy you did last night with my mother's paintings? I know it's kind of a long shot, but maybe it will reveal something helpful."

Gabriel focused on the painting. He reached his hand forward and beckoned forth the colors. Particles of paint drifted off the canvas toward his fingers and hovered in mid-air to reveal a smeared landscape saturated in crimson tones. The image moved in a fragmented motion—like an old black and white film that had been soaked in blood. A steep dirt road bordered by the ghostly outline of pine trees was barely recognizable in the tenebrous night.

"I sense Mother," Coco said quietly. "She's somehow a part of this painting."

The scene faded, and the particles of paint seeped back onto the canvas.

"There's not enough here we can use," Gabriel said. Coco's

eyes filled with tears. He placed an arm around her trembling shoulders. "Next time, Colombina."

She shook her head. "I'm an artist who happened to get up in the middle of the night and paint."

"Do you truly believe that this is a random act?" he asked.

"For a moment, I thought I'd painted something significant. But I didn't. I'm not my mother and hardly a member of the Allegiance."

"You do not get to choose to be in the Allegiance—the Allegiance chooses its members, for their talents and courage."

"Then you screwed up—I can't help you!"

She pulled away from him and turned to leave. Gabriel gently took hold of her elbow. "For centuries, great artists have lived in the shadows of the masters, and there is a reason for this. They are the artists who are not afraid to paint intuitively—from their hearts and souls. Their paintings bring beauty and solace to us all. They are the Creatives… artists who are born to bring important secrets to us. Your mother is one of our best. We believe she holds a valuable secret."

"What secret?"

Gabriel let go of her elbow. "The identity of an important leader. One who will help bring balance to this world."

"And who else knew that my mother would one day receive this information?"

"Everyone in the Allegiance."

"So whoever betrayed her, betrayed the future of the world as well?"

"Not all is said and done. But you're right, she was betrayed so that Kenan could kill or turn the future leader."

"Maybe my mother doesn't hold this information?"

"We've thought of that."

"Will Kenan kill her, if he—" Coco looked away. "Is that why he tried to kill me? Did he threaten her with my life?"

"It seems that way."

"Why did you wait until now to tell me this?"

"Because we hoped you would have faith in yourself," he said. "It is the task of the Allegiance to protect and support this new leader. We will not stand by and witness the world spiral into chaos—it already shows signs of doing so."

Coco turned and faced him. "Why do you have faith in me?"

Gabriel placed his hands on her shoulders. "Because I sense your fearless courage. Your defiance."

Coco looked away, but Gabriel's hand caught her chin and turned her face to his. She stared at him for a second, and then pushed his hand away. "I'm so sick of doing what everyone tells me to do, all the time. I'm fed up with the prodding, the maneuvering, and the mind games. I'm done with all of it! I'm thirty-two, for God's sake. Please... let me make some mistakes." She stepped away from him. "Do you know that since you showed me what happened to Mother I've relived every bit of pain that little girl of four went through—over and over again? I can't eat, I constantly suffer from nausea, and I'm frightened all of the time. So this is my fearless courage, Gabriel, and it hurts. But you know what? If my mother saw her own demise into misery, and had faith that I could rise above all of this shit, then nothing will stop me. I'll do my best to find her, even if it means I die trying. You got that?"

Gabriel stood perfectly still.

She walked to the bedroom door and opened it. Her breathing was fast and shallow. Her whole body trembled and she knew what she had to do. She slammed the door, and turned around to face him.

"Take the mind block thing down," she said. "Do it now, please."

"Are you sure that's what you want? You may be surprised at some—"

"I've seen the worst, and now I need to feel the good stuff. To feel loved. Please, Gabriel."

He nodded, and walked to her.

"Will it hurt?" she asked.

"No, in fact it may feel quite peaceful after everything else you've seen."

He pulled a rune from his pocket and took hold of her hands. He held the rune against her forehead, closed his eyes and breathed in and out slowly.

Coco gasped and then closed her eyes. Tears cascaded down her face. After a few minutes, Gabriel took away the rune and let go of her hands. She opened her eyes and stared into his.

"I knew then," she spoke quietly. "I knew I would fall in love with you. I saw it."

She flung herself at Gabriel and kissed him. Her body tingled the moment their lips met and a torrent of joy flooded her body. She grabbed his hair while his tongue hungrily explored her mouth.

O

When their lips parted, Gabriel trailed kisses across Coco's cheek, finally resting above her right ear. "*Mia bella musa*," he whispered.

He lifted Coco into his arms and sat her gently on the bed. One quick glare at Thalia and Max, accompanied by a click of his fingers, had the two animals scurrying across the floor toward the door that opened with a wave of Gabriel's arm. The click of the lock confirmed him of the privacy he wanted.

The winter sun had dropped behind the hills leaving the valley shrouded in a charcoal wash. The air felt chilled like the ash of long forgotten fires. Another sweep of his arm brought life to the dead embers in the fireplace, and in seconds, warmth and ambience swirled through the room. He placed his hand on the back of her neck and brought her mouth to his.

He breathed in Coco's scent of arousal; the wild geranium that lingered amongst the orange blossoms and lavender had intensified. He found it intoxicating. He kicked off his shoes and slowly lowered her to the bed, captivated in the warmth of her mouth.

He lavished his time and enjoyed the fragrance of her freshly washed hair, which smelled to him like cherries and almonds. His hand slipped under her T-shirt and travelled down her body. He caressed the muscles and dimples at the base of her spine and explored the curve of her hips. In one motion, he undid the buttons on her jeans and found the wetness between her legs. Her moans evoked a deep groan of satisfaction from him. With one hand he lifted her T-shirt above her head and then kissed her breasts until her nipples strained beneath the constraints of a white lacy bra. His tongue explored the curves of her collarbone while she writhed in motion to his fingers.

He loosened her bra, and aroused her nipples with his tongue. Her breath quickened and he covered her mouth with his. As he kissed her deeply he felt her body peak and then tremble in release.

Her eyes brimmed with tears. "Why are you crying?" he asked.

"I'm overwhelmed."

"By what?"

"Freedom—and you," she said, as she pulled at the shirt he was wearing and hauled it over his head. Gabriel followed her gaze as it wandered over the symbols tattooed across his chest and shoulders. His fingers ached to touch her as she kissed the symbol above his heart: the rune, Dagaz.

Coco wriggled out of her jeans. Seconds later they lay together, skin against skin. Muse and Warlock. She straddled him and ran her fingers over his body. He caught her left hand and kissed it, but she pulled her arm away and lowered herself forward. His body reveled in joy as she kissed every defined muscle on his body.

They played for hours before he entered her. Their bliss ascended, until passion fused with the unending coil of love, and they lay satiated in each other's arms.

He held her against his body while she dozed over the next hour. When she finally opened her eyes, he looked at her with concern. "You're hungry. Let me cook for you."

Coco looked up through lustful eyes and dramatically waved her hands around the room. "All of this, and you cook too?"

"Yes, I cook, and I eat too."

"Good, because right now, I can tell you without a doubt that I'm ravenous."

His laugh was infectious. "*Buono… perfetto.*" He felt her body shiver. "You're cold."

"A little," she said.

He lifted her up and carried her into the bathroom, placing her on her feet under a hot shower. They explored each other again, before he felt Coco's hunger making her weaker. He dried her hair with a towel.

"How about we cook together?" she said.

"I'd like that," Gabriel kissed her. "I'd like that a lot."

○

They made their way to the kitchen and Coco took a seat at the island.

Gabriel poured them both a glass of champagne. "*Brindiamo all'amore.*"

"If you want me to translate then you will need to speak a little slower."

"A toast to love," he said.

"*All'amore*." Coco leaned across the marble counter and kissed him.

"Because you're a guest in my villa, I'd like to cook an Italian dinner for you." He walked over to the refrigerator and pulled out a bunch of basil. "You're a vegetarian."

"I am, yes, but I eat dairy… and if you need to eat meat I'm okay with that."

"Vegetarian is fine—sometimes I prefer it too."

"I can help—dice or slice. Just give me directions."

Gabriel looked up while gathering ingredients, bowls, and saucepans, and noticed Coco grinning at him. "What's so funny?" he asked.

"Am I dreaming? I never thought I would feel like this with any man."

"What do you mean?"

"This—being here with you—preparing food together. It feels comfortable. I'm extremely happy right now."

He lifted her onto the counter so she was at eye level with him. "You've brought joy to my heart." He kissed her and handed her a knife. "For the tomatoes." She pushed herself off the counter and he passed her a bowl of tomatoes.

"Thanks." Coco began slicing. "How old are you?"

"588."

Coco paused the knife midway through a tomato. "Shit! That's old."

"No kidding," he said.

"Can you read my mind?"

"Sometimes."

"Now?"

"You need to eat, Colombina, don't tempt me." He stared at Coco's lips.

She gazed at his hands. "Who is your father?"

"Would you like to know the story of my birth?"

"Yes."

"My father's name is Stefan Lazarevic. During his mortal life he was an important ruler—a Serbian prince, and later a despot. He'd been placed in an arranged marriage, but his heart always belonged to Prudence. For many years he and my mother were lovers and at that time, she acted as a nurse for his forces. The frescoes painted during this time did not display his wife's image, but there are many that show a woman who resembles my mother.

"She had a premonition about his death, and together they made the decision that he would return to a new life as an immortal. Shortly before he took his final breath she used her magic and cleared the room of others. His maker entered and drained my father's body of blood, and then forced Stefan to drink from him before leaving. He awakened to his new life as a vampire with Prudence standing beside him.

"The moment he opened his eyes his craving for blood overcame him. Prudence quickly cast a spell to calm his thirst. This diverted his need to feed into lust. I'm the product of a starved and virile newborn vampire," he said with a smirk.

"But how could Stefan father a child when he was no longer human?" Coco asked.

"The sperm left in a man's body after he makes the transition from human to vampire has a short lifespan. Once a new vampire takes his first drink the sperm is no longer fertile. Mother knew this and foresaw the importance to the sequence of events that night."

"So, Prudence is also immortal... but not a vampire. Is that correct?" Coco asked.

"Yes, because of my mother's bloodline she is immortal. That night she drank some of Stefan's blood so they would be intuitively connected forever. Prudence knew she would give birth to a son, and Stefan asked that I carry on his legacy and be raised, like her, to protect those who are creative."

"What a story," Coco said. "You carry your father's DNA, and so you must have predatory instincts. Have you killed innocent people?"

"Have you?" he said.

Her mouth fell open.

"Like you, my mother's DNA gives me self-control, and no, I have not killed an innocent being."

"But you've killed people?"

Gabriel's silence gave Coco her answer. She took hold of his hand, stood on her toes and kissed him. "I trust you," she said, and went back to slicing tomatoes. "So, just to clarify, and I mean this purely in scientific terms... you're able to procreate?"

Gabriel put down the bunch of basil he held in his hand and turned to Coco. "I don't think I've seen you so coy before, Colombina. I find it extraordinarily sexy. And for the purely scientific research that you are conducting, the answer is yes. I can procreate. Let me know when you would like to practice again."

"I've never been with an older man," she said.

"And how are you finding it so far?"

"I think I'm the luckiest woman in this universe. I've found the perfect mix of Eros and wisdom."

CHAPTER 31

Gabriel's playlist ranged from the Italian classics, to the Beatles, and Jack White. But it was the silence between songs that made Coco wonder where Christopher and the others were. "The villa seems unusually quiet. Where did everyone go—and your pack of dogs?" she asked.

"Christopher and Layla are spending the evening at the farmhouse—so is the pack—and Prudence and Maria are staying with Eduardo."

"You planned this?" she asked.

"No. Wished—yes."

"Do you know how lucky you are to live here, in this place?" she asked.

"I never have until tonight." He picked up an aged bottle of port and two glasses and offered his other hand to Coco. "I promised to take you up to the turret. Come on, the view is beautiful."

"It's dark outside."

"I hadn't noticed." He guided her to the back of the villa and toward an archway. Its weathered keystone triggered a memory in Coco's mind, and she paused beneath it. Reaching up, she touched the stone with her free hand and noticed the corners of Gabriel's mouth turn up to form a smile. "What are you grinning at?" she asked.

"When you and Christopher were little, you would both jump up and down every day to see who would be the first to touch the keystone."

"He did it first, didn't he?"

Gabriel nodded. "Of course he would have, you were four and he was seven. He practiced jumping for hours but could never make it. Then he noticed how light you were. He put you on his shoulders and jumped, and you touched the stone."

"But then he lost the game."

"That's what I told him, but he insisted that he won as well because you two accomplished the task as one."

"He did that for me?"

"Yes."

He gave her a gentle tug toward a looming spiral staircase built from stone. At the top of the stairs an icy breeze touched her face. She turned to Gabriel. The light of the moon gave warmth to his pale skin, and this reminded her of a quote from Michelangelo. *"I saw the angel in the marble and carved until I set it free,"* she said.

"*Il Divino*," Gabriel said.

"Was he a Creative?"

"Yes, but he didn't make it easy for me to get to his paintings. Murder on my back."

"The Sistine Chapel... how did you... you knew Michelangelo?"

"Yes."

"Anything else you'd like to share? You must have known Lorenzo too?"

"Ask Prudence about Lorenzo. They were great friends and got up to all kinds of mischief together."

Coco gazed up at the night sky—dark as black velvet and alive with stars. Gabriel placed the bottle and glasses on a slab of stone between two crenellations and pulled her close to him, her back against his chest. "You have another question."

"Oh, I have more than one," she said.

"Let me have it, then."

"Can you fly?"

"Yes, but it derives from magic. Like my mother, I have tele-portation abilities. Flying is Alessandro's talent. He can travel farther than me. He's also unnervingly fast."

"And your father, can he fly?"

"Yes, he is exceptionally talented because he carries my mother's blood and the blood of his maker. But it is my father's sword that gives him his fearless reputation."

"Remind me to keep on his good side," she said, staring up at the stars. "How does this look through your eyes?"

He kissed the top of her head. "Every star is encircled with multiple colors that pulsate—as if they each beat with their own heart. It's quite miraculous."

They stood silently under the illuminated heavens until Gabriel felt Coco's body tire. "You need to sleep." He handed her the port and glasses and picked her up. "Another night," he said, and whisked her off to her bedroom.

○

They lay tangled together. Coco became lost in pleasure, as Gabriel's fingers traced the outlines of each muscle on her back. Her entire body felt numb with exhaustion, but she didn't want to give in to the euphoria of the past few hours. "Are you using your magic to draw me to you?"

"No. What you and I are feeling is very real, although it does feel magical," he said. "Do you need me to leave so you can sleep?"

"Never," she shook her head. "Do you ever sleep?"

"Every so often, but not tonight, your questions are relentless."

"Can you tell me any more about your father?"

"My father's story is not conducive to sleep."

She delved further. "You said he's a vampire." She slid back so she could see his face.

"It's difficult for me to think of anything else when you're laying naked beside me, Colombina."

She grabbed his T-shirt and pulled it on. "There. Now, where does he live? Is Prudence still married to him? Do witches and vampires actually hold marriage certificates? Are you close to him?"

Gabriel took in a deep breath that seemed to take forever, and then exhaled slowly. "My parents have multiple villas. Yes, they're married. No, they don't have a piece of paper alerting everyone of their marriage—they are bound by blood. A bond that can never be broken."

"You're acting like a four-year-old at a pre-k show-and-tell. Why the aloofness about this man? And you didn't answer my last question."

"My father is a warrior and a vampire. My mother is bound by her birth to honor the beauty of art. One fights with a sword, the other with her emotions. At times I find it difficult to honor my vampire side—the fear of giving in to that much power takes constant restraint."

She leaned on a hand. "So you hold it in. You do to yourself what you preach against. From what I've seen in history—and feel free to tell me if I'm incorrect—whenever anyone refuses to at least confront their dark thoughts, then you can bet they'll eventually explode. We all have a shadow side, Gabriel. Suppressing it will kill you. Or worse... maybe someone else."

"Are you suggesting that I need some father-son time with Stefan? A weekend away together—camping, perhaps?"

"It may take longer than two days," Coco said. "What's stopping you anyway?"

"The image of you posing naked in front of a group of students comes to mind."

"Jealousy," she said. "Go work it out."

"I'll think about it." He kissed her with fervor, then whispered in her ear. "You look extremely seductive in my T-shirt."

"Is there anything about you... what you are, that is in any way unsafe to me? It's not like I've ever been with a vampire-warlock before."

"Christ, I hope not, or I'd be forced to commit murder! Entering into this relationship is a deep commitment... for both of us. You've always been under my protection, but now you are mine."

"Yours?"

"When I say you are mine... they are the words a vampire uses to pledge himself to another. I'm not asking you to give up your autonomy. Your fierce independence is one of the many traits I love about you. Perhaps the closest definition is that it would mean death to anyone who attempted to hurt you."

"Define 'hurt'."

"Physical pain of any kind is intolerable. Emotional and verbal abuse are no different," he said. "Does this make sense to you?"

"Am I supposed to feel the same way about you? Because I don't know if you've noticed, but I'm not exactly a lethal weapon and I don't like violence."

"There will be times when you may need to fight."

Coco snuggled in beside him. "I've been told repeatedly that this property is protected. Yet, if this is so, then how did my mother get taken? And who is Kenan?"

"Kenan is a vampire of the worst kind. He's known in our world for wanting power, and taking anyone, or anything he desires—no matter the cost. He believes that the Church must approve all forms of art. In short, he's a madman with archaic beliefs."

"But surely, in this day and age, no one can possibly take him seriously? And the current Pope seems open to change."

"You're right, this Pope brings hope. But there will always

be those few within the Catholic Church who support Kenan's agenda. In our world there are rules. We cannot kill another vampire without proof they've committed a crime, unless we're in battle. When you completed Chantal's unfinished painting in her studio and I saw what was beneath the façade—we had the confirmation we needed that Kenan had taken her. For thousands of years these grounds have remained sacred. But the day Kenan stole Chantal, we were betrayed by one of our own."

"Who?"

"Caprecia—Eduardo's wife."

"Louisa's mother?"

"Yes."

"But... how does the Professor go on? How can anyone deal with such loss?"

"Because to do anything else, is to disregard the gift of life," he said. "You must understand this—any disregard for life is difficult for our kind to accept. Chantal adored her mortal life. Kenan stole it from her. We do not know Caprecia's reason for betrayal, but, sadly, she unknowingly signed her own daughter's death sentence. Chantal must have foreseen that your curiosity and natural commitment to the arts would eventually bring you back to us."

"I'm exhausted," Coco said. "I don't want to go to sleep but I'm not sure I can stay awake any longer."

○

Gabriel pulled Coco to his body. "You are a Creative—here to bring beauty and stories to the world through art." He felt her breathing slow. "Everything you paint has a message painted underneath the outer layer—you've seen this through your mother's paintings and now your own." Coco's breathing deepened, telling him that she had fallen asleep. As he watched her his mind drifted.

He thought of the first time his mother had walked him through the villa's orchard as a small child. She had showed him trees filled with pink blossoms. Months later they walked the same path, but the trees stood with their branches bent toward the ground and heavy with luscious fruit. Prudence had instructed him to pick one peach and run his fingers over the velvety skin and take in the sweet-smelling scent. He followed her request. His nose tingled when he held the peach up to his face and inhaled deeply. This triggered the desire to taste the fruit. But she told him to wait, and he thought this would make him crazy. Finally, she nodded her head, giving him permission to eat and he bit into the soft fruit. The fuzzy outer texture tickled his lips, but the second his teeth touched the juicy flesh and the nectar slid down his throat, a rush of pleasure flowed throughout his entire body. He wanted more.

"Enough," Prudence said. Gabriel had felt angry, he wanted more of the sweet nectar. "Wait, my son," she said. "Savor this moment so that your sensory memory can place this occasion into your brain. This is a moment you will want to remember."

His mother had been correct.

Gabriel leaned down and kissed Coco's forehead. "This evening is forever embedded into my memory, sweet Colombina." He carefully removed his arm from around her, put on his clothes, and walked to the library.

The slightest sound from Coco had Gabriel bounding up the stairs to be by her side. This made it difficult for him to concentrate on his work. Finally, he took his laptop to her bedroom and set himself up by the fireplace at the foot of her bed. A few hours later, he sensed a subtle change in her sleep pattern. Her eyes blinked open. Oblivious to his presence, she rose from the bed and padded into the studio. She picked up a new canvas and placed it on the easel, squeezed paint from tubes onto a palette, and picked up a brush and began painting. Gabriel leaned against the wall and watched her paint. Her slender muscular body draped in his T-shirt. He felt he was in the presence of an angel. "Botticelli would have loved you," he said in a hushed tone.

Coco completed two paintings and then simply placed the brush on the table, got into bed, and fell back to sleep. Gabriel stretched out beside her, his mind concerned with the images she had painted. He noticed a sketchbook that lay under her computer and extracted it with the guile of a cat burglar. On the first page Coco had drawn a portrait of a young man. She had repeated the same image on many of the following pages. He traced the young man's face with his fingers, leaving it engraved on his mind. With a gesture of his hand, the book returned to the exact position he'd found it. Coco stirred, her arms searching for his embrace. He gently stroked her hair, and her body relaxed.

An hour later, she awoke fully and looked up into his eyes. "So I wasn't dreaming after all," she said.

Gabriel leaned down and kissed her. "I've been dreaming about last night for many years." She pushed a strand of his hair off his face and noticed the paint splattered on her hands. She jumped up and ran to the studio. Gabriel stood by her side.

"Did I paint these last night?"

"Yes."

"You watched me?"

"Yes."

"So you know what's beneath the façade of both of these, don't you?"

Gabriel nodded.

Coco swore and Gabriel was reminded of her rich vocabulary.

"Would you like me to show them to you?" Gabriel asked.

"Of course."

"There is always a sequence." Gabriel picked up the painting that Coco had done first and placed it on the easel. "I'm intrigued by the amount of magic around you." He took her left hand in his. "If my intuition is correct, then you can do this on your own." With Coco's hand in his, he reached out toward the painting. Particles from the top layer dissipated from the canvas toward Coco's fingers.

"How is this possible?" Coco asked.

Gabriel shook his head. "I'm not sure."

"It tingles."

"You'll get used to it."

The image revealed a desolate place.

An architecturally modern house sits on the edge of a cliff surrounded by wooden decks balanced high above dark water. Multiple levels with long windows are built around large boulders. A heavy mist creeps over the water. It slinks into the forest of tall pine trees that stand draped with light green moss like beacons of predetermined doom.

A thick wooden door opens to a hallway lit with dim lights. The floor is made up of sections of cement embedded with pebbles, smooth and bordered with dark wooden frames. Three steps lead down to a large living area walled with windows that frame the bay and the forest.

At the opposite end of the hall a staircase descends to bathrooms and bedrooms. An open door reveals a bed with an adjoining bathroom. Beside this room is another door—its heavy sliding bolt and lock rusty from the damp air. The scene is immersed in crimson.

The paint flowed back onto the canvas. Gabriel pulled Coco into his body and stroked her hair. He could feel her anxiety rise. "One more painting, *tesoro*." She nodded and extended her hand toward the final painting.

Chantal sits on a small bed in a cement cell. She looks up at Coco and speaks to her telepathically: "Tell Alessandro that the scent reminds me of my twenty-fifth birthday, he will remember."

Coco gasped as the scene disappeared. "I need to see my father."

"He's on his way." Gabriel sent a text to Prudence telling her to call the others to an urgent meeting.

Coco's body shook and her face paled. Gabriel placed a hand on her forehead and a calmness spread over her. "I'm so sorry for the pain you've had to endure, both physically and emotionally—"

"I understand… it's okay," she said, snuggling into him.

"If I could have taken the pain for you, I would have. Do you want to tell me what Chantal shared with you?"

"After I've told my father." She lifted her head and met his golden eyes.

His lips met hers as he gently massaged around the base of her neck until he felt her body completely relax. He pulled back—his body alert. "Alessandro's here. You are covered in my scent and he's a vampire with protective issues even stronger than mine—although I doubt that's possible when it comes to my feelings for you. Perhaps it would be wise to rinse off and put on some fresh clothing."

Coco grabbed clothes from the closet and ran into the bathroom where she quickly showered, cleaned her teeth, and brushed her hair. She arrived back in the bedroom a few minutes later.

Gabriel pushed back his inherent need to hold her, and instead he picked up his laptop and opened the door. Alessandro greeted him. In a show of friendship the two men grasped each other's elbows. Gabriel stepped past his friend and into the hallway. Alessandro walked into Coco's room and closed the door behind him.

CHAPTER 32

The image of the gallant man that the Professor had painted years ago was gone. In his place stood a forsaken soul. If one stared upon this man long enough then perhaps they would catch a flicker of his life force, but it would just be a glimmer, hanging on by a single thread of hope. Alessandro's eyes were dull, tired, and somber. Deep lines ran across his brow, his face looked gaunt, and his body hunched.

When Coco looked into her father's eyes she instantly understood his suffering. She sensed his sorrow for having left her, and the grief he held for the loss of her mother, his beloved wife. She had never felt such intense sadness radiate from anyone before this moment. Now she understood what Prudence meant when she'd said that Coco may regret the words she had spoken about her father.

"Forgive me, Colombina," he said.

His voice, raspy, and full of pain, tore at her heart. She fell into his arms and he embraced her. She heard him inhale, taking in her scent and stroking her hair just as he had done when she was a child. After a few minutes, he spoke. "You have many questions."

"Yes, I do. But time is not on our side, and I have something important to tell you."

"About Gabriel and you? He is a good man, and my dearest friend—"

"Dad, no, not about Gabriel and me." She stepped back, unable to keep her pent-up emotions in check. "You left us—two small children. All this time, I thought you and Mother were dead."

Alessandro reached into the pocket of his coat and pulled out three stalks of lavender. In an offering of peace, he handed them to her.

"It was you, at the hospital," she said. "You brought me the lavender."

"Yes, and I saw you the day of your accident, before I headed off to pursue one of Kenan's assassins here in Italy. Gabriel and Stefan would cover for me so I could visit you at the hospital. I hoped the lavender would help you heal and perhaps remind you of your past."

Coco ran the lavender under her nose. "You were at the masquerade in Florence too."

"Yes, both Gabriel and I were there," he said. "Over the years, I have been around you and Christopher whenever I was not searching for Chantal."

Coco's demeanor softened. "I've been painting... like Mother. Last night I finished another piece, and somehow Mother spoke to me... intuitively, through an image I painted. She asked me to give you a message." Alessandro's head turned to her in anticipation. "She said, 'Tell Alessandro the scent reminds me of my twenty-fifth birthday... he'll remember.' Does this make sense to you?"

Alessandro's eyes glistened and he nodded. "Yes," he said. "Chantal wanted to see the whales off the San Juan Islands, in Washington State. She loved the smell of the pine trees mixed with the salt of the ocean. I took her to Lopez Island." He grasped Coco's hand and walked with her toward the door. "You have done well, little dove," he said, as they descended the stairs, and entered the living room where the others were gathered.

O

Coco ran straight to Christopher. "I can't begin to fathom the burden you've had to carry all of these years—they asked too much of you."

Christopher brought her into a hug. "In all honesty, for a long time I thought Mom and Dad were both dead too. And for a while I wasn't that nice to Dad and Gabriel either."

"I've been such a bitch to you. I'm so sorry," she said. "When we have time I need to hear your story."

"If that's what you need, then yes, of course," Christopher said.

"No more secrets," Coco said.

"No more secrets."

CHAPTER 33

Coco felt a surge of warmth flood over her. She turned around and met Gabriel's gaze, golden and full of passion. Since he had freed her childhood memories, an intrinsic connection to him had ignited within her—as if an invisible lasso had wound around their hearts and bound them as one. She walked to him and he clasped her hand in his.

"Are you alright?" he asked.

"I am now," she said, and gave his hand a squeeze. She turned to Alessandro as he stepped toward Prudence and Gabriel.

"Colombina has gained vital information from Chantal," Alessandro said. "I believe she is being held on Lopez Island. It is one of the San Juan Islands off the coast of Seattle in the United States. That is where we need to search."

"How fresh is this information?" Prudence asked.

"Colombina painted the images a few hours ago," Gabriel said.

"Then we must leave immediately," Prudence said.

Gabriel strode to his desk and in seconds had his laptop open. "I'll contact our members in Seattle. Christopher— call Eduardo and Maria. I'll feel better if they stay here while we're gone."

"Of course," Christopher said, taking out his cell phone.

Gabriel waited while Google Earth zoomed in to the area he had typed in to search. He scrolled over the coast of the island and stopped abruptly. "This is the house Colombina painted—this must be where Chantal is being kept."

"I can be ready in a few moments," Coco said. She turned toward the stairs.

Gabriel planted his body in front of hers and placed a hand firmly on her arm. "You can't come with us," he said. "You will stay here with Christopher and Layla, Eduardo, and Maria."

"But mother gave the message to me. What if I paint tonight? Maybe she'll speak with me again."

"It's not possible for me to take you on this journey." He went to embrace her but she pulled back from him.

"You can either take me with you now, or I'll find my own way to get to Mother—but Christopher and I need to be there."

Gabriel dropped his arms to his side. She continued, "I can paint the location and you can do your magic and get us all there quickly."

Gabriel turned to Prudence for assurance. She gave him a nod. "Fine, but you must stay close to Alessandro," he said.

"Agreed," Coco said.

"How long do you need to paint the images?" Gabriel asked.

"Give me thirty minutes... alone." She took off up the stairs.

Gabriel turned to the others who were all staring at him. "She definitely inherited your stubborn temperament, Alessandro."

"Perhaps a few of my language skills too."

Christopher ended his call with Eduardo and then guided Layla into the kitchen. He offered her a chair at the counter and sat opposite, taking her hands in his. "When were you going to tell me?"

Layla blushed and she stared at the floor. "How long have you known?" she asked.

"When you met me at the airport yesterday, I noticed something different about you," he caught her chin and lifted her face to his. "And last night... your body felt different." He shook his head and grinned. "It wasn't until I caught Alessandro staring at your stomach that my initial theory was confirmed. When's our baby due?"

"I'm just a few months along. I wanted to tell you but there's been so much going on, and—"

"Nothing in this world is more important to me than you, Layla." Christopher pulled her into his embrace. "God, I love you so much." His lips found hers and for a few minutes their lives were perfect. "I want you to stay here, so I'm not worried about you while we're gone."

"I understand," she said.

"This isn't just about you and me anymore." He stood up, "Can we tell the others?"

"I think most of them already know," Layla said. "But yes, we can make it official."

They walked hand-in-hand into Gabriel's office. Alessandro, Prudence, and Gabriel looked up at them. "Layla's pregnant," Christopher announced.

"You finally told him—thank God," Alessandro embraced them both. "I am so happy—for all of us."

"It will be wonderful to have a child around us again," Prudence said. "Now, let us bring Chantal home so she can share in this joy too."

Gabriel walked across the room to Christopher. "I understand if you need to stay here," he said.

Christopher looked to Layla for confirmation of his

decision. "You need to go and help bring your mother home," she said. "Our child will need both sets of grandparents to help navigate through this world." She tugged at Christopher's hand. "Let's tell Coco."

Layla waited while Christopher changed into darker clothes and work boots. When Coco emerged from her bedroom, they shared their news with her. "Wow, that's… amazing! And what a great surprise for Mother." She placed the paintings on the floor and hugged them both.

"We'd better get back downstairs," Christopher said.

O

Gabriel's office had transformed into a small armory. Alessandro, Gabriel, and Prudence were busy strapping knives and silver daggers to their legs and across their backs. Alessandro tossed Christopher a knife. He caught it by the handle and placed it inside his right boot.

Coco stared at him. "Jeez—"

"A sharp silver blade stabbed directly into a vampire's heart slows it down," Alessandro said. He handed her a belt with a sheath attached, but she stepped back.

"I… I can't do that… there's no way," she said.

"You will, if it means the difference between your life or the vampire who wants to kill you," Alessandro said. "You chose to be a part of this, Colombina, so you will carry a knife." He held the knife out to her and this time she accepted it and allowed him to tie the belt around her hips, securing it with a leather strap around her thigh. She slid the knife into the sheath.

Prudence lifted her head toward the entrance in expectation. Eduardo and Maria entered, followed by Stefan. He walked directly to Prudence and embraced her. Thalia loped into the room and promptly shifted into a mountain lion. She found Stefan and nudged his thighs with her head. He bent down and patted her. "I have missed you too, sweet lady." He looked across at Coco. "Colombina, I am Stefan, Gabriel's father and husband of Prudence." He walked toward her and lowered his head in a small bow. Coco held out her hand to him. "As much as I would sincerely like to embrace you, my dear, perhaps this is not a good time. My son's protective instincts are currently running on high alert," Stefan said with a wink.

Gabriel stood beside Coco and placed his arm protectively around her. "I am honored to meet you, Stefan," Coco said.

Gabriel took the paintings from Coco's hands and set them up against the sofa. "Tell us about these images," he said.

The group gathered around Coco. "This first painting shows the exterior of the house from across the bay." She pointed to the next image. "This is the interior—the living room to be precise, and this last painting is the small room where Mother is being held."

Gabriel stepped forward and took control. He pointed toward the first painting. "This image will get us through to the first location so we can meet our comrades from Seattle. From here, Prudence can sense how many troops Kenan has with him, then we'll decide on our strategy and get into the house via this second painting." He turned to Coco. "You and Thalia must stay with Stefan, Christopher, and Alessandro. Once we're inside the house, your job is to guide them to where Chantal is held. Any questions?" He handed the second and third paintings to Coco and pulled her aside. "Are you alright?"

"Yes," she said. "And thank you."

Gabriel kissed her hard on her lips. "If it were Prudence, I would want to be there. But recognize that your decision comes with a price. Use the knife if needed. Is that understood?"

Coco nodded.

Christopher embraced Layla. "I love you, fairy princess," he said.

"*Ti amo,*" Layla said. Maria placed her arm around Layla as Christopher joined the others.

"Stefan, you go through first," Gabriel said, pointing to the first painting. "Christopher, you next, then Colombina, Thalia, and Alessandro. Prudence and I will follow."

"How do we get back here?" Coco asked.

"Leave that to me, my dear," Prudence said.

Gabriel placed the painting on the easel and held a hand toward it. The air became charged with energy and the still scene on the painting began to move. Mist drifted above dark water, the sound of waves crashing onto a beach, and the scent of the sea wafted into the room. Stefan stepped forward and disappeared into the mist. The others followed.

CHAPTER 34

Lopez Island, Washington State, U.S.A.

The modern house, made of steel and wide wooden beams, stood out like an avant-garde bastion on the edge of a cliff overlooking the cold waters of a desolate cove. There were no lights from the mainland to be seen through the dense fog that saturated the Puget Sound.

Kenan lay on a plush sofa speaking on his cell phone. The glow from his laptop reflected back on his pale face. He looked up at Caprecia when she entered the room. Although she was a young vampire, and somewhat frail, her body tempted him, reminding him that not all of his needs had been met that evening. He tossed his phone onto the table and in seconds slammed her body against the wall.

"Perfect timing. I need to fuck," Kenan said, as he tore the shirt from her body and ripped her skirt. "I chose you well, Caprecia, you are a good whore and the spicy scent that your body exudes when you crave me is quite delicious." He entered her quickly and pulled her hair back to expose her tantalizing neck.

"You only fuck me when you don't have young boys to tease,

Kenan, and you should know that this is how I always smell," she said, her honeyed voice purred in his ear. "I love to fuck."

Kenan ignored her words. He knew she loathed everything about him and that she did what she needed only to keep on his good side. He threw back his head as she taunted him with the veins that pumped in her neck. He felt drunk with power when his hand hit her face. He felt her body brace expectantly for the next beating.

Kenan breathed in her scent and ran his fingers over her femoral artery. He wondered if he should tell Caprecia about Louisa's death but the scent of another vampire on her body distracted him. He slapped her hard across the face again. "You allowed another to feed off you!"

He felt her leg wind seductively around his hips. "But you were not here, and I needed more. Surely you would not deny me that which I crave. It is *your* blood that I carry in my veins so you must know when my sexual hunger has not been met."

"Yes, we are a horny little family aren't we?" He grabbed her by the neck and shoved her face against the wall, then pumped her hard in the arse.

O

Kenan had made Caprecia an immortal. He was her maker—her lord, as he preferred to be called. The constant exploitation of her sexuality and the brutality of this creature was not something she had foreseen. But she was bound to him forever. Even if she escaped his confines it would take hundreds of miles between them, or some kind of magic, to keep her from returning to him. The physical abuse, although violent, was something her vampire body healed from quickly. But the verbal abuse haunted her, and his next words hit her harder than any blow from his fist.

"Ignacio enjoys his time with your daughter," Kenan said. "He says she knows how to please him. I hope for her sake that she has the strength to endure him—he seems to be spending a little too much time with her. Mortals are such weaklings."

Caprecia prayed that Ignacio not be as barbaric a lover as Kenan. Not a day had gone by since she betrayed the Allegiance that regret filled what was left of her cold heart. She loathed what she had become, and abhorred everything Kenan did to Chantal. She wanted him dead.

After years of enduring his abuse, she had devised a plan to help her friend. If Kenan caught her it would most likely mean her death. But she had no desire to live the life she was currently living—filled with guilt and shame.

Kenan's obsession with power had kept him distracted. He was unaware that Caprecia had tempted the vampire who guarded Chantal's cell. She had learned quickly that her sexuality acted as her best weapon. She prayed on the weaknesses of the vampires around her—blackmailing them to get what she needed. Kenan saw her as needy and stupid. And that worked for her.

She had easily seduced Chantal's guard, and now he was addicted to her. Once under her spell she had suggested that he show her the prisoner. Caprecia had boasted to him that she'd been the mastermind behind kidnapping the Creative. This sickened her, but so did her self-loathing for what she had done to Chantal.

She remembered the night the two women first came face to face after they had been turned into immortals. She had expected more hatred from Chantal, but instead she only felt empathy. Kenan hated Chantal because she represented balance—a trait he would never have.

Caprecia had played the mocking slut to perfection, managing to pass a note to Chantal while keeping the guard occupied.

I want to help you—what can I do?

Chantal had mouthed her answer.

I need something that is living—if only for a few moments.

The guard's inflated sense of self had been his downfall, and this made it easy for Caprecia to lure him into submission with her sexual tricks. She'd thought for months about what to smuggle in for Chantal. An object filled with life that would not raise alarm should the guard see it. When the answer came to her, she began putting together the pieces she needed for her plan to succeed.

Caprecia waited until Kenan went on an extended hunting excursion. She slid the bracelet over her wrist and checked that the locket was attached safely. She sauntered down the steps where the guard hungrily awaited her. In her hand, she held a bottle of blood that Kenan had told her to give Chantal.

If there is a God and you are listening—then please help me tonight.

She felt the guard's desire but teased him until she knew he had reached his weakest point. "Kenan requested that I give the bitch this blood. Let's get the business out of the way so we can play." In desperation the guard had clumsily unlocked the door.

Chantal sat on the edge of the bed. Her hunger was displayed through hollowed eyes and pale skin that exposed her starved veins. When Chantal brought her hand out for the bottle of blood, Caprecia slipped open the locket and let the contents fall into Chantal's hand.

She willed silent prayers to Chantal that she say nothing of the gift she handed her. Caprecia slammed the door to the cell and turned her attention back to the guard. "Come, my sweet, the freak has her food. Let's have some fun."

Chantal waited momentarily before removing the bottle of blood and observing the object that Caprecia had slipped into her hand. She thought of Shakespeare's Cordelia…

So we'll live,
And pray, and sing, and tell old tales, and laugh
At gilded butterflies, and hear poor rogues
Talk of court news; and we'll talk with them too—
Who loses and who wins; who's in, who's out—
And take upon 's the mystery of things,
As if we were God's spies.

She felt the life of the chrysalis beating in her hand…

CHAPTER 35

Gabriel perched on a boulder overlooking the modern house that held Chantal prisoner. The damp evening air hung thick with mist, constantly creeping in and out of the forest, like a ghost haunting a graveyard. Ancient Douglas firs dwarfed the madrone trees with their smooth red trunks, and the green moss hanging from their limbs emitted an eerie fluorescent glow.

Along with his group were five other vampires, each with varying talents and all with an instinctive will to honor the Allegiance. The head of the Seattle chapter, Lida, was known for her speed and accuracy. She introduced her companions as David, Cheveyo, Kai, and Ahiga.

Prudence stared across the bay. "I sense Kenan, ten other vampires, and three mortals."

Gabriel nodded and turned to Coco. "Once we're all inside the house you must use your skills and quickly find your mother's cell."

"What?" she said. "I can't do——"

"You're a Creative—this is what you do, and trust me, your adrenaline will help." He turned his focus to his father. "Stefan—lead Alessandro, Christopher, Colombina, David and Kai. I shall fight alongside Prudence, Lida, Cheveyo and Ahiga.

Colombina's painting showed Chantal in a tightly enclosed room. Kenan's strongest will be guarding the door. We'll meet up again in the rendezvous location and return immediately to Florence."

He jumped down from the boulder, and the others followed. "Do not attack the humans without reason. We're here to rescue Chantal. Work quickly and decisively."

Prudence held an arm toward the house. "Caprecia is with him," she said. "Let me bring her home, Gabriel. Eduardo has lost enough and I cannot believe that she is all evil."

Gabriel turned to Alessandro for his answer.

"What happens to her is up to you," Alessandro said. "My priority is rescuing my wife and bringing her home."

"Then Caprecia is yours, Prudence," Gabriel said. "The wind is close to turning and we cannot risk Kenan catching our scent." He took a moment to look into the eyes of those around him. They all bent their heads and said in unison. *"sine virtute omnia sunt perdita."*

O

Kenan held Caprecia by the neck, her blood dripped from his greedy mouth. "Tell me again how much you enjoy being fucked this way," he demanded.

"You know what I like, Kenan," Caprecia said.

With his free hand he slapped her hard across her face. "Actually, I don't give a fuck what you like, you Portuguese whore. I just enjoy watching you suffer." He whipped her around so that she faced him, and felt her muscles tighten in anticipation of his next assault.

As Kenan lifted his arm to strike her, he froze. His nostrils flared. He heaved Caprecia through the air as if she was a ragdoll, then turned and faced Prudence and two other vampires.

In seconds, he fled outside only to be met by Gabriel and Lida. His mouth turned to a sardonic grin. "I feel so honored," he said. "The high Pooh-Bah himself calls on me." He gave a mocking bow before delivering a hard kick toward Lida.

○

Lida flipped back and rolled out of Kenan's reach. Gabriel leapt forward and grabbed one of Kenan's legs, then hurled him against a thick steel girder. Gabriel and Lida watched as Kenan's body quickly transformed. His bony fingers tapered off into pointed and filthy fingernails. Slowly he turned toward Gabriel, his face looked decrepit with yellowed teeth and blood-shot eyes. His body expelled a foul stench of sulfur.

When Kenan spoke, his strident voice grated on Gabriel. "Still the protector? Sprinkling little dollops of honor over this god-forsaken planet. You really need to change your game plan, Gabriel. You've become so fucking predictable."

"There is strength in ritual," Gabriel said as he stared at Kenan's sunken glare. He grasped the residue of composure that rippled through his veins—the precursor to the rush of adrenaline about to engulf him.

Kenan continued, "Chantal has proved herself useless. Becoming a vampire didn't go over so well with her... creative abilities. She has no idea who the *chosen one* is and trust me—I did everything I could to force that information out of her, but to no avail. She's a feisty little wench—but doesn't take well to being slapped around." He walked toward the edge of the balcony. "Now that other one, Caprecia, she's a delightful whore... revels in being beaten to a pulp. Not quite what she was used to with the Professor—I doubt he took her past the missionary position. Maybe I need to abduct him next time—I could teach him a thing or two."

Kenan hurled a knife through the air, aiming it at Gabriel's heart. He flipped his body out of the way and flung one of his own knives at Kenan. The blade struck the jaundiced skin of his neck and slowed him down long enough for Gabriel to swing his body around and kick his opponent in the head.

As Kenan staggered backward he wrenched the blade from his neck and dropped it on the ground. He let loose with an angry grumble, pulled another knife from a boot and hurled it at Gabriel. The blade pierced the skin above his heart. He yanked it out and tossed it into the darkness of the cliffs below the balcony. The wound soared with a burning pain that spread quickly like fire through his veins. It was then he realized Kenan's blade had been tainted with something more than silver.

A new scent alerted Gabriel to another vampire about to attack him from behind. He willed forth a burst of energy and spun around. In a second he sliced his blade through his enemy's neck and flung the beheaded body over the cliff. Kenan used this opportunity to throw another knife at Gabriel. This time he made a direct hit to his femoral artery. Gabriel looked over at Lida as she fought one of Kenan's men. She flung the body to the ground, yanked back his head and ripped it from his body. Her next attacker met the same quick death.

○

Prudence held a knife in her hand and moved to defend Caprecia. A young vampire that flew at her landed headless on the floor. She looked around and saw a female vampire throw a knife at Cheveyo's heart, but he quickly had her by the throat on her knees. "Where are they keeping the woman?" he demanded. The woman spat at him. "Fuck you." They were her final words.

Prudence grabbed hold of Caprecia, but a sudden jolt of pain shot through her body. This was what she feared most. She knew, without doubt, that her son had suffered a fatal blow. She yelled to Cheveyo. "Hold on to this woman—do not let her escape. Kenan is her maker and therefore in control of her." Cheveyo took Caprecia in a tight grip.

When Prudence reached the balcony, she saw the remains of Ahiga's decapitated body in front of her, and Lida about to strike a fatal blow to her opponent. The scent of Gabriel's tainted rage filled every particle of her being. Kenan's hands were around his throat. She pulled out her sword from under her cloak and hurled it into the air toward Kenan's neck. But his keen sense of smell had preceded Prudence's arrival. He let go of Gabriel, pulled out another knife from his belt, and turned to face Prudence.

The sword Prudence threw went deep into Kenan's chest— a direct hit to his heart. "You should have joined me when you had the chance, *Prudenza.*" His words were filled with hatred. He pulled out the sword. "You might get what is left of the Creative back tonight, but I will pick off your precious female members of the Allegiance one by one and torture them until they break. The power I have behind me is so much more than you have ever imagined, my angel." He thrust his knife quickly, his aim perfect.

Kenan's heinous laugh was the last thing she heard before she staggered and collapsed beside Gabriel.

○

Coco followed Stefan as he led the way through the house in search of Chantal's cell. His sword was drawn and the first of Kenan's vampires to confront him died a quick death. She went to scream but Christopher covered her mouth with a hand and whispered. "Coco! This is your new reality. Focus on finding Mother. There will be time to process everything later."

"I don't know how to do that!" She felt her adrenaline rising.

"Yes, you do!" he said.

She closed her eyes: *what the hell am I doing here?* Seconds later the image of the scene she had painted of the house the night before emerged in front of her. She remembered the hallway, with the stones embedded into cement. She looked at the floor and grabbed Christopher's hand. "This way," she said.

Stefan stayed by her side and Alessandro followed with David and Kai. When they reached the top of the stairs that led down to Chantal's cell, Coco pointed to the door. "She's down there. The door's padlocked."

David and Kai nodded to Stefan, and the three vampires jumped over the banister and raced down the steps with Stefan in the lead. Alessandro turned to Coco. "I need to get into Chantal's cell." He took the painting from her and leaned it against the wall. Coco held out her arm just as she had done with Gabriel. The scene began to move and her fingers tingled. Alessandro took a step forward and disappeared.

Christopher went to follow but a sound distracted them. They turned and saw two humans. One had a pistol pointed at Coco. Christopher's telepathic words to her were loud and strong—*Don't move!*

Thalia leapt out of the darkness, knocked the gun out of his hand, and brought a quick end to his life. Christopher kicked the other human in the groin and he fell to the ground. Coco grabbed her brother's arm just as a popping sound rang through the air. Christopher dropped to the floor.

The human who fired the shot stood in the hallway. He turned to run but David leapt over the staircase and struck him with a fatal blow. Coco grabbed her brother. "Christopher!"

○

Stefan had just killed the vampire that guarded Chantal's cell when he heard Prudence's scream rip through the night. He felt the sharp blade enter her heart. He closed his eyes and focused on her. She was gasping for air and drowning in her own blood. He saw Gabriel leaning over her, forcing his mother to drink from a cut in his wrist. Stefan immediately realized what was wrong with Prudence and why Gabriel's blood could not heal her.

In seconds he was kneeling beside her. He saw Gabriel stumble back. Stefan worked quickly. He freed the blood from his wrist and placed it against Prudence's lips.

"*Bevi, amore mio,*" he whispered, as he placed his other hand behind her neck to support her while she drank.

The moment Prudence recognized his scent she latched onto the blood flowing from his wrist. All the while he kissed her face and encouraged her to drink. When her eyes flickered open she released her mouth. "*Sono in paradiso?*" Prudence whispered.

Stefan shook his head. "No, *tesoro*—this is not heaven." He lowered his mouth to hers, and when they parted, he placed her head gently on the ground and turned to Gabriel. He was conscious but fading quickly.

"Bring Colombina immediately!" Stefan yelled to Lida. He turned to Prudence. "Was this Kenan's doing?"

"Yes," she said. "His knives are cast from the coins used to cross the River Styx—Charon's abol. Once this has pierced my skin, your blood is the only way of saving me, and because Gabriel carries my blood the same poison will eventually kill him." She moved over to be near her son and laid a hand on his forehead, and the other on his belly. "This will slow down the poison until Colombina arrives."

Stefan picked up the knife covered in Kenan's blood.

"This stinks of that fiend. I wish I had killed him when I had the chance."

"Kenan is different now... much stronger than before," Prudence said. "By the time I arrived here he looked aged and twisted. There is dark magic in his blood. This is how he eluded us for so many years."

Stefan placed a hand on her shoulder. "Be careful, *tesoro*, you and our son stand between Kenan and the Creatives. Make no mistake—he will use Charon's abol against you both until he gets what he wants, and he will go after everything the Allegiance holds dear. Kenan and others like him must be destroyed!"

"Is killing him the answer?" Prudence whispered.

"This is no longer about Kenan versus me and you, Prudence, this is the Allegiance against the deranged power-hungry demons, who for centuries have used the Catholic Church as a façade for their need to control a submissive culture. Kenan is their puppet. He is evil and dangerous." He shoved Kenan's knife down the side of his boot.

O

When Alessandro stepped into the cell and saw Chantal laying in a fetal position on top of a cement slab, he sliced open a vein in his wrist and held it against her mouth. Her tongue found his blood on her lips. As if waking from a dream, her eyes flickered until she was able to focus on his eyes.

"*Cara*... my beautiful, Chantal," Alessandro said. "At last we have found you." Chantal's instincts took over and she drank his blood.

Kai kicked open the door to Chantal's cell and Alessandro immediately caught the scent of Christopher's blood. So did Chantal. She released her mouth from his wrist. "Christopher..." she said, her voice frail and scared.

Alessandro folded her into his arms and fled up the stairs. They found Coco sobbing over her brother's unconscious body, her tears falling onto his pale face.

Chantal had enough strength to understand what was going on around her, but her senses were on overload and she felt confused and scared.

Coco raised her head and saw her mother and father. "He's dying," she said. "He saved me."

Alessandro passed Chantal to David. "Do not let her go." He knelt beside his two children and gently removed Christopher from Coco's grasp. "He needs my blood, Colombina."

○

Coco nodded and stood. She placed a hand on the side of Chantal's face. Her mother closed her eyes and leaned into her daughter's hand. Her cold skin felt so different to the warmth that Coco remembered from her childhood, and the scent of lavender and rosemary seeping from her skin had grown stronger. Coco took her mother's hand in hers and turned back to her brother.

She watched as Alessandro slashed open his wrist and forced the blood into Christopher's mouth. When Coco saw the dark red liquid running from his open lips, she turned away and fought back her nausea. Seconds later Lida appeared. "Colombina, Stefan needs you," she said.

Coco turned to Alessandro for guidance. "Go to him, Colombina," Alessandro said.

She followed Lida toward the deck but stopped in her tracks when she overheard a conversation between Stefan and Gabriel.

"You know better than to go into battle without feeding and gathering your strength," Stefan said.

"There was no time," Gabriel said. Coco hardly recognized his voice—it made a rasping sound.

"You are drenched with the scent of Colombina, why did you not drink from her?" Stefan asked.

"I didn't want to frighten her..."

Another gasp and then silence.

Coco ran through the living room mortified by the horrific scene in front of her. A river of dark blood ran across the floor. It fell over the balcony, like a waterfall, and into the sea. But she pushed back her fear when she saw Gabriel lying on the ground. She ran to him and dropped to her knees. "What does he need from me, Stefan? Tell me!" she screamed.

"He needs to drink your blood, Colombina."

"I don't know how... what do I do?"

"Give me your wrist," he said.

Coco held out her hand and in one easy, painless movement, Stefan scraped a sharp fingernail across Coco's wrist and blood began to flow from her vein.

"Hold your wrist firmly to Gabriel's mouth," he said. "He will resist at first, because he does not want to force this on you. But without your blood he will die."

Coco lifted Gabriel's head onto her lap and did as Stefan suggested. She felt his mouth latch on to her wrist and suck. The sensation felt calming and somewhat erotic.

"It only feels like this because you are lovers," Stefan said. "It is not like this for everyone."

Gradually a pinkish glow returned to Gabriel's skin, and his cuts and bruises disappeared in front of Coco's eyes. She felt dizzy. Stefan reached across and pulled his son's mouth off of Coco's wrist. "Enough, my son. Your beloved has done well, but you will make her weak if you take any more."

Gabriel's eyes sprung open and he flung his arms around Coco.

She pushed him away. "Don't do that again—if I'd have

known we were walking into such a bloodbath I would gladly have given you my blood!"

Gabriel grabbed her and kissed her hungrily. When he broke away he bit into one of his fingers bringing blood to the skin's surface. He placed it over Coco's bloodied wrist and her skin quickly healed.

"Christopher's injured... we have Chantal..." Gabriel caught her in his arms as she passed out.

○

David appeared, but Gabriel had already read his mind. "How bad are his injuries?"

"He was shot," David said. "He's not responding to Alessandro's blood."

Moments later, Prudence sat by Christopher's side. She placed her hands where the bullet had gone through his body, closed her eyes, and slowed her breathing. She looked to Stefan. "We need to get him home." Stefan lifted Christopher off the floor.

Prudence turned to Chantal, who lay in Alessandro's arms. She placed a hand on her face. "It is good to see you, my dear friend, but I am sad that we meet like this. Christopher will live, but we need to move quickly." Prudence spoke to Gabriel. "I want to take Caprecia with me."

Gabriel nodded to Kai. He returned moments later with Cheveyo who was holding Caprecia. She stared at Gabriel. "I beg your forgiveness. Kill me if you must, but I would rather fight alongside the Allegiance and kill Kenan."

Prudence took Caprecia from Cheveyo. "We do not have time to discuss this now. You will come with me."

Caprecia lowered her eyes like a cowering dog.

"Gabriel, leave Coco with Maria at the villa," Prudence said. "Then bring Layla to Christopher. His mind is frantic for her."

Coco stirred in Gabriel's arms. He placed his fingers gently on her eyelids and she fell back into a deep sleep. "We will be with you soon," he said.

Stefan nodded to his son. Prudence gave Gabriel a soft smile. "Be safe, my son." She closed her eyes and a mist enveloped the small group. When it dissipated they were gone.

Lida and Cheveyo approached Gabriel. Lida carried the remains of Ahiga. "A noble warrior deserves a hero's burial," she said.

"I am sad for your loss, Lida," Gabriel said. "Ahiga's courage will be remembered."

David returned to the others, in his hands he held Kenan's laptop and cell phone. "These are Kenan's." He placed the items beside Coco's paintings on the ground next to Gabriel. "It has been an honor to fight beside you."

"The honor is mine," Gabriel said. "We will meet again."

Gabriel watched Lida and her companions walk away. He closed his eyes, lowered his head and began taking deep, slow breaths. On his third breath the laptop, cell phone, and paintings, rose into the air until they came to rest above Coco. The image of the living room at the villa formed before him. He stepped forward with Thalia beside him.

CHAPTER 36

Casa della Luna Crescente

Gabriel carried Coco upstairs to her bedroom and placed her gently on the bed. Thalia returned to her regular cat form and curled up beside her. A quick glance at the clock on the bedside table told Gabriel it was one o'clock in the afternoon. He took out his cell and called Prudence.

"How's Christopher?"

"He is weak, but will survive," Prudence said. "Are you at the villa?"

"Yes, Colombina is sleeping. I'm about to go and speak with Layla. How does Chantal seem?"

"She needs time to adapt. Kenan starved and beat her. When Chantal insisted that she did not have the information he wanted, he ordered Colombina's murder. After the hit and run failure, he wondered if Chantal had told him the truth, and changed his tactics to capturing Colombina."

"So he believes she holds the information," Gabriel said. "Has Caprecia shared anything?"

"I shall speak with her shortly. Hopefully, she has information to share that will help me understand from where Kenan draws his strength."

"What were Kenan's knives tainted with?"

"The blades were forged from one of Charon's coins."

"And this can kill us?"

"Yes… it is deadly to both of us," she said. "Once Charon's abol has pierced our skin, the blood of our beloved is the only thing that can save us. You lived tonight because of Colombina."

"I am aware of that. How did Kenan gain this knowledge?"

"I have a theory and will share it with you once I am certain of its truth."

"Be careful, Mother, there was a moment tonight when I felt Kenan's strength. It came directly after my first attack—a kick to his body," Gabriel said. "He fell, but did not rise to defend himself. It was then he transformed into the ancient figure that you saw."

"Dark magic is in his blood," Prudence said.

"I shall bring Layla to you." He ended the call and went downstairs in search of Maria, Eduardo, and Layla. He found them in the kitchen.

When Layla saw Gabriel she threw her arms around him. "Thank God you're back safely. Are the others here too? Where's Christopher?" Gabriel explained what had happened and asked Maria and Eduardo to watch over Coco while he transported Layla to *Casa della Pietra*.

O

Coco is standing amongst a group of people dressed in cocktail attire. She's searching for a young man. When she sees him, she walks over and guides him past the reception area to a door that leads to a concrete stairway. They move past the door and run up the stairs and exit at the sixth landing. At the end of a long hallway, Coco yanks open a heavy oak door. She pulls the young man inside the room and locks the door behind her. Thalia is waiting in the dimly lit room beside the bookcase. Coco searches for a particular book title: Democracy in America. *She pulls the book back and places her index finger on the back of the bookcase where the book rested. A small section of the paneled wall opens up. Coco and the young man slip inside, and the panel closes behind them.*

Coco woke abruptly, and then visions of her brother in a pool of blood came flooding back to her. She jumped up and was greeted by Maria. "Where's Christopher?" she asked.

"He's safe. The others are at *Casa della Pietra.* Gabriel brought you and Thalia here," Maria said. "He has taken Layla to be with Christopher."

"But he's coming back? I need to be with Christopher and my mother—"

"Of course, he will be here shortly, but he wanted to make sure that you rested and gained your strength," Maria said. "Shall I bring you some tea?"

"That sounds good, thank you." The second Maria left the room, Coco grabbed her sketchbook from the bedside table. On most of the pages the face of the young man whom she'd just dreamt about stared back at her. She placed the sketchbook on her desk and opened her laptop. The icon telling her that she had mail bounced up and down at the bottom of the screen, but she ignored it.

Who are you? Coco thought as she closed her eyes, willing the vision to return.

Gradually, she pulled the image into her conscious mind. She recognized the location—Christopher's office building in D.C. The large room filled with people came to life and one person caught her attention: a tall man dressed in a tailored suit that bore a slight sheen. He had dark slicked-back hair and a scar that barely missed his right eye. She had seen this man once before. She remembered her mother's blood dripping from his mouth. This was Kenan. He turned in the direction of a group of interns. The young man from her sketchbook reached into his pocket to retrieve his cell phone. Coco searched the room for clues as to the purpose of the event. She saw a display board that read:

The Legal Offices of Faye, Lenning, and Rhodes, are proud to honor the following graduating interns into the Centre for Environmental Justice.

Coco opened her eyes, and her fingers sped across the keyboard. She punched in the words she had seen on the display board and browsed through the top hits until she found what she needed. It was a story about a cocktail party to honor five undergraduate students who had volunteered their time to the Centre for Environmental Justice. The date and time of the function was for this evening in D.C.

Coco checked the time.

Suddenly Thalia morphed into a lynx and leapt at the window. Coco turned and gasped when she saw two beady eyes staring directly at her computer screen. Thalia hissed and scratched at the window incessantly. Coco knew instantly that the predator was no ordinary bird of prey. She unlocked the window and pushed against it, forcing the large bird off the ledge. It flew up into the sky. Coco slammed the window shut and drew the heavy curtains. She put her hand on Thalia's neck. The cat's fur stood on end.

"What the hell was that?" Coco said, turning her laptop away from the window and returning to the task at hand. She perused the names of the students being honored. One name resonated with her: Jeremy Lange. She Googled his name and found him on a few social media sites and clicked on one. His face stared back at her. It matched the portrait she had drawn many times. The seriousness of his eyes met with a determined strength. She had seen these eyes before. The icon bouncing at the bottom of the screen reminded her why Jeremy's eyes were so familiar.

Coco walked over to her duffel bag and felt around until she found what she wanted. In her hands she held the wooden box from her childhood. She opened it and pulled out the small piece of paper with the portrait she had drawn many years ago. She tucked it into the pocket of her jeans, returned to her computer and scrolled down the mountain of unopened emails searching for one name in particular. Her heart pounded as she clicked on one of Arianna's recent emails.

Hi Coco—I have so much news to tell you. I have a brother and he contacted me— actually he's my twin. You're like a big sister to me and right now I could really do with some sisterly advice. Hope you're okay and happy,

Call me xo

Coco opened Arianna's most recent email.

Coco—why haven't you answered any of my emails? Are you okay? I can't believe you've just vanished off the radar. I'm really worried about you. Please call.

Arianna xo

"Shit!" Coco grabbed her cell phone and dialed. Arianna picked up immediately.

"Coco, are you okay? I've been trying to get ahold of you for months—"

"Arianna, I'm fine, but please listen to me, this is important. Does your twin brother work for my brother, Christopher, in D.C?"

"Yes, he——"

"Where are you now?"

"I'm at home in L.A."

"Listen to me. You and your mother need to come away with me for a few days. Pack whatever you need and meet me at my loft. I'll be there in a couple of hours. I'll explain everything when I see you. Can you do this?"

There was silence between the two women.

"I don't understand—what's happened?"

"Arianna, listen to me! Jeremy's life is in danger." It was the only thing that Coco knew would make Arianna listen to her.

"Oh my God—what's going on?"

Coco sounded desperate. "I've known you for six years. I've guided you and always been honest with you. Now I'm begging you to trust me. I don't have time to explain everything right now. Please, will you do this for me?"

Arianna hesitated for a moment.

"Alright. I'll do it."

"One more thing, don't tell anyone else about this. Explain to your mother that I'm back in town and want to take you both on a short holiday—tell her it's a delayed surprise graduation present. I'll text you my security code—it will allow you access to the front gate of my building and the garage. Park your car in the garage, don't leave it out on the street. There's a key to my apartment hanging on a hook beside the side door. Wait for me inside my apartment and don't turn on any lights."

"Okay," Arianna said.

"I'll see you soon."

"Please keep my brother safe."

"I will." Coco ended the call and sent the text with her security code to Arianna.

Maria entered her bedroom with Max. The large dog ran directly to Coco, and she bent down and patted him.

"Have you heard from Gabriel yet?" Coco asked.

"Yes, he expects to be here within the hour," Maria said. "Are you alright?"

"I have to grab a few of my belongings from the farmhouse before we leave, will that be okay?"

"Of course, but I'll come with you. Gabriel would want that."

"Let's go," Coco said, as she walked to the door followed by Maria, Max, and Thalia.

○

As soon as they entered the farmhouse, Coco sprinted up the stairs to her childhood bedroom. Maria waited for her in the living room. Coco eyed the old wooden trunk that sat on the floor at the end of her bed. The lid opened easily and she let it fall gently against the bed. The small leather-bound sketchbook sat on top as if it had been waiting for her. She picked it up and opened it.

She stared at page after page of portraits of Jeremy Lange. When she closed her eyes and touched the pages, an image of herself as a child sitting in her bed at night drawing, flashed in front of her. She remembered the last time she had drawn in the sketchbook, her mother had entered her bedroom. Chantal had looked at the drawings, then kissed young Coco on the forehead and told her that she loved her. That was the day before her mother's abduction.

Coco flipped through the pages until she found what she was looking for. She lifted the small portrait of Arianna from her pocket and inserted it into a spot where a page was missing in the small sketchbook. It fit perfectly. This was the confirmation that she had been searching for. Now she knew that as a child she had also kept a secret, even from her mother. All along it had been hidden in a little wooden box.

"Oh God," Coco whispered. "Arianna, it's you."

Coco ran to her mother's bedroom and opened her closet. She pulled out an elegant black cocktail dress, shoes, purse, and evening jacket, and then opened the top drawer of the dresser. Inside she found a silver chain with a pendant made from glass and marcasite, and engraved with the same symbol tattooed on Gabriel's shoulder. She placed the necklace over her head and tucked it under her shirt. The necklace lay close to the symbol of the Allegiance that had recently appeared above her left breast. She grabbed the bag and ran downstairs.

"Do you have everything you need?" Maria asked.

"Yes, let's go."

When they arrived back at the villa, Coco excused herself from Maria and went to the studio off of her bedroom. She pulled a blank canvas onto the easel and began painting. She showered and dressed in her mother's black dress and heels, and placed the items she needed into her mother's evening purse.

How does Kenan know about Jeremy? It had to have been the falcon. But like so many things that had transpired in her life over the past few months, it made no sense.

She needed Gabriel.

Kenan stood atop an abandoned watchtower on the outskirts of Florence. Shards of light from the sinking sun peeked through dark thunderclouds and caught the neat scar above his eye.

The predator began its silent descent toward Kenan's outstretched gloved hand. He tossed a live bat into the air and the falcon caught it midair. She landed on Kenan's gauntlet, and gently folded her inky black feathers around her prey. Kenan stroked the bird's proud chest and stared at its beady dark eyes.

"You have done well, my lady."

With one swift movement, he drained the falcon of blood and life. When Kenan opened his eyes, he discarded the falcon and the leather gauntlet over the high wall. Seconds later, he heard the familiar beat of heavy wings before he saw the pale skin of a ghostly woman dressed in shreds of black chiffon. She landed on the tower beside him. He pulled out his cell phone. His lips turned into a menacing grin. The image of Jeremy appeared fresh in his mind along with the quick flash of information on Coco's laptop. The woman in black brought Kenan's lips to hers and then she vanished, leaving behind a single black feather floating in the air. It landed in Kenan's outstretched hand. He leapt onto the highest part of the watchtower and disappeared into the stormy sky.

CHAPTER 37

The door to the bedroom flew open and Gabriel entered. He ran to Coco and embraced her. "Are you alright? I had to make you sleep—I apologize, but I didn't have time to explain."

"I'm fine and I understand," Coco said. "How are Christopher and Mother?"

"Layla's with Christopher, he's going to be fine. Chantal is relieved to be back in Alessandro's arms." He took her by the hand. "We can leave now." He eyed her up and down. "Why are you dressed like this?"

"I know who the new leader will be," she said.

Gabriel stopped in his tracks. "Explain."

"Things that have seemed inconsequential in my life are starting to make sense. Earlier, while I slept, I had a dream, well, more of a vision."

Coco told Gabriel everything about her dream.

"What time is this event?" he asked. "I want to cancel it and keep the boy safe."

"It's too late for that. Jeremy's already there and the event begins in less than an hour," she said. "There's something else. I think I know one of the ways that Kenan's been keeping one step ahead of the Allegiance. A large bird of prey, a kind of black falcon, sat at my window tonight, and Thalia went berserk. It stared at the screen of my computer. As crazy as this may sound, I think the falcon saw the image of Jeremy that I'd drawn, and information about the event tonight on my laptop. Does that sound insane?"

Gabriel let out a string of profanity. He grabbed his cell and was set to call Prudence, but Coco stopped him.

"Gabriel, I have one more piece of information to share with you," she said. He looked up from his cell phone. She opened her purse and showed him the image of Arianna that she'd drawn when she was four years old. "I did this drawing the night before Mother was taken, twenty-eight years ago. After I drew it, I tore it out of the sketchbook and kept it hidden in a little box Mother had given me. I know this girl—her name is Arianna. I met her about six years ago at the farmers' market in Santa Monica, and we became friends. I tutored her. She was adopted as a baby by her parents. She found out recently that she has a twin brother."

"Jeremy," Gabriel said.

"Yes. What if I've known since my childhood who she is, but kept it a secret? I mean, the twins weren't even born when I drew this. I can't believe it's all a coincidence."

"There are no coincidences. Everything we do has a purpose," Gabriel said. "Prudence believes that Kenan figured out recently that you were the one who held the secret and not Chantal. Which explains why he has not attempted to kill you since the hit and run. Where is Arianna now?"

"I told her to go to my loft and wait for me. Her adoptive mother, Isabel, is with her."

Gabriel guided Coco along the hallway, up another flight of stairs and into his bedroom. He took out his cell phone and began an animated conversation with Prudence in the language of the Allegiance. He looked at Coco. "I need to change and then we'll leave for D.C." He handed her his cell phone. "Prudence wants to speak with you."

"Hello?" Coco said.

"Colombina, you have done well, and I am proud of you," Prudence said. "We shall all be together again soon—stay safe." The call ended and Coco heard water running in the bathroom. This was the first time she had been in Gabriel's bedroom. She looked around. On the walls were framed photographs. They were all of her. From her graduation at UCLA to a few weeks before the car hit her.

Gabriel stood beside her, and when he spoke it startled her. "I'm ready, let's go."

Coco grabbed his arm. "Who took these photos?"

Gabriel's gaze shifted to the photographs. "I did," he said. "I've been in love with you for a very long time." He eased his arm from Coco's grip and placed it around her shoulders. "We can talk more of this later, if you like. But Alessandro and Stefan are waiting for us in Christopher's office." Thalia morphed back into a cat and stood beside Coco. Gabriel raised his arms and a wind formed around the trio.

CHAPTER 38

Alessandro paced up and down Christopher's office while he waited with Stefan for Gabriel, Coco, and Thalia to appear. The door opened, and when Michelle greeted them, she spoke directly to Alessandro. "Is Christopher ill?" she asked. "What happened to him?"

"He will be fine," Alessandro said. "He has a high fever and so he thought it best if he stayed away… no need for everyone to get ill. And his uncle and I are happy to take his place tonight. Coco and her… fiancé will arrive shortly. Did you get the information he requested?"

"Yes, three waiters called in to the caterer today saying they were sick, here's the name of the replacements he hired."

Alessandro stared at the names. "Thank you."

Michelle turned to leave. "Did you say, Coco's fiancé?"

"Yes, they met while she was in the hospital," Alessandro said.

Michelle smiled. "Lucky her! I'll see you downstairs. Don't be too long, people are asking for Christopher." She closed the door behind her.

A few minutes later, Gabriel appeared with Coco and Thalia. Coco ran to Alessandro and hugged him. She noticed that his general grim appearance had changed. He stood taller, and tenderness befell his poise.

"How are they?" Coco asked.

"Prudence removed the bullet from Christopher's chest and he is recuperating well," Alessandro said. "And Chantal is weak, but as beautiful as ever." He turned to Gabriel. "Is there any reason why we can't pull Jeremy out now, rather than put him through this whole ordeal? Dreams can be conceived as warnings."

"Agreed, but I believe this vision has a defined purpose," Gabriel said.

"Then we need to move forward," Stefan said, as he turned his attention toward Coco. "In your dream, did you recognize anyone else with Kenan?"

"There were others with him but I didn't recognize them."

"Because this is a private event, he is limited to how many of his men he can bring into the building," Gabriel said. He spoke to Stefan. "You and I will distract Kenan so that Coco can get Jeremy back down here. Alessandro, you work with our other members to get Kenan's combatants out of here quickly."

Alessandro placed a hand on Gabriel's arm. "Gabriel, you are my dearest friend and I honor your place in the Allegiance. But I must ask that you give me this night to revenge Kenan. Do not ask me to stay back—allow me this justice."

Gabriel stared at Alessandro and nodded. "Of course, I understand. We'll keep your back safe." He pulled Coco aside. "Remember that no matter what happens you are to continue on with our plan. Do you understand the importance of this?"

Coco nodded, and they followed the others down to the floor where the event was taking place. Thalia stayed in Christopher's office.

○

When they entered the banquet room, the reception was in full swing. The room shared a similar view to Christopher's office, showing the Monument and Capitol building aglow with lights. Aged bricks lined the interior walls and an open ceiling revealed strong wooden beams. The design integrated well with the slick modern furniture that decorated what was normally the firm's open conference room.

Coco clutched her mother's purse slung over her shoulder. Once she had Jeremy safely in the secret passageway, she would move on with the rest of her plan. Her heart quickened, but she pushed her fears aside to focus on the task at hand. She grabbed Gabriel's elbow, and he turned toward her. "Promise me that you will explain about the Allegiance, and everything regarding our unusual members to Jeremy and Arianna."

"I'll talk to them when the time is right," he said. "You have my word."

She surveyed the room. "Do you see Kenan?"

"Not yet," he said.

Coco did another quick sweep of the room. "I'm going to walk around—he must be here somewhere." She walked toward the center of the room and looked around the sea of guests. Suddenly, an icy wave descended down her spine and spread, like a virus, over the rest of her body. She remembered this feeling from her childhood.

She turned around and faced Kenan. He smirked back at her. Coco fought back her nausea and searched the room for Jeremy. When she saw him, she quickly walked over and took hold of his elbow. "Walk with me, Jeremy," she said. A confused look spread across his face. "Your life and many others are in danger."

Jeremy looked at her in disbelief and shrugged off her hand, "Who the hell are you?"

Coco stood firm. "Christopher Rhodes is my brother. He sent me here tonight. I don't have time to explain, but I'm begging that you walk with me."

"You're Coco?"

"Yes."

"Okay," he said. "Let's go."

She steered him through the crowd to the back of the room and out the door to the stairs. They sprinted up five flights of stairs to the door labeled with the number six and entered. Jeremy sounded out of breath, but Coco grabbed a tighter hold of him and ran down the hallway toward Christopher's office. She opened the heavy oak door, they fell inside and she turned the lock. She walked over to the bookcase. Her eyes stopped at a familiar book. She pulled it forward, then placed the tip of her index finger on a small indentation carved into the wood where the book had been, just as she'd done in her dream. The secret door sprang open and Thalia darted in ahead of Jeremy and Coco. The door closed behind them.

Coco remembered Christopher's words. *"You will always be safe in here."* He had shown her this place on her first trip to D.C., explaining that it was the entrance and exit used by members of the Allegiance.

She grabbed for flashlights that she knew would be on a small table to her left and handed one to Jeremy. They ran down the staircase and stopped at the next landing.

○

Members of the Allegiance were placed strategically along Coco's route. They made quick work of Kenan's men the minute they entered the door behind Coco and Jeremy. Stefan shadowed Kenan, knowing that neither the Allegiance nor Kenan would dare break the rules of the code of all creatures and fight in front of a room full of humans. He stood behind Kenan, in the hallway that led to Christopher's office where Alessandro stood poised and ready to fight.

"You will die for what you have done to my wife," Alessandro said, his voice strong and full of vengeance.

"I did what I could to bring out the worst in her," Kenan said. "But she does not respond well to a beating." He turned his head slightly. "You cannot defeat me now, Stefan, and certainly not without your witch."

"What else do you want?" Alessandro yelled.

Stefan moved in closer behind Kenan, his sword drawn and ready.

"It seems that I took the wrong woman—I want your daughter, Alessandro—and the boy. Jeremy… ah yes, that's his name. The little peacemaker."

"You will have neither," Alessandro said.

Kenan sprung without warning into the air and kicked back at Stefan, but in his normal vampire form his reflexes were slow compared to the Serbian's. Alessandro yielded his sword across Kenan's back and watched him fall to the floor.

Gabriel strode toward the three men and tossed his runes into the air. "Isa," he yelled. Kenan could not move.

Stefan threw Alessandro the knife that Kenan had left on the deck in Washington. "Kill him," Stefan said. "Take your revenge and end this."

"Release your magic, Gabriel," Alessandro said.

Gabriel held his hand out toward the runes and caught them as they fell.

Alessandro forced Kenan's body around so it faced him, and then plunged the knife into his heart.

Kenan screamed an unearthly, guttural sound. Alessandro twisted the blade and then yanked it out.

"So, Charon's abol affects you also," Stefan hissed. "But who is your beloved, Kenan—who will come running to save you now?"

"You will meet her soon enough!" Kenan screamed. His

head fell back. Alessandro brought the knife down, but Kenan had vanished.

Stefan stood ready for an attack but none came. In the place where moments before Kenan had stood, a single coin now spun in the air. It slowed and fell to the floor in what remained of Kenan's blood. Stefan, Alessandro and Gabriel watched as it fizzled and melted into nothingness.

"Charon's abol…" Stefan whispered.

Gabriel snapped his fingers, and all evidence of fighting and blood vanished. The three men ran to Christopher's office and entered through the secret door. It closed behind them.

O

Coco heard the fighting in the hallway. She stopped on the second landing and turned to Jeremy. "What's your sister's name?"

"Can we start with what the fuck is going on?"

"Jeremy, you are in danger. I need to get you out of here but you must give me information."

"How do you know I have a sister? I only found out myself, recently."

"I know what it's like to suddenly find out you have family," she said. "This will sound crazy, but I've known about you since before you were born, and I believe that it's my job to protect both you and your sister." Coco pulled out her cell phone and showed Jeremy an image on her phone. It showed a photo of her with Arianna. "This is your sister, Arianna, correct?"

"What's this about?"

"I don't have time to explain. Please—is Arianna your sister?"

"Yes! Okay, Arianna is my sister!" Jeremy said.

"You have to trust me." Coco pulled out the canvas she had in her purse and placed it on the ground. With one hand she reached out to the painting, with the other she grabbed onto Jeremy's arm. "All you need to do is take a step with me."

"What the——?"

Coco heard noise behind her, and at the same time she felt Jeremy struggling to get out of her tight grip. She stepped forward with Thalia beside her.

Gabriel raced down the first flight of stairs, followed by Alessandro and Stefan. Jeremy looked up at the three men hurtling toward him. Gabriel brandished his arm into the air and Stefan threw the collapsing form of Jeremy over his shoulder, and followed Alessandro and Gabriel into the painting just as it began to disappear.

CHAPTER 39

Casa della Pietra

Prudence and Layla sat beside Christopher while he slept. Layla placed her hands over her stomach, grateful for the life growing in her womb. But her concern for Christopher did not go unnoticed by Prudence.

"Christopher has great courage, Layla," Prudence said. "And he possesses a strong will to live. But I have given him a remedy to make him sleep. We both know that he is not one to rest. Something else troubles you, though, what is it?"

Layla couldn't hold back her tears. "Is it right to bring a child into this world?" she asked. "I am not ignorant of the darkness that lurks beneath so many people, and it scares me."

Prudence put a hand over Layla's. "I asked myself the same question when I carried Gabriel. I think that perhaps most mothers think these thoughts, and always have. Your child will be well protected. I need to check on Chantal and Caprecia," Prudence said. "But if you need me, a whisper will be fine, I will hear."

Layla nodded. "Am I safe here, being human… with Chantal so vulnerable?"

"I have surrounded this part of the fortress with a charm to keep you safe," Prudence said. "And Stefan made sure that there is plenty of blood available for those who require it. But perhaps you would do well to stay away from the refrigerator in the main kitchen… it may make you nauseous."

She went to join the others downstairs.

Layla sat on the bed beside Christopher and gently placed his hand on her belly. "We need you, *amore mio*."

○

The black jaguar loped along the passageway and down the stairs beside Prudence. They joined Chantal and Caprecia in the living area. Both women were still fragile but were slowly gaining their strength.

"How is my son?" Chantal asked quietly.

"He is resting. When Alessandro returns you may go to him," Prudence said. "The others will join us soon. We are safe here. *Casa della Pietra* is a place that Kenan is not familiar with, and the entire property is hidden under myriad concealment spells."

"He only has to get close enough to Caprecia or myself and he'll figure out the puzzle," Chantal said, her words full of sadness.

"We will keep him away from you both," Prudence said. "He has no idea about the girl, Arianna, and we need to keep it that way."

Caprecia broke her silence. "Make no mistake, Kenan will do what he must to get to Coco and Jeremy. He does not value any form of life."

"Who is he working with, Caprecia?" Prudence asked.

"I don't know," Caprecia said, her voice weak and taut. "In all of the years we were held captive, I never saw him meet with anyone."

"Did he ever leave you for extended periods of time?"

"Once, yes. It was not long after he turned Chantal and I. We lived in an ancient castle. When I first laid eyes on the place, I thought it was deserted. But underneath the ruin a series of rooms had been built, and that's where we lived. The wind howled most days and nights, and the rain pounded like nothing I have ever heard before or since. Snow and ice kept us inside most of the time we were there. And I remember that the days were either very short or painfully long," Caprecia said. "When Kenan returned he kept to himself, and shortly after, we moved again. After this he became even more brutal and cruel, and obsessed with falconry… it seemed like such a strange thing for him to take on."

Prudence's body language did nothing to give away her alarm at hearing Caprecia's words. "This information is vital, thank you," she said. "And now I need to tell you something, and I wish with all of my heart that I did not have this to share with you."

Caprecia stiffened. "No! Please don't tell me that anything has happened to Louisa or Eduardo. Please."

Prudence moved closer to Caprecia and gripped her hands while she broke the news of Louisa's death. Caprecia's screams echoed through the house in a deluge of anger and pain. Her hysteria erupted into the still air of the approaching dawn. It magnified the never-ending stabbing pain that only a parent can know after hearing of the death of their child.

Caprecia wailed her mourning cries until long after the sun had risen, and all the while Prudence held her in her loving arms. The ancient witch sang incantations until the young vampire finally collapsed from exhaustion.

Later, when Caprecia awoke, Prudence placed her in a warm bath and washed the dried blood from her body. Caprecia's skin and bones had healed from the beating Kenan had given her prior to their arrival on the island, but Prudence also saw scars that she sensed he'd marred her with before turning her immortal. No doubt he wanted her to remember the power of his brutality.

The Portuguese beauty stared with dazed eyes at the bathroom's mottled stone walls. Prudence dressed her in fresh clothes and muttered healing enchantments to the young vampire, who seemed empty of any emotion. When Chantal entered the room, Prudence left the two women alone. She knew they harbored deep emotional wounds that needed to be aired before their healing could begin.

○

Chantal picked up a brush and drew it through Caprecia's hair with long, gentle strokes. Caprecia grabbed her hand, and laid it against her cheek. This simple action was all she could do to give an apology to the woman whose human life she had allowed to be taken away without her consent. Chantal placed the brush on the table and gently stroked the woman's hair while she spoke.

"There were times when I lay in that damp cellar and planned your death," Chantal said. "I hated you for what you had done to my family and the Allegiance. At first I thought Kenan had killed my little muse, but then, when my focus returned, I knew she lived. I felt the essence of her life force tugging at my soul.

"Years ago I had foreseen my death. I planned ahead and wrote the children letters. I gave them to Prudence, and she gave me her word that Christopher and Colombina would receive them on the required dates. But I did not know who would betray us. If I had known, I would have tried to stop you. So, we both have our burdens, Caprecia. Perhaps if I'd shared everything with Prudence and Gabriel none of this would have happened."

Caprecia stared at her reflection in the mirror. "I was jealous of Eduardo's talent. I didn't understand his dedication to his work and his love of the arts. It sounds so stupid now."

"How did Kenan find you?" Chantal asked.

"I was in Paris, in a restaurant on my own. At first, I didn't know what he was. He preyed on my loneliness and naiveté. He bought me flowers and dresses and made me feel special—something that I longed for. I was besotted. He seduced me, and after that first week in Paris we met in different destinations. Eduardo seemed oblivious and this only fueled my self-destruction. I became enamored with the sensuality of being with a vampire, and the thought of being immortal intrigued me, while the thought of becoming old was terrifying.

"But all of that changed the night he made me a vampire. He wanted nothing more to do with me. You fascinated him and I became nothing but his whore. But Kenan taught me well, and without that talent we would both still be stuck in that house."

Tears tinged with blood fell down Caprecia's face.

"I heard what he did to you," Chantal said. "His words and your screams echoed through to the walls of my cell. But the night you gave me the chrysalis I began to have hope. When it hatched, the butterfly's life gave me enough energy to find my daughter. I imagined myself at the lake. I felt Colombina there. I hoped that if she saw me, it would give her hope and courage. Illusions sometimes do that." Chantal kissed Caprecia's hand. "You risked your life to give me one brief moment of hope, Caprecia. Kenan may have taken our human lives but he did not steal our hearts."

"I have no heart. I *chose* this life. How could I have been so stupid?" Caprecia said. "I betrayed the Allegiance, and now I have lost my beautiful Louisa, my only child. How can I go on?"

"You will go on because you are a woman of the Allegiance and we protect our own and everything that is ethical about this planet. You will go on because your husband needs your support." Chantal stared into Caprecia's eyes, which were overflowing with tears. "You will go on because you and I must destroy the one whose blood runs through our veins, for only with him dead will you and I ever be free. Do you understand this, Caprecia?"

Caprecia nodded and kissed Chantal's hand. Kenan's blood would forever unite them.

CHAPTER 40

Westwood Village, California, U.S.A.

When Coco fell into her loft with Thalia she heard nothing.

Silence.

She looked around and saw Arianna sitting on the sofa with another woman whom she guessed to be Isabel. They both stared in disbelief as Gabriel, Alessandro, and Stefan, who was carrying Jeremy, leaped toward them out of thin air.

Isabel stood and ran to Jeremy.

"Coco!" Arianna shouted. "What's going on?"

"These people are my friends and family, Arianna," Coco said. "Please don't be alarmed. I know how strange this must seem, but please, listen to us."

Gabriel bowed his head toward Arianna. "My name is Gabriel, it's a pleasure to meet you." He turned to Jeremy, clicked his fingers, and the young man woke up. "My apologies for forcing you to sleep, Jeremy, but we needed to get moving quickly." He reached for Coco's hand.

"Jeremy—are you alright?" Isabel asked.

"Isabel? Where are we? And no—I'm not alright. I'm pissed," Jeremy said. "What the hell just happened?"

"The explanations will have to wait," Stefan said. He looked to Gabriel. "We need to return to the fortress."

"I'm not going anywhere un—"

"Jeremy, listen to me," Arianna interrupted. She turned to Gabriel. "I will agree to go with you if you answer one question."

"What is your question?" Gabriel asked.

"Who chose the numbers for the security code to this building?" she asked as she turned to Coco. "The numbers you texted me."

"I did," Coco said. "When Christopher set it up he asked me for a set of numbers. I chose them randomly, why?"

"When were they set?" Arianna asked.

"When we moved in, and I've lived here for fourteen years— they've never changed."

"That code isn't random," Arianna said. "It's mine and Jeremy's birthdate." She turned toward Jeremy and Isabel. "I trust Coco. She supported me throughout my senior year in high school and all through college. Until we know more, I think we need to do what she says."

Jeremy lifted his shoulders in submission.

Isabel turned to the three men. "I am Isabel, Arianna's adoptive mother. You have my trust."

Gabriel stepped forward. "Isabel. You have my word that once we arrive at our next destination, we shall share more information with you." He turned to Coco. "Do you need anything?"

Coco took the painting that she had done many months ago down from the easel. "Just this," she said.

Stefan and Alessandro picked up Arianna and Isabel's bags and gathered the group together.

"One moment," Arianna said. "I almost forgot something." She walked over to the sofa and picked up her purse and the wooden box Katja had given her. She turned and joined the others.

Coco caught Stefan's reaction when he saw the box Arianna held in her hands. Tears brimmed in his eyes, and a look of admiration fell over his face. She also felt something shift in the air around them. The wood seemed to wake up, bringing with it an emotive sense of wonderment, as if exhaling a sigh of relief, or finally letting go of a secret it had been holding.

"I have a box just like that," Coco said. "Where did you get it?"

"My birth mother, Katja, gave it to me before she died," Arianna said.

Stefan placed a hand on the wooden box. "Do you know who gave this to Katja?"

"It was a gift from our father," Jeremy said.

"And who is your father?" Stefan asked.

"Mom would never tell us his name," Jeremy said. "But she said all of the information that we need about him is in her diaries."

"And the diaries, have you seen them?" Stefan asked.

"No. Arianna and I are going to get them the next time we're back east. Why?"

Stefan looked up at the twins. "This is a story for my wife to share with you," he said. "We need to return to her immediately."

Coco looked to Gabriel and saw moisture glistening in his eyes; the gold flecks caught the light from her small flashlight, making them sparkle like moonbeams as his ambience embraced her. His hand tightened around hers and he commanded the wind to take them all to *Casa della Pietra*.

CHAPTER 41

A s soon as the small group arrived at *Casa della Pietra*, Stefan left to find Prudence. He traced her essence to their bedroom, where he found her waiting for him by the window. He wrapped his arms around her, kissed her, and then whispered in her ear.

"I have much to tell you, my love. I gave Alessandro Kenan's knife, and when it pierced Kenan's skin he could not transform. I asked him where his beloved was to save him with her blood, and he answered, 'You will meet her soon enough.' But there is something else, my love. When he vanished, a coin from the boatman hung in the air."

Prudence closed her eyes and leaned her head against Stefan's chest. "When my mother told me the story of her rescue she said that she heard the call of the ferryman and felt Freyja's presence." Prudence looked into Stefan's eyes. "I spoke with Caprecia, and from what she has told me, I believe that Freyja is behind Kenan's dark magic. Perhaps my father bought me time on this earth in exchange for another life. Maybe my time is running short."

Stefan tightened his arms around her. "I will find your father and demand the truth. I will never let you go."

"It is no accident that you saw the coin tonight, the Goddess planned it. But this is one time when I cannot afford to be fearful of anything Freyja brings forth. Last night I dreamt of my mother. She handed me a rune."

"Which rune did she give you?"

"Raido. Journey… reunion, I suspect she means between me and her," Prudence whispered.

"Your journey will not be alone," Stefan said. "I will be with you."

Stefan kissed her and Prudence fell into his embrace. He was reminded of the strength in their love for one another, and of the many challenges they had faced together. But he could not ignore the impending veil of darkness that crept over her.

"You have more to tell me," Prudence said.

"I think it best if I show you." Stefan guided her to the hallway. Prudence stopped suddenly. He looked at her face. Her eyes had glazed over, and her mouth turned into a faint smile. "The twins… could they be Elion's children?"

CHAPTER 42

gnacio lay on the bank of the river. Time passed, he did not care. The branches of the trees in the forest around him stood gray and mostly bare. A breeze caught a single leaf and its neighbors surrendered to the melancholy of winter and danced along with the cadence of the moving air. Threads from spider webs glistened between branches and billowed like sheets on a clothesline as the wind howled. Ignacio's mind and body were caught in the grips of hunger and madness. The icy water lapped around him, splashing and dripping. He thought of Ophelia…

And the poet says you come at night
To gather flowers in the rays of the stars;
And he has seen on the water, lying in her long veils,
White Ophelia floating, like a great lily.

Ignacio felt the wind brush past his face. He opened his eyes and prayed that he was no longer alive—that death had taken hold of his miserable existence. But then he heard her call his name.

Ignacio… Ignacio…

He forced himself up and rested on his elbows. His beloved

Louisa… she stood on the other side of the river. Her arms stretched out to him, beckoning him to her.

Ignacio…

He pushed himself up and stood in the water, but when he looked at Louisa the image that he had seen moments before had changed. She looked drained of life with blood dripping from two small punctures on the pale skin above her heart. Her tears were blood-red.

"I loved you, Ignacio, I loved you."

Ignacio ran across the river and dragged himself up the muddy bank to her. "Where are you, Louisa? I swear I did not do this to you… please believe me. I love you."

"I'm lost," Louisa whispered. "It is dark and cold. I'm so cold, Ignacio. Please, find me… I need you, my love."

Ignacio sank to his knees. "I will find you, Louisa, I will find you, my love."

He watched as Louisa's image faded away…

Epilogue

Casa della Pietra

One look at the interior gray rock walls, and Coco knew Gabriel had delivered them somewhere incredibly old. Above a grand fireplace hung a Rembrandt she instantly recognized. Huge tapestries depicting angelic creatures adorned the walls, and ancient bronze statues, and ceramic vessels gave the place a masculine ambience. Coco knew this room belonged to Gabriel. Splendid and ornate, yet comfortable, the decor seemed like a curious paradox to her 1960s-styled loft apartment.

She was aware before looking at Gabriel's face that his gaze was upon her. It had not gone unnoticed to her that since they had consummated their love an intuitive feeling between them had increased tenfold. Each nuance he emitted, she shared. Each thread of magic he yielded, she felt. They were complete together.

She turned to him. "I know this place."

He kissed her tenderly. "Yes, you were here many years ago. You loved it then, too."

Coco's mind drifted to forgotten memories of pain, sadness,

and deep love. She remembered a long carpet runner, and images of dragons, peacocks, unknown portraits, and dogs flashed before her.

She felt the familiar form of a mountain lion nudge against her legs. "Sweet Thalia. My muse and protector."

The deep longing for her mother crept over her, but unlike most of her life, she now allowed the emotion into her heart.

Soon, Mother, I will come to you.

The End

ACKNOWLEDGEMENTS

RESEARCHING AND WRITING *A Secret Muse* has been an extraordinary journey of learning. My eternal thanks to my parents, Dr. Bill and Doris Jackson, who encouraged my passion for the arts, and instilled in me their belief that education is not defined by one's ability to memorize facts and figures.

To my dear friends who have traveled along beside me while I wrote this story, I am grateful for your friendship. To my beta readers, Trudie Town, Donna Jackson, Wanda Cecchi, and Maggie Causey, thank you for your patience and thoughtful comments regarding the early manuscript. To Lupo Benatti and Wanda Cecchi, many thanks for your Italian translations. To Katherine Odesmith, MFT, thank you for keeping my feet anchored to the ground, and encouraging me to write and paint; I remain "eternally Jung." To my art students, thank you for your dedication, courage, and willingness to participate in my classes, and for encouraging me to stretch my own wings. *Viviere!*

Thanks to Dan Peel for patiently poring over and editing hundreds of pages of my early material, and counseling me to slow down and enjoy the magic of storytelling. To my editor, John Hudspith, thank you for whipping my writing into a tight story, and for doing it with your delightful and witty English humo(u)r. To my copy editor, Josh Sindell, thank you for your expertise.

My heartfelt thanks to authors Prue Batten and Siobhan Daiko for sharing their insightful knowledge, experience, and advice regarding the book publishing industry. And to Steve Sann for sharing with me his informative research on the history of Westwood and the W Hotel.

To Anna Milioutina, my book-cover designer, thank you for your creativity, talent, and willingness to explore endless possibilities. To Alexandra Mooney, thank you for the laughter during our photo sessions. Thanks to Megan Smith for your elegant website design skills.

Gratitude to my sister, Suesie Shaw, who, in the midst of the sadness of losing our dear mother, arrived with her paints and brushes, and encouraged me to "get to work" on the book's cover art. And my brothers, Jeremy and Russ, thank you for your support and love.

To Bettelu Beverly, my darling American Mom, thank you for your unyielding devotion to our family, your much-needed hugs, and your maternal love. You are amazing!

But not one word of this book would have been possible without the three men in my life: My husband, Brian Beverly, and our sons, Angus and Jack. Thank you for encouraging me to write, your never-ending notes of reassurance and support, the flowers, chocolate, and coffee. But mostly for your unconditional love, patience, and constant faith in my creativity.

Photograph by Alexandra Mooney

Mandy Jackson-Beverly was born in the bustling town of Pyramid Hill, Victoria, Australia... Population: 419. This remote childhood kick-started Mandy's imagination, as did the rugged coastline and rolling hills of Tasmania, where her family relocated when she was four years old.

In 1982, Mandy moved to London, where she discovered the importance of the creative collective: The 1980s fashion scene. In Los Angeles, she found her own creative freedom among the thriving, no-holds-barred visionaries of the music video world. As a costume designer and stylist Mandy worked for photographer Herb Ritts, and directors Joel and Ethan Coen, David Fincher, and Julien Temple, and music icons David Bowie, Madonna, and Tina Turner, to name a few.

Mandy has taught Advanced Placement Art, written and directed high school theatre productions, and writes blogs for *The Huffington Post* and *Tasmanian Times*. She resides in Ojai, California, with her husband, Brian Beverly, a crossed-eyed cat, Luna, a dog named Cash and, sometimes, her sons, Angus and Jack.

www.mandyjacksonbeverly.com

CPSIA information can be obtained
at www.ICGtesting.com
Printed in the USA
LVOW04s1355140816
500337LV00037B/1233/P